A HIKER'S GUIDE TO PURGATORY

MICHAEL NORTON

A Hiker's Guide
to Purgatory

A Novel

IGNATIUS PRESS   SAN FRANCISCO

Cover photographs courtesy of the author

Cover design by Enrique J. Aguilar

ISBN 978-1-62164-518-4 (PB)
ISBN 978-1-64229-213-8 (eBook)
Library of Congress Control Number 2021940975
Printed in the United States of America ⊗

For all the holy souls in Purgatory,
that they may swiftly see the face of God.

I

To die would be an awfully big adventure.

—J. M. Barrie, *Peter Pan*

The trailhead was exactly what Dan Geary had expected. Which meant, strangely, that it looked like nothing he'd ever encountered before.

He was standing at the base of a long, grassy hill that rose gently to a cloud-sprinkled sky. Nothing else—just green grass stirring in the breeze and a blue, blue sky flecked with brilliant white. A minimalist landscape, but one saturated with intense color. All around him was music: the songs of hidden birds and a light wind sighing as it went.

Turning around, he saw that he stood at the edge of a vast rolling steppe, an endless grassland through which the wind moved much more vigorously, in sweeping waves like the billows of a great green sea. He felt it on his face and in his hair, tugging gently at him. His heart, frozen in torment only a moment before, now lifted in unexpected joy.

Seconds ago, he had been thrashing and fighting for breath, surrounded by noise, distraction, and turmoil. All of that was gone now: the glaring lights, the white walls, the masked faces leaning above him . . . the anxious professional voices, the beep and hum of monitors and suction pumps, the brief but searing pain.

All of it. Gone now.

"Thank you," he breathed. "Oh, thank you."

He'd been dreaming of this place for so long that he couldn't even remember when it had first begun to take shape in his mind. Probably years ago, after the children had grown and gone, just as he and his wife had started settling down into a gentle middle age. He'd encountered it fleetingly at first, in his sleep, and eventually it started to recur in quiet waking moments when he was taking a walk or resting his eyes from a book.

It was like a memory, vivid and precise in all its details, even though he could not recall ever having been to such a place. He'd found it oddly comforting, especially during the last few years of his life as he'd learned to say goodbye to so many beloved people and places, to accept his faltering talents and abilities and the gradual narrowing of his world.

And now I'm here, he told himself, squinting in the sunlight as he turned back to the grassy summit. *I guess we know what that means.*

It meant, obviously, that he was dead—at least in the conventional sense. He found this hilariously ironic since he couldn't remember ever having felt so completely and perfectly alive as he did right then. He smelled the sweet scent of earth and grass. He felt the firm soil under his feet, the heft of a hiking stick in his hand, and the solid weight of the well-balanced pack on his shoulders. And he felt something more: an upsurge of eager impatience that made him smile.

Trailhead fever, he thought. *Just like old times.*

As trailheads go, however, this one had a few deficiencies—most notably, the lack of a trail. The grassy slope in front of him certainly looked inviting, but it bore no sign that anyone had ever walked this way before. And while he could understand the absence of a parking lot —cars would simply be out of place in this roadless landscape—he saw none of the other amenities one usually encountered: no helpful signboard, no map, no listing of rules or other pertinent information.

Guess I'm pretty much on my own, then, he thought.

Signage or no signage, Dan didn't intend to spend eternity standing around waiting for instructions. He was dressed and equipped for a journey, and that obviously meant he was expected to start journeying. He even resisted the temptation to take off his pack and see what kind of gear he'd been issued.

The truth was that all of this was perfectly fine with him, especially after what he'd been through during his last few years on earth. If he'd ever had any reservations about the idea of an afterlife—quite apart from the usual concerns about hellfire and damnation—they'd involved a nagging suspicion that after a life of passion and challenge it was all going to be terribly boring. Clouds and harps sounded like a tedious way to spend eternity.

Well, he knew better than to think this was Heaven, and he was relieved to see that it didn't look like the Other Place either. This was a trailhead, and he knew from long experience what that meant. The adventure wasn't over; if anything, it was just beginning. Like a runner at the starting line, he could feel the old anticipation thrumming in his legs like the note of a bass guitar. He may not have had much of a grasp of metaphysics, but he knew how to hike.

Gripping his hiking stick, he stepped out on a gentle diagonal across the face of the hill. The grass brushed lightly against his boots, his lungs filled with clean air, and he settled into a steady rhythm. It felt good to stand straight, stretch those muscles, and feel the strength returning to his arms and legs.

Somewhere a dog barked—a single joyful note, not very distant—then, moments later, another bark. And another. It was a familiar, friendly sound, and it made Dan smile. This had to be a pretty decent place if it had dogs.

His smile widened to a full grin when a stocky Labrador retriever appeared at the top of the hill, paused briefly, and charged headlong toward him, parting the grass like a ship plowing the sea. He recognized that wedge-shaped head with its silly grin, that lustrous chocolate coat, that dangerously enthusiastic tail. In any other place he wouldn't have believed it for a moment, but here it was —marvelous, true, and utterly fitting.

"Buddy!" he yelled. "Here, boy!"

Not that there was any need for him to call out— within seconds, Buddy was all over him, barking, jumping, whining, and insisting on his undivided attention. Dan knelt on one knee, took the dog's head between his hands, and stared into its bright, moist, excited eyes. He could feel the tears in his own.

"Good dog!" he said, scratching behind the floppy brown ears. "So good to see you, pal."

Buddy hadn't been Dan's first dog, but he had been the last. For twelve years, he'd been the family clown and playmate, a gentle guardian to the children and a tireless companion on innumerable walks. You couldn't leave him alone with food of any kind, and he refused to accept the truth about skunks and porcupines, but he'd been a beloved member of the Geary household—and it had been a sad day when they learned about the inoperable cancer and made the decision to have him put down. After that, Dan never had the heart to get another dog.

But here was Buddy again—strong, healthy, and filled with all his old carefree canine excitement. Dan was surprised at how good it made him feel.

He stood and took a firm grasp on his hiking stick. There might not be signboards at this trailhead, but he'd evidently been provided with a guide of sorts.

"I hope you know your way around here, pal," he said, "because I certainly don't."

In answer, Buddy gave another happy bark. The two of them began to climb the hill, carving a trail of their own through the waving grass.

It wasn't a particularly steep ascent—just enough to give Dan a light sweat and a welcome sensation of long-deferred exercise. Before long, he and Buddy were standing at the top of the slope, which ended abruptly at the edge of a high escarpment. Spread out below them, as far as they could see, was a landscape of wild and astonishing beauty.

2

A good way of testing the calibre of a philosophy is to ask what it thinks of death.

—George Santayana, *Winds of Doctrine*

Far below them, a wide valley opened out, enclosed by towering sandstone cliffs that glowed red and gold in the sunlight. Vast stretches of open country and thick tracts of forest rose and fell gently in a mosaic of green; lakes and streams glittered under the sky. Sunlight and cloud-shadows waltzed slowly and silently across the country-side.

In the far distance stood a range of soaring, jagged mountains, their snow-capped summits almost painfully bright. The sight of those peaks made Dan's heart suddenly beat faster, and he knew he wanted to climb them. Had to climb them.

Gazing out over the boundless landscape before him, he thought of his wife, and a sharp pang of longing shot through him.

How Anna would have loved this, he thought.

They had been constant companions for most of their lives and had hiked thousands of miles of trails together through some of the most majestic places in the world. This was more imposing and more beautiful than any of them, and he wished he could share it with her.

That was impossible, of course. They had talked wistfully and often about the parting that death would one day bring, knowing that one of them would inevitably be left alone while the other journeyed on. But those discussions had always focused on the sorrow of the one left behind; he hadn't considered that there would also be sorrow—even loneliness—on this side.

Oh, Anna, he thought. *Don't wait any longer than you have to. You're going to love this place.* And he found himself suddenly making a fervent prayer for her and for their children, that all of them would one day be able to make this journey and arrive safely at its end.

Strange. They taught us to pray for the souls of the departed, but I never gave much thought to the idea that the departed might also be praying for us.

He stood there for a long time, his heart filling with the awe and splendor of the scene below him—a place of wonders, all waiting to be explored as though for the very first time.

Buddy was waiting impatiently off to his left, where the cliff was broken by a narrow chasm that cut between tall slabs of tawny sandstone. With a last glance at the wide panorama below, Dan followed his dog down into the ravine. It was an easy walk, and they quickly established a brisk rhythm as they picked their way among smaller rocks and underbrush.

Dan couldn't help enjoying himself. It felt splendid to be walking without aches, pains, or weakness, freed from all the debilities and hitches of age. He hadn't given much thought to it until now, but if this was the afterlife, he wasn't feeling particularly ghostly. This seemed to be his familiar self, tuned up and repaired, and it felt perfectly comfortable. Wonderfully comfortable, in fact.

The last few years had been difficult ones for a man as active and restless as Dan had always been. He'd had to come to grips with a series of physical limitations —arthritis, weakening vision, flagging stamina, and one frightening encounter with cancer. Worst of all, he'd gradually been forced to admit that his mind was beginning to deteriorate. Small failures of memory and judgment had started to increase both in frequency and severity, until there was no way to deny or explain away the slow, inescapable creep of senility.

That was all gone now. His step was firm, his vision was clear, and he felt infused with more strength and energy than he'd known in years. Best of all, his mind was refreshingly clear, sharp, and quick. This might not be Heaven, but it definitely had its perks.

The sun-warmed stone ravine they now walked through was balmier than the open hillside above them, and a steady breeze blew up from the valley beyond, carrying with it the perfumed scent of grass and wildflowers. Sunlight reflected off the ravine walls, bathing everything in a soft buttery glow. Canyon wrens and ever-cheerful chickadees flitted in and out of nearby shrubs. Dan could hear occasional scurrying noises from the underbrush—geckos, field mice, jackrabbits, or other small creatures, he assumed. He was surprised that a place so majestic and vast could feel so familiar.

So, he thought, *this has to be Purgatory . . . It certainly can't be either of the other two alternatives.*

Still, it wasn't a bit like the Purgatory he'd learned about during his rambunctious years at Saint Ignatius Elementary School, where the teachers had often reminded them to pray for all the poor souls who'd been condemned to suffer there as punishment for the many bad things they had done during their lives.

That had been his earliest impression of Purgatory—

that it was a sort of otherworldly jail. Not as permanent or horrible as Hell, maybe, but pretty darned unpleasant just the same: a place where bad boys and girls would find themselves if they didn't sit up straight, stop fidgeting, and pay better attention in class. Only people who did seriously evil things would go straight to Hell; but if you'd committed a few lesser offenses (and after all, who hadn't?), you were going to have to spend some time in Purgatory working off your sins unless God could be persuaded to grant you an early release through the prayers of your anxious friends and relatives.

To a ten-year-old delinquent accustomed to frequent lectures and warnings from adults, this all made a kind of sense, of a piece with the blue-collar immigrant Catholicism that had surrounded Dan during his childhood. *Don't do the crime if you can't serve the time.* On the other hand, it didn't seem like the sort of system a benevolent God would set up for his beloved, if wayward, children. Years later in his earthly life, he would include "that whole Purgatory thing" in his extensive list of the many cruel doctrines that had led him to leave the Church, shrug off organized religion entirely, and become an assertive cocktail-party atheist.

It wasn't until his career as a freethinker ended in a colossal, heartbreaking fiasco that he reluctantly "returned" to Christianity—only to encounter a God, a Church, and a reality that were radically different from the things he thought he'd walked away from as an adolescent. As he hungrily began reading and studying every book, tract, and sermon he could find, he began to see how shallow and cursory his early religious education had been.

Warnings and admonitions that had once seemed arbitrary and loveless now appeared reasonable and even kindly. Rituals and traditions he'd dismissed as outdated and embarrassing now seemed astonishingly beautiful, rich with meaning and filled with light. Doctrines and dogmas he'd once despised and belittled now appeared completely sensible.

And that included the idea of Purgatory. What he had viewed as some kind of extraterrestrial penitentiary gradually began to resemble something compassionate, even gentle: a place of preparation and anticipation, set up not for punishment but for purification and the cultivation of excellence. He'd tried thinking of metaphors—dozens of them—as he wrestled with the idea. Olympic training center? Fitness camp? Outward Bound program? They all seemed clumsy. But the more he'd thought about Purgatory, the more convinced he became of its utter necessity.

He'd been relieved, then, when thoughts of this place had begun to reappear more and more insistently during his waking and sleeping hours at home and in the hospital. At the very least, Purgatory seemed to promise that he'd have some prep time—and if there was a little pain involved, so much the better. As they said at the gym: no pain, no gain.

And now, here he was, doing the very thing that had always given him so much joy. No ethereal, airy-fairy afterlife for him—hiking stick in hand, he had a full pack on his back, and a trusty dog trotting along beside him.

Well, not exactly beside him. In typical doggy fashion, Buddy was meandering down the ravine on a scouting expedition of his own, sniffing in odd corners, growling at lizards, and watering the occasional rock. Looking ahead, Dan saw that the ravine turned abruptly to the right in what he hoped was a gentle switchback that would lead them down the cliff face. As he rounded the corner, he caught glimpses of distant mountain peaks on the far horizon.

Suddenly, he heard a familiar, dreadful rattle.

"Buddy!" he yelled in his most commanding voice. "Come here! Now!"

But it was too late. Buddy had already seen the snake, an enormous timber rattler that was coiled in the shadow of a cliff wall. It was as big around as Dan's arm and had to be several feet long, and it didn't seem to be in a particularly good mood. Tail wagging, the dog ambled up to investigate.

"Buddy! No!"

To his amazement, nothing happened. The dog sniffed the snake with canine curiosity, the snake eyed the dog with reptilian disdain, and that was that. Satisfied, or bored, Buddy turned away and wandered down the ravine in search of other diversions.

Dan sighed with relief, feeling more than a little foolish.

Well, that was interesting, he thought, edging circumspectly past the snake's lair. *Apparently, some things are very different here.*

As the descent continued, he noticed more changes in their surroundings. The sparse alpine scrub they'd been walking through since leaving the summit was being supplanted by more plentiful vegetation—flowering shrubs, bushes, and even a few small trees. He could hear a faint sound of water trickling into the ravine, and moments later he spied its source: a modest rivulet flowed out through a fissure between two slabs of stone and was making its way down the mountainside ahead of them.

Buddy stopped to lap loudly at the water for several seconds, allowing Dan to catch up. He scratched the thirsty dog behind the ears, and a new thought struck him.

Animals apparently didn't attack each other here, but it seemed they still got thirsty. Presumably they still got hungry too. Which natural instincts and behaviors applied here, and which ones were no longer in effect? If a lion didn't kill and eat the occasional antelope, could it still be a lion in any meaningful sense of the word?

It would be splendid if there were lions here, he thought, especially the kind that didn't feel obliged to kill and eat the occasional hiker.

That thought led quickly to others. Why, for instance, hadn't he encountered any other people? Given the state of the world he'd just left, he'd have expected Purgatory to be fairly crowded, but he hadn't seen even the faintest footprint of another person. He'd occasionally been irritated by the congestion on some of the park trails he and Anna had traveled, and he couldn't say that he felt particularly lonely now. But he had to admit that it was more than a little eerie to find himself alone.

He passed the next few miles in such thoughts, speculating about the various ways in which a place that looked, smelled, and felt so very earthlike might at the same time be quite different from the world he had known. It was an idle exercise—but exercise was exactly what his mind hadn't been getting during the last few years.

The ravine was visibly widening now; he could see more of the sky, and the little stream had grown more respectable in size and sound. Small birds darted back and forth above him as he and Buddy made the next turn. *Swallows*, he thought. *They must nest in these cliffs.* He began to keep a lookout for other birds—not to mention the peaceful mountain lion he'd already conjured up in his imagination—but the rock-strewn floor of the ravine still demanded a certain amount of his attention. He was fairly sure that if you twisted an ankle here, it would still hurt, and he had no desire to test that hypothesis.

The sun had been nearly overhead as they began their descent, but Dan was beginning to notice some lengthening of the shadows around him. Buddy wandered back and forth, returning regularly for head pats and scratches, and Dan's thoughts began to wander again too.

This is a lovely place, he thought. *If this is life after death, why would anyone be afraid to die?*

It was a perplexing thing, he reflected, the way human beings seemed hardwired to cling to earthly existence in all but the most appalling situations. He'd known a few elderly men and women who were ready for death— some because they were eager to be reunited with loved ones who were already gone, others because their lives were filled with pain, loneliness, or ennui. But there were so many others—his own mother came immediately to mind—who seemed obsessed with the idea of prolonging their lives, willing to spend huge sums of money for an extra year, an extra month, an extra week.

Was it simply a matter of wanting to stay until one's work was done, one's lessons learned, one's journey well and truly ended? In some cases, perhaps. But Dan suspected that the more likely motive was fear, the unacknowledged but nevertheless terrifying conviction of one's own guilt, one's own unfitness for happiness.

Enormous energies had been channeled into the work of persuading people that there was no afterlife at all— or that if it existed, it would be an utterly judgment-free place, presided over by a grandfatherly and not terribly bright deity who could be easily manipulated and cajoled. A place where one's crimes were not forgiven but merely overlooked. Instead of judgment you got a pat on the head, and Grandpa would say, "There, there, now. It doesn't matter."

But at some deep, inescapable level, people knew better. It *had* to matter how you lived your life—because if none of it mattered, then you didn't matter either.

In spite of the vast amounts of noise, ridicule, and hate that were expended to create and sustain that comfortable myth, it was a fragile fabric that tore easily, fraying and unraveling before the inescapable approach of mortality. No matter how often it was proclaimed on talk shows and websites, inserted into the plotlines of novels and films, embedded in the lyrics of songs, and preached from the pulpits of churches that everyone's sins were small and everyone's offenses insignificant, no one really believed it. Not with any confidence, anyway.

In the dark reaches of the night, only a sociopath could avoid the nagging suspicion that it was all a lie, that once the party was over, a terrible bill was going to be presented for payment. Under the circumstances, then, maybe you couldn't blame people for reacting with such chill dread, such frantic anger, such desperate efforts to fend off death at any cost.

Well, he'd been spared *that*, in any case. Here he was— walking through Purgatory carefree as you please, without any particular sense of apprehension. If there was something here to fear, something he had not yet encountered, he couldn't seem to muster up any unease about it.

That was another thing Dan was beginning to notice

in himself: an absence of anxiety. Anna had always called him a "control freak," and he couldn't deny it—he'd spent a lot of energy trying to plan and manage every circumstance and situation he encountered—but now he didn't feel any interest in worrying. He wasn't really in control of anything anymore, and he probably never had been. Fretting about the future seemed like a waste of time.

It was an agreeable feeling—in its way, maybe as invigorating as his restored physical strength and health, and he was enjoying the sensation. Immensely.

As he negotiated another turn in the long switchback, the tall sandstone cliffs gradually fell away on either side, and he saw that he and Buddy had now reached the mouth of the ravine. They stood at the head of a sloping, grassy alpine meadow, leading to a valley that stretched out far below, looking just as beautiful as it had from high atop the escarpment where they had first viewed it.

The wind carried an astringent, bracing fragrance of mingled sage, thyme, and juniper. A few hundred yards ahead, Dan got his first view of some good-sized wildlife; a small herd of elk, their graceful bodies lithe and cinnamon brown, was grazing in the meadow below. The antlers of a massive bull gleamed in the sunlight as he raised his head to look at Dan, then returned calmly to his meal. They were magnificent animals, and it gladdened Dan's heart to see them.

The stream he and Buddy had been following continued on ahead, tumbling and gurgling insistently over the rocks. It had widened considerably now. Although Dan didn't feel particularly thirsty, a lifetime of hiking had taught him that you never passed up an opportunity to rehydrate. He didn't know if there was a water bottle in his pack, but the stream was right there, and he figured he had nothing to lose by drinking from it.

Why not? If the rattlesnakes aren't dangerous, I don't suppose the water will kill me either. Especially since I'm already dead.

He knelt by the brook, splashed his face and neck, and drank a few mouthfuls of cool water from his cupped hands. It tasted fresh and clean, just as he'd expected. Refreshed, he stood and took a long, careful look at his surroundings.

At his back were the steep sandstone cliffs he and Buddy had just descended. The cliffs extended to the horizon on the left and the right, towering above him and glowing in the afternoon sunlight. Ahead was a rough country of grasses, shrubs, and low-growing trees punctuated by weathered spires and knobs of pale red stone.

From the top, this landscape had all seemed rather flat, but now he realized that the terrain before him was actually quite rolling and rugged. There were thickly forested hills far ahead, dark with trees of various shapes and sizes, and beyond them the snowy peaks of those distant mountains, still beckoning him forward.

Buddy, who had bounded ahead as soon as they were in the open, now turned and gave a happy bark of anticipation.

"Good boy," Dan said. "You lead, and I'll follow."

Their journey down the meadow was a pleasant, undemanding ramble. The stream seemed to be leading them toward an alpine lake folded in among several low peaks. Silvery and wind-riffled, it shimmered gaily in the afternoon light, and Dan estimated it was two or three miles ahead.

The sun was definitely lower in the sky now and was beginning to shine in his face. He found himself squinting a little as he peered ahead and was glad to be wearing a cap with a decent brim. It would be evening in a few hours, and that lake might be a good spot to bed down for the night.

Buddy ambled happily down along the stream bank, doubling back every few minutes to make sure Dan was still following. And Dan *was* going a bit more slowly now, stopping more often to look around and enjoy the scenery. This open terrain provided a lot more opportunities for sightseeing than the ravine that had brought them down from the rim.

Now he could spot several herds of grazing animals scattered around the meadow on either side, although they were too far away to identify. Pronghorns, perhaps. Overhead, some sort of eagle or large hawk soared effortlessly in the sky, riding the high thermals of the air. Smaller birds darted in and out of the thickets by the stream and made brief forays into the open. In the way of small birds, they did a lot of chirping and twittering, and it was a merry sound.

An hour's brisk walk brought them down to the place where the stream emptied into the lake, which was sheltered on three sides by lovely half-timbered hills. Dan was glad to see that he'd guessed well: this was the perfect spot for a campsite. The lake was surrounded by a belt of low-growing trees, mostly pine and spruce. Almost everywhere, the vegetation grew right down to the shore, but there was one small, sandy clearing that looked as if it would make a fine bivouac. Aside from a few smooth boulders, the spot seemed clean, dry, and free of stones.

He shrugged out of his pack and sat down beside it to take an inventory of his supplies. They were exactly what he would have brought if he'd assembled everything himself: a lightweight tent, a sleeping bag and blanket, a backpacking stove and mess kit, a flashlight, a pair of water bottles, various necessary toiletries and sundries, three pairs of his favorite merino wool hiking socks, extra T-shirts and boxers, and a blue hoodie that proclaimed *Heaven Can Wait.*

Someone has a sense of humor, Dan mused. There was a nice assortment of freeze-dried food too—which was fortunate, since he was already starting to feel hungry. Noticeably missing from the pack were bug spray, Band-Aids, or anything for blister care. *Well, apparently this is to be a pest-free, problem-free sort of hike,* Dan thought.

Buddy wandered over to sniff at the pack but didn't seem particularly interested in any of the food—a distinctly un-Buddy behavior, Dan thought. After a few minutes and some judicious ear scratches, the dog wandered off toward the lake to do his own exploring while Dan set up the tent.

It didn't take him long to make camp and heat some water on the stove for dinner—a pouch of beef stroganoff and some instant fruit drink. As he sat down to eat, he said the familiar blessing he and Anna had always recited with their children on camping trips when they were all much younger.

> Thank you for the world so sweet.
> Thank you for the food we eat.
> Thank you for the birds that sing.
> Thank you, God, for everything!

It was a bittersweet exercise. He had been blessed with a wonderful family and some wonderful years, but this was a journey he could not share with them. That made him more than a little sad.

It had always been that way with him. This was the time of day when he had always been most vulnerable to loneliness, regret, and homesickness, as the light softened and the world prepared itself slowly for the gentle approach of evening. There was only one cure: shake it off and find relief through useful work. He washed and rinsed his dishes, put the stove away, and wandered down to the shore to see what had become of Buddy.

There was still plenty of daylight left. The wind had died down, and the lake had grown still. Ducks were cavorting on the water, splashing and quacking and diving for food.

"Nice spot, isn't it?"

The voice startled Dan. He turned, and there at the edge of the clearing, leaning against a large granite boulder, was a park ranger dressed in khaki and green, regarding him with a broad open smile. Buddy was lying on the ground at his feet, looking not at all penitent about having failed to announce this new arrival.

"You must be Dan," said the ranger, waving to him in greeting. "Welcome to Purgatory."

3

The angel replied, "I will go with you; I am familiar
with the way."
— Tobit 5:6

"Thanks," said Dan to his visitor. "It's good to be here."

"Yes, it is," said the ranger. "Believe me, it's *very* good
to be here, considering the alternative." He was an inch
taller than Dan, well-tanned and lean, with warm brown
eyes and curly brown hair that poked out from under his
green ball cap. The cap bore an embroidered logo that
read *Fear Not!*

"I'm Rafe," he added.

"Glad to meet you," said Dan as the two shook hands.
"Apparently I don't need to tell you my name. And I see
that you're already good friends with my dog too."

The stranger glanced down at Buddy, who favored him
with some enthusiastic tail thumping. "Yeah, Buddy's a
good fellow. Aren't you, boy? I hope the two of you had
a good hike down from the trailhead."

"We did. This is magnificent country."

"Glad it agrees with you. By the way, congratulations
on picking a good campsite for your first night. This is
one of my favorite spots."

Dan studied the ranger for a few seconds. "I'm going
out on a limb here, but I assume you're an angel of some
kind, right?"

"Yep. I am." Rafe gave a nod and a boyish grin. "An archangel, in fact. Hope you're not disappointed by the lack of wings."

"I really wasn't thinking about it."

"Some people complain. They want us to look . . . well, more angelic. But in most social situations a set of wings can be really distracting, and on the trail they're more trouble than they're worth. Really useful when you're in a big hurry, though."

"I don't mind at all," said Dan. "Wings or no wings, it's all perfectly fine with me."

"Good," Rafe said with a wry smile. "I appreciate that. Anyway, I just stopped by to say hello, see how you were settling in, and give you the standard orientation talk. I imagine you have a lot of questions about this place, and I'll do my best to answer them."

"That would be great," said Dan.

This brought another smile. "Why don't we sit down, relax, and have a little talk? After all, you've been walking since you got here."

They sat beside each other on the ground, their backs against the sun-warmed rocks. Dan couldn't help stealing glances at his new companion, although it made him feel a little disrespectful to be giving him the once-over. This was the first angel he'd ever met, and he wasn't sure how to act.

Rafe seemed unfazed by the attention. "So . . . questions?"

"Well . . . hmm . . . I'm still trying to get oriented here. I don't suppose you have a map?"

The angel shook his head firmly. "Everybody asks that one. But no, there are no maps, and you won't find a compass or a GPS unit in your pack either. This isn't that kind of place, and you're not on that kind of journey."

Dan nodded. "I guess we're back to the basics, then. What kind of place *is* this, and what kind of journey am I on? Where am I going, and how do I get there? What are the rules?"

Rafe laughed. "Where are you going? I should think that would be obvious by now. You're going to Heaven. And like any good hiker, you'll get there by putting one foot in front of the other. As for the rules, well, you should already know those. Don't litter. Don't leave your campfire unattended. Clean up after yourself and be courteous to your fellow hikers. What else do you really need to know?"

Dan was surprised. "Fellow hikers? So there *are* other hikers, then? That's news to me. You're the first soul I've seen since I got here. I haven't even come across any footprints."

"First soul," Rafe repeated with a smile. "I like that. Oh, there are plenty of other travelers—they're all over the place. You just haven't noticed them yet. I promise that'll change as you get farther along."

"And how long will this journey take?"

"How long? Are you in a hurry or something?"

"I was curious, that's all."

"All I can say is that it will take as long as it takes. And that's pretty much up to you."

"Up to me? That sounds like the sort of thing the warden tells the new inmates in those prison movies, and everybody knows he's lying."

"This isn't a prison," said Rafe. "And it's not a waiting room or a holding tank or even the celestial boot camp

29

you seem to have been expecting. You have nothing to atone for here, and nothing to prove. That's already been done for you." He looked sharply at Dan. "You understand that, right?"

Dan nodded.

"Good. That's really important. No matter what you may have been told, you're not here because you were a bad person. Oh, and in case you're tempted to congratulate yourself, you're not here because you were a particularly good person either. You're here because at some point in your life, in some clear moment of grace, you understood that a great gift was being given to you, and you were willing to accept that gift instead of throwing it back in the Giver's face."

"I totally get that," Dan said.

"Great. Glad we got that out of the way. But here's the thing. To be perfectly blunt, you're not ready for Heaven yet."

Dan found himself smiling. "If you were expecting an argument from me, you won't get one," he said. "If we're talking about meeting the Creator of the Universe face-to-face, I'm absolutely not ready."

"Good to know," said the angel, nodding. "More than anything else, Heaven is a place of blinding truth, blinding light, and blinding love. I'm sure that sounds perfectly wonderful to you. And it is—it's unimaginably beautiful. But unless you're prepared, it can also be unimaginably terrifying."

Dan frowned.

This doesn't sound like clouds and harps, he thought. *And that's a relief. But it doesn't sound very encouraging either.*

"Okay," Dan said. "You're the local expert. But you're

going to have to walk me through this metaphysical stuff because I'm having a tough time wrapping my head around any of this."

Rafe nodded sympathetically. "I understand. We have plenty of time to talk about these things, and maybe we should save that discussion for another day. Right now, all you need to know is that you still have a lot to learn. And you have a great deal to forget."

"So . . . this is a kind of school, then?"

The angel waved his hand dismissively.

"You really love your metaphors, don't you, Dan? Okay, it's like a school. Or you could think of it as a hospital, a rehab center, or a detox program, if any of those things help. It's Purgatory, man! The main point is that here you'll have time to clear away the clutter of a lifetime—all those old habits, cravings, wounds, and scars that have collected on you like barnacles—and to strengthen yourself for the Great Adventure ahead."

"Okay. I think I'd like that."

"Most people say that. And most people also find it . . . uncomfortable." Rafe tipped his cap back and squinted up at the sky. "You may already have noticed that some things are different here."

"Well, yes," said Dan. "Apparently snakes don't bite, and dogs don't beg for food. At least this dog doesn't, and I thought I knew him pretty well."

Rafe chuckled, scratching Buddy behind the ears. "Very, very undoglike, isn't it? But convenient for you too, since it means you won't have to carry a ten-pound bag of kibble in your pack. But I think you'll begin to notice even bigger differences pretty soon—most of them in yourself."

"Such as?"

The angel glanced over at him with what looked to Dan like sympathy.

"Look, I don't have to tell you that the world you came from is not a peaceful place," he said. "It's a battlefield, where good and evil are constantly at war in the souls of men and women, and nobody emerges from it undamaged. Nobody. But as far as you're concerned, that war is over now. Evil has no power here. Nor does any lie or evasion or deception. You've left all of that behind."

He paused, and they both stared out over the tranquil lake and the mountains behind it. The sun was low in the sky now, and its light had taken on a reddish radiance.

"I'm glad," said Dan. "I don't think I'll miss any of that."

"Don't be so sure. What I'm trying to tell you is this: you're about to discover how much you've been depending on lies and evasions to get by in the world, and how difficult it can be to give them up. Truthfulness—being truthful in everything—is a skill that doesn't come easily to most people."

Dan nodded. "All right," he said. "But if it's all the same to you, this place suits me just fine for now."

"It won't suit you for long," said the angel firmly. "It isn't meant to. After all, nobody's supposed to stay in school forever. You're training for something much better than this."

"Okay, but how do I know where I'm going? I've got no map, remember?"

"You have a compass," said the angel. "Its name is Desire."

Dan stared at him, baffled. "Desire? I thought that was one of the things I was supposed to stay away from."

Rafe shook his head.

"No, Dan. The problem isn't desiring things—it's desiring the wrong things. Like most people, you spent most of your energy wanting things that weren't worthy of your desire. For the believer, there is only one question worth answering: How much do I want to reach Heaven? Enough to give up everything? Ask yourself: Has that ever been the uppermost question in your mind? Be honest. Has it?"

Dan shook his head sadly. "No, it hasn't. I admit it."

"Of course not. Things got in the way. You pursued other goals, competed for other prizes, followed other voices. Heaven was just a nice idea that you planned to investigate sometime in the future, less urgent than all the other things that were demanding your immediate attention."

"Guilty as charged," Dan said. "I wasted a lot of time."

"Here you're going to see all those things in their proper light and realize how insignificant most of them were. And if you spend your time profitably, your attachment to those things will gradually fade away, and you'll feel your True Desire burning ever brighter. In the end, you will want to be with God more than anything —maybe almost as much as he has always wanted you to be with him. And that's what will lead you onward. Desire will be your compass and your star."

Dan picked up a flat stone and tried to skip it on the water, but it sank with a faint plop instead. It all sounded a bit obvious to him.

33

"Don't overthink this," said Rafe. "Just hike. Enjoy the scenery; savor this opportunity. All those competing voices have been silenced. You finally have the freedom to reflect on things that are really important. Take advantage of it."

Rafe got to his feet. "I should go now," he said.

Buddy jumped up, his tail wagging furiously. Rafe shook his head, and the dog sat down again.

"All right." Dan stood up too. Somehow, he couldn't help feeling he was being abandoned. "Thanks for stopping by, Rafe. I hope we'll meet again soon. I was getting used to your company."

"Don't worry. I'll check in every so often to see how you're doing." He pointed across the lake, where the sun was just sinking past the tallest of the low peaks, bathing its bare stone summit in soft purple light. "For starters, if you're not sure where to head next, you might think about exploring what's on the other side of those hills."

Dan nodded. "Thanks, I will."

"You're going to be fine. Really."

"I'm sure," Dan said. "I can't wait to see more of this beautiful place. I'm so glad Purgatory isn't the way I heard it described when I was a kid. All that smoke and fire and suffering."

The angel stared at him intently.

"There is no evil here, Dan," he said. "And there is no falsehood. But I never said that there wouldn't be suffering."

He turned and walked into the trees.

4

The more one longs for a thing, the more painful does deprivation of it become. And because after this life, the desire for God, the Supreme Good, is intense in the souls of the just . . . the soul suffers enormously from the delay.

—Saint Thomas Aquinas

Dan stared after the angel long after his footsteps had faded into the distance, struggling with a sudden wash of emotion.

"Well . . . okay, then."

The sense of loneliness he had felt before Rafe's appearance was returning with even greater force, and he wondered now if it was more than the usual evening blues, more than a predictable nostalgia for the places and people he had left behind. Those parting words had been strangely disquieting.

He walked down to the lake and stared across the water, listening to the soft rhythm it made as it washed the pebbled shore. The sky had begun to take on a pastel glow of mingled blue and apricot as the sun slowly made its way behind the hills, and a few tentative stars were already appearing. Buddy had followed him, and they stood together silently in the gentle light.

Somewhere up the trail, back in that wide sloping

meadow they'd come down on their way to the lake so many hours ago, a bull elk bugled: a strange, eerie, whistling cry that echoed from the stony heights. Dan wasn't sure what that sound meant to an elk, but to him it spoke of sorrow, loss, and deep regret. It struck him to the bone, and he felt a sudden, painful tug of homesickness.

What am I homesick for?

He knew that feeling from many a campout. You began with a beautiful evening, a crackling fire, good companions, and the languorous relaxation that creeps over you at the end of a satisfying day. And then, in the middle of it, for no discernible reason whatever, you got stabbed with a pang of melancholy so pure and strong it made your heart ache. You were lonesome, but for whom? Homesick, but for where?

Maybe for your real home. The one you remember only in scraps of dream. The one you're always returning to but never reaching.

Quite unexpectedly, he felt an urge to pray. It was an uncomfortable impulse, since prayer had always made him feel clumsy and self-conscious, but he plowed ahead anyway.

"Hello, God," he said. "You know I've never been very good at this, but I'm feeling a little blue right now, and a little overwhelmed by all the things ahead of me. I want to thank you for loving me, even when I was at my most unlovable. Thank you for the good life you gave me, and for this new life that's ahead of me now. I know I don't deserve any of this."

He sighed in frustration, feeling foolish, and kicked at the ground.

"But honestly, I still don't really know what I'm supposed to do here. All I know is that I'm going to be facing some hard things. That's fine with me. But help me to be brave, and show me where I'm supposed to go. Make yourself more real to me, so that I can love you as much as you deserve. Strengthen my desire. Please. I want it to be the way Rafe described it—my compass and my star."

Buddy whined faintly, and Dan reached down to pat his head.

I could use a few head pats myself, he thought ruefully. *I wonder if that's what I'm really asking for.*

"Come on, Buddy," he said. "Let's take a stroll."

They wandered along the pebbly shore in the soft evening light, and Dan let his thoughts run free. He'd never seemed to get the hang of prayer, and even here in the afterlife it wasn't much different.

After his return to the Church, he'd come to know many men and women who prayed so naturally and unpretentiously that it made him envious. It was as though they had an open line to God—as if they walked and talked with God every day. And what's more, God talked to *them.* They could feel his presence, hear his voice, carry him snugly in their hearts through the day.

Dan had never had any of that. Not as a wide-eyed kid in Sunday school, and not as the sneering know-it-all teen who stomped out of church when he was sixteen, or the sheepish penitent who returned years later, or the stalwart Christian husband and father he'd tried to be for the rest of his earthly life. Only once in all that time, just once, had the silence been broken.

As for his own prayers, they'd usually sounded contrived and pretentious in his own ears—and the more he'd tried to be sincere, the more unnatural they'd felt.

It was as though he were talking into a deep void, a dark well from which no answering echo ever came.

He knew what his old sneering self would have said: *It's because there's nobody there—nobody who's particularly interested in you, anyway. You're just faking it, talking to yourself. And so are all those other delusional people around you.*

He'd hated that sly voice. It had belonged to a life he had put behind him long ago, but it returned with distressing persistence, and it always sang the same song.

Come back to us, sterile and cheerless as we are, because we're the cool kids. We're the smart and sophisticated people. You know you miss us. Come back, because the universe is blind and deaf, and nothing means anything. You don't belong with these church-going chumps. You can be one of us again. You won't have to pretend you're someone you're not, and nobody will make fun of you anymore.

Sometimes he'd wondered if he was doing something wrong—if there was a technique of some kind that he hadn't mastered, or if he'd always been too busy talking at God and not enough time listening for the things God was trying to tell him. Finally, he'd gone to his parish priest for advice.

"Relax, Dan," Father Nick had said. "It's okay that you don't hear God talking to you. It's not a punishment for your sins or a flaw in your technique. This is a discipline. Long ago the Lord cured you of your wandering, faithless heart, and now he's teaching you another kind of skill—how to stand firm and steadfast. He is teaching you how to wait, and that's a hard lesson. I think it's especially hard for you."

That was certainly true, he admitted. Waiting had never been his strong suit. But eventually he'd made a sort of peace with the silence. He'd spent a good deal of time meditating on the role of the watchmen who seemed to be mentioned a great deal in the Bible—lone sentinels posted on the walls of the ancient cities to warn the inhabitants of approaching danger.

It must have been lonely, tedious work, standing up there through the cold starry nights, trying to stay alert. Not a glamorous job. But Dan had done his four years in the Army, and he'd understood the principle: you go where you're told to go, and you stand your watch until you're relieved. He'd memorized a line from one of the psalms to get him through those times: *I wait for the Lord, my soul waits—and in his word I hope; my soul waits for the Lord more than watchmen for the morning, more than watchmen for the morning.*

He found it comforting to see how often the writers of the New Testament epistles—Paul, Peter, James, and John—urged new Christians not to give in to boredom or fear, not to be distracted by novelties or fall back into old habits but just to hang in there and keep the faith.

My prayers may be shallow and unimaginative, but I will pray anyway, he'd told himself over and over. *I may feel as if I'm just going through the motions, but I'll keep going through the motions, because the alternative is even worse. Someday I'll see him and hear his voice, and I'll finally get it.*

But here he was, in a reassuringly benign afterlife—he'd just had a conversation with an angel, for Heaven's sake—and his prayer life still didn't seem to have improved much. He'd expected to feel more . . . spiritual or something. But mostly what he was feeling was this ache, this longing. This incompleteness.

There were more stars now. They glowed in the sky,

and their reflections danced on the luminous surface of the lake. He could hear the soft murmuring sounds of birds settling down for the night among the reeds and grasses.

"It's probably time we headed back," he told Buddy.

Quietly, they returned to the campsite in the fading twilight. There was a mingled scent of pine and balsam poplar in the air, a comforting smell that reminded him of his childhood in the northern forest country.

He thought of Anna again, and all the many camping trips they'd shared. Those had been wonderful times, and he thought of how much she would have loved this spot by the water.

But those days belonged to the distant past, he reminded himself. The kids were taking trips with their own children now, and Anna's hiking days were far behind her. Memories were sweet things, but you couldn't cling so tightly to them that you missed what was coming next.

I always knew I'd be taking this journey by myself, he thought, *but I never expected to feel so lonely. Once a watchman, always a watchman, I guess. God, please take care of my sweet wife and my children; I can't watch over them now, but I know you've always been better about that than I ever was.*

Buddy pushed his way into the tent—wet fur, sandy paws and all—as soon as Dan unzipped it, settling down contentedly beside his sleeping bag. Dan was more fastidious—he took his boots off and left them outside.

"Let's get some sleep," he told the dog. "Tomorrow will be another big day."

5

She was truthful when lying was the common speech of men; she was honest when honesty was become a lost virtue; she was a keeper of promises when the keeping of a promise was expected of no one.

—Mark Twain, *Joan of Arc*

Dawn came with a thunder of wings, as thousands of waterfowl rose from the lake into the rosy sky. Awakened, Dan emerged from the tent and stood up to look around; across the water, the hilltops glowed softly in the sunrise, but the rest of the land around him was still in shadow.

"Good morning, God," he said. "Thank you for the good night's rest, and for this beautiful day!"

The night had been cool—good for sleeping—and the air still carried a chill, so that his breath steamed a little as he set up the camp stove to heat water for coffee and breakfast. Buddy trotted off to a nearby tree, and Dan walked down to the lake to wash up. Stripping off his clothes, he plunged into the water and gasped at the bracing cold of it.

Hearing a heavy sloshing noise behind him, he turned to behold a sight that made him catch his breath. Down the shore, not more than twenty yards away, a huge bull moose with impressive antlers was wading majestically through the shallows, dunking its head into the water to scoop up big dripping mouthfuls of vegetation. Dan had encountered a few moose before, but never one so enormous or so close. It was a sight that lifted his heart but also made him more than a bit nervous.

The creature grunted a testy good morning to him, but didn't seem particularly disturbed at his presence. He watched for several minutes, then slowly and carefully made his way back to the shore to towel off, dress, and return to the campsite. A moose might be perfectly harmless in this place, but he knew it was never wise or polite to disturb a wild animal at breakfast.

Hot coffee and instant oatmeal did a lot to energize him and clear the remaining cobwebs from his brain, and it was a quick job to clean up the dishes and put things away. By then the moose had moved on. The sun had risen over the cliffs he and Buddy had descended the day before, and the air was noticeably warmer. He set about breaking camp, rolling up the sleeping bag and shaking out the sand Buddy had brought into the tent before stowing it all in his pack.

"Okay, pal," he said to the dog. "What's the best route around this lake? Right or left?"

Buddy looked at him happily, barked twice, and wagged his tail, but those were his only contributions. Apparently, no magical canine directions would be forthcoming.

"All right, then. You had your chance. Left it is."

There was enough stony beach above the waterline to make passage around the lake relatively trouble free, though they had to splash across several modest creeks and skirt a small marsh along the way. As the morning continued to brighten, Dan found himself glancing up to the peaks that rose above the opposite shore. Now completely illuminated by the sun, their lower slopes were covered with trees, ascending to form gently rounded granite domes that emerged from the greenery and into the sky.

It was a beautiful morning, and the sun felt good as they made their way along the shore, stopping to admire a heron fishing in the shallows and a flight of cranes that passed high overhead, making their weird rattling cries. Buddy was displaying some of his Labrador pedigree, splashing through the water and swimming after sticks that Dan threw for him.

It took several hours for them to reach the far side of the lake. Looking across the water now, Dan could see the stand of trees that marked their former campsite, and the long rocky meadow rising beyond it to the cliffs. Ahead of him, a faint game trail led up from the shore through a maze of low bushes and into the pine-covered foothills.

Somewhere off to the left, he could hear a persistent rustling sound. Searching the hillside, he noticed that one of the larger bushes near the game trail was shaking. And for a moment he assumed he'd come upon a bear or some other large and potentially fearsome animal. Instead, to his astonishment, a young woman suddenly stood up at the edge of the path, beaming with excitement.

"Good morning!" she said brightly. "I found blueberries! Lots of them!"

"And good morning to you!" he replied, nonplussed. "I have to say, you're quite a surprise."

"Seriously, these are amazingly delicious! Oh, hello, Buddy." The dog had bounded ahead at the sound of her voice and was already standing beside her, looking up and wagging his tail exuberantly. "You're Dan, aren't you? I've been watching you two coming along the shore for quite a while now. Isn't this just the loveliest day?"

Her good spirits were infectious, and Dan found himself smiling back as he approached. She was tall and auburn haired, in her late teens or early twenties, dressed in jeans, a sky-blue polo shirt, and light hiking boots, and she carried a nylon day pack. All in all, she seemed confident and friendly . . . and for some strange reason, unsettlingly familiar.

"You know my name," he said. "Have we met before?"

"No, I'm afraid we haven't." Her smile faltered, but only for an instant, and she held out a berry-stained hand. "Everybody calls me Amy. It means beloved, you know."

Dan chuckled. "No, I didn't know that. But I can see why it would suit you. I'm pleased to meet you, Amy."

"I'm very pleased to meet you too! Sorry about the sticky hands. Really now, try some of these before I eat them all myself."

He looked, saw that the bush was loaded with fat, cloudy blueberries, and had no trouble plucking a handful that he popped into his mouth. "You weren't kidding," he said. "They're really tasty."

"I never kid," Amy said solemnly.

Dan looked at her more closely. "If you don't mind my asking, what are you doing out here all by yourself? Are you an angel too?"

She giggled. "Nope, not an angel. Just a girl out for a hike. But I'd love to walk with you for a while, if that's okay."

44

"We'd be glad for the company, wouldn't we, Buddy? As soon as you've finished your snack, that is."

"Oh, I've had more than enough. Just give me a second to wash up, and I'll be ready." She stepped down to the lakeshore, rinsed her hands in the water, and looked up at him. "Which way would you like to go?"

"You seem to know your way around here," he said. "I was hoping you might have some suggestions."

"I may not know as much as you think," she said, settling the small pack more securely on her shoulders and looking up at the granite outcroppings above them. "You were already starting up this hill, weren't you? I think that would be a nice way to go."

They headed up the faint trail, with Buddy in the lead and Dan taking up the last place. As they climbed the gentle slope, the scrubby vegetation gradually gave way to an open forest of pine and aspen, filled with flickering light and freshened by the morning breezes. The air was cool and fragrant with the fresh scent of the trees, and they soon fell into a comfortable rhythm.

Amy was a confident, energetic hiker, and he found himself working to keep up with her. She also proved to be an enthusiastic observer of their surroundings, eagerly pointing out each of the many things that delighted her—a flight of birds winging their way through the forest understory, a massive rock that reminded her of a crouching bear, a clearing carpeted with tiny sweet-scented flowers.

"Isn't it beautiful?" she exclaimed over her shoulder. "I'm so grateful for this lovely day, and I'm so glad to be sharing it with you. Right now, my heart is so full that . . . so full that just saying 'Thank you, God' doesn't seem like enough. But thank you, God, anyway!"

What an unusual young woman, he thought. Not at all the way his own kids had been at this age—so cool and unimpressed, wary of betraying any enthusiasm that had not already been approved by the stern jury of their peers. It was a pleasant surprise.

The sun was nearly overhead by the time they broke through the tree line and found themselves near the summit: a scattering of broad granite domes rising from the forest like the skyline of some fabulous city from the *Arabian Nights*. Below, a panorama of woods, plains, and lakes surrounded them on all sides. In the far distance, the high snowy peaks he'd first glimpsed from the cliff top reared up against the deep blue sky, shining in the midday light.

Here on the bare rock, there was room to stand side by side. Amy turned to him and smiled as he caught up to her. *Does she ever stop smiling?* In silence they looked out over the landscape around them. Buddy, who had run ahead as soon as they emerged from the trees, came back and sat beside them, panting contentedly.

"It's beautiful country," Dan said appreciatively.

"Yes, it is. And I think it's also time for some lunch." She scanned their surroundings briefly and pointed to a spot on a nearby dome, off to the right, where the rock bulged out to form a natural bench shaded by shrubby twisted pines. "That looks like a good spot for a rest."

"Lead on, and I'll follow," said Dan. Gingerly, they made their way down the slope, hopped across a small fissure, and climbed to the spot Amy had chosen. It felt good to be able to shrug out of his pack and sit for a while. He handed Amy his water bottle, and she accepted it gratefully, taking deep appreciative swallows as he watched in fascination.

"Let me see what I can find here," he said, rummaging through his pack. "I think there's some trail mix and granola bars in one of these side pockets."

"Oh, I think we can do better than that," said Amy with a mischievous grin. "I brought sandwiches."

"For both of us?"

"For both of us. And I promise you'll like them."

She was right, of course. They were his favorite: fresh whole-grain bread, dark and fragrant, with thin-sliced ham, smoked cheddar, pickles, and mustard.

"I'd have been happy with peanut butter and jelly, but this is glorious," he said happily. "Thank you, Amy!"

She beamed at him.

"You're very welcome!" she said. "And since I brought the food, you can say the blessing."

And so he did. As he repeated the familiar words, looking up across the lowlands toward that glittering range of distant peaks, he felt her hand come to rest lightly on his own. Startled, he glanced over and saw that she was watching him; somehow it didn't feel strange or inappropriate. As he recited the threadbare table blessing he'd learned as a child, he noticed that the prayer seemed somehow more *resonant*.

Naturally, the sandwiches were every bit as good as they had looked. Buddy even accepted several bits that Amy offered him, though Dan suspected the dog was just being polite.

They sat on the ledge in contentment, gazing out at the scenery below them as they ate, and Dan found he was having difficulty trying to start any kind of casual conversation. None of the usual opening lines seemed appropriate with this young woman.

"So, Amy," he began tentatively, "tell me a little about yourself."

"There's not very much to tell," she said brightly. "Honestly, there isn't. I'd much rather hear about you."

"All right, then. I'm seventy-seven years old—at least that's how old I was until very recently. I have to say that I really don't feel that elderly. I wonder if these numbers even mean anything now. Do they?"

She shrugged. "You're asking the wrong person, I'm afraid. But they obviously mean something to you."

"Well, seventy-seven was as far as I got. I was born in Minnesota and lived there almost all my life, except for a four-year stint in the Army and some time away at school. I was an attorney, and by the time I retired, I was a partner in a large Saint Paul law firm." He glanced at her and saw that her eyes had returned to the landscape again. "I'm already boring you, aren't I?"

"Well . . . none of those things really means anything to me," Amy said apologetically. "I'm sorry, Dan, but they don't."

The angel said there would be no lying here, he reminded himself wryly. *Guess I can't say I wasn't warned.*

"I want to hear about your family," she said, with a sudden eagerness. "Tell me about your wife. Tell me about your children."

"My wife's name is Anna. We were married for, gosh, more than fifty-five years. She's a wonderful, kind person, and she was my best friend in the whole world. A great hiker too. Not as tough as you, maybe, but you'd have loved her."

"I'm sure I would," said Amy, as though she really meant it. "Tell me more. How did you meet? How did you decide to get married? What was your life together like?"

Dan held up his hand, laughing. "Whoa!" he said. "That's a lot of questions. The first one is the easiest: We met in high school. I sat behind her in chemistry class, and after the first couple of weeks Anna started helping me with my homework. She could see that I was really terrible in that class. She always used to say that my personal chemistry made up for it."

Amy laughed.

"She was very pretty—thick chestnut hair and a sweet, round face—and she had a cheerful personality." He smiled, shaking his head. "But I have to admit that what attracted me the most was the way she looked at me, as though I was the most important person in the world. Anna boosted my self-confidence, and I think I really needed that. One day I worked up the nerve to ask her out on a date, and that's how it began. We went to a football game, and I took her out for a hamburger afterward."

"And then?"

"Then . . . well, we dated on and off all through high school. My family loved her, and her family seemed to like me. When I enlisted and had to leave Saint Paul for training, we decided we couldn't stay apart any longer, so we got married. Not in a church—that wasn't a part of our lives back then. But it was a nice little wedding, and we were happy together."

Amy shot him a penetrating look.

"Happily ever after, then. Like in the fairy tales?"

Dan shook his head slowly. *All right*, he thought. *No lies, no excuses.*

"No, not like that. Not at all like that. We were happy for a decent interval, and then I began to act like a selfish fool. There was a long, terrible, painful phase in our marriage that brought us to the brink of divorce—and I'm sure it would have been over between us if Anna hadn't been such a patient, faithful, forgiving wife."

She was still staring intently at him, nodding, and he flinched from her eyes, staring instead at the ground.

"I don't like to think about that time now," he said. "It's frightening when I realize how it could have ended, how much I would have lost. Thank God, things turned out very differently."

"Yes," she said. "Thank God."

"I do, Amy. I thank him every single day." He stood up, dusted his hands, and reached for his pack. "Shall we get started again?"

6

Every saint has a past, and every sinner has a future.

—Oscar Wilde

Amy looked up at Dan, and he could see she was disappointed. "There must be more," she said. "How about children? You haven't even mentioned your children."

"Oh, there's much more," he said with a smile. "I guarantee, once you get me talking, you'll never be able to shut me up. But I'm an attorney, and we do all our best talking on our feet." He looked around at the rocky heights that surrounded them. "Where should we go now?"

"That way, of course," she said, rising to her feet and pointing west toward the distant mountains as if this were something Dan should already have known. "But I'm not really sure how we get down from this place."

Dan reached down to scratch Buddy behind the ears. "Let's ask this guy," he said. "He's always had a good nose for this kind of thing. What's your opinion, pal?"

The dog barked, happy to get started again, and they followed him across the rocks, scrambling over the bare domes and squeezing through the overgrown passages between them until they found a dry gully that led gently downward. It would become a good-sized stream during rainy season, Dan thought.

"We have three children," he began as they picked their way among the stones and boulders of the wandering streambed, "but they're not really children anymore. Brendan is the oldest; he's living in Florida. Sara is our middle child; she lives in Minneapolis with her husband and two grown kids of her own. And Paul, our baby, is also married and living in Arizona; he and his wife have one son."

"They're pretty spread out, then?" said Amy. "Did you get to see them often?"

"Not as often as I would have liked," he admitted. "Except for Sara, who stayed pretty close to home, they did seem to migrate away when they got the chance. I guess that's how the world works now, and I certainly didn't try to discourage them. But it would have been nice to have had them around a little more often."

She nodded thoughtfully. "I'm sure I would feel the same way if it were me. But tell me, what was it like for you when you first became a father? Can you remember when you first found out?"

"Oh yes, of course," he said with a chuckle. "It was a long time ago, but I remember it very well. I had never expected to be a dad—the truth is, I'd been altogether against the idea of children for many years. Anna and I had our careers and a comfortable lifestyle, and I was full of nonsense I'd picked up in college about my responsibility to do something about overpopulation. So we got a dog instead."

"Dogs are nice," said Amy, scratching Buddy's neck. "But they're not people."

"No, they're not," he agreed. "Looking back, I can see

that I just wasn't ready to grow up. Being responsible for another person's well-being—even my wife's—seemed like a huge burden, and the idea of children terrified me. But then . . . well, something happened. Something huge and frightening. And when it was over, everything had changed. Everything."

To his surprise he found he couldn't speak anymore, and for once Amy didn't press for more details.

They hiked in near silence for the next hour or so, as the sparse vegetation of the summit gave way to taller, thicker forest and ever-deepening shade. Finally, they found themselves at the bottom, in a vast wooded hall of evergreens whose massive trunks rose around them like the pillars of a great cathedral.

Pine needles carpeted the forest floor, interspersed with tall, glossy ferns. A light mist seemed to float close to the ground; dim spears of sunlight pierced the canopy overhead and lanced down through the trees. Ahead was a wide trail—almost a road—winding its way through the woods. This was a quiet place, its silence broken only by an occasional burst of birdsong.

"How enchanting," said Dan, his voice very soft and subdued. "How magical."

Amy nodded. Together, they followed Buddy into the forest.

"Now," she said solemnly, "tell me about your children and how it was when they were growing up."

The trail was wide enough for them to walk comfortably beside each other, and the pine needles muffled the sound of their footsteps. It was a much better venue for conversation than the trail down the hillside had been. He still found himself speaking in hushed tones, as though they were in church, but somehow that seemed appropriate.

"You have to understand, Amy, that by the time Brendan arrived in our lives, I was no longer the same man I had been," he said. "I wasn't perfect, and I'm still not perfect—but I had changed. It was as though something dark and cold inside me had died and something else had begun growing in its place, getting brighter and stronger every day."

"I think I understand," said Amy. "New life was growing in Anna, but it was growing in you too."

"Well, yes." He glanced at her, surprised. "Yes, it was. And I still remember the night my son came into the world. It wasn't an easy birth—Anna was in labor for hours on hours, and finally she was so exhausted that the doctor decided to do a C-section on the spot. I was there in the room, praying like I'd never prayed before, when they opened my wife's abdomen and brought my son out into the light. It was terrible and wonderful all at the same moment—fear and joy mixed together—and praying was all I could do."

Amy said nothing, but he could feel her attention growing as she walked beside him.

"Brendan was kind of gray and blue, all covered with blood and mucus—but he was breathing, and he was beautiful! Afterward Anna was still sedated from the surgery, so they brought him to me to hold, wrapped in a little blanket. I sat there, rocking my son and looking down into his tiny peaceful face and thinking to myself, 'You fool, you almost missed this. You almost missed all of this.' And I blessed him, and thanked God for him."

He glanced over at her and saw that there were tears in her eyes. *For whom?* he wondered. *For me?*

"Don't stop," she said. "Tell me more."

And he did. In fact, he talked himself almost hoarse during their long journey into the forest, describing the births of all three children and every milestone he could remember in their lives together—including dozens of stories he had long forgotten: the birthdays, the school days, the baptisms and First Communions, the music recitals and basketball games, the long walks, the camping trips and beach vacations, the quiet winter evenings reading together by the fireplace.

He talked of watching as those three youngsters emerged from childhood into adulthood, adopting the distinct personalities that became their own, and about the pride and the unavoidable sorrow he and Anna had felt over those changes. He spoke of his children's triumphs and their heartbreaks, the commencements and marriages, and the peculiar grief that parents endure when they must watch their children struggle and suffer and are powerless to intervene.

He felt it all flowing through him as he spoke, a parade of memories and emotions that had blurred and faded over the years and were now much clearer, brighter, and more intense. It was invigorating to relive them again.

Amy was an attentive listener, carrying his monologue along with questions and comments, laughing when he remembered a funny story and growing quiet when he spoke of a tragedy.

"They're grown now," he said finally. "They're leading their own lives, in other places and with other people. That was probably the hardest thing Anna and I had to learn—that it's not just the children who grow. We had to teach ourselves to say goodbye to one part of our parenthood so we could embrace another part, and to say that goodbye over and over again, no matter how much it hurt. To accept that they didn't belong to us, and had never really belonged to us. That they belonged to God, who could love them and guide them much better than we had."

They walked on. Hours must have passed already; even in the shadow of this tall forest, he could feel the change. Evening was coming.

"Thank you for sharing all this," said Amy at last. "They were very lucky to have you as their father."

He shook his head. "No. It's just the opposite: I was lucky to have *them*. I never deserved any of this, Amy. To be this happy. To have had so much joy. It should have gone to a better man than I was."

"That's not how he works," she said quietly.

"No, it isn't." He glanced up at her, brightening. "Now look what I've done! I warned you that I could talk a blue streak—see what happens when I have a good audience? And you haven't told me a single story about yourself. Did you ever marry, Amy? Did you have any children?"

She shook her head and smiled.

"It's like I said when we first met. There's really not much to tell."

"Everybody says that, but nobody really means it."

"I really do." Briefly, her eyes flashed. "I suppose that makes me a pretty boring conversationalist."

"Not at all. The best conversationalists are people who let everyone else do the talking. But it does make you a very mysterious young woman. All day, I've been feeling that I know you from somewhere, that we must have met before."

"No," she said. "We've never met."

He took several steps before realizing that she had stopped in the middle of the trail. Buddy was standing beside her, gazing up at her face.

"It's getting late," she said. "You'll need to set up camp soon, and I'd say this looks like a pretty good place."

They had reached a small clearing in the forest, where the light was bright enough for a few small trees and bushes to take root and grow. She was right—it did look like a good spot to spend the night. Dan looked at her, puzzled.

"What about you?" he asked.

"I have to move on. It's time for us to say goodbye now."

He felt a sudden and unexpected sadness that surprised him by its intensity. "Can't you stay a little longer? I'll cook dinner. We'll talk more."

"No." She looked even more deeply at him, and there was something new, something tender, in her eyes now. "I'm sorry. I really have to go."

"But we were just getting to know each other."

"It was a wonderful day," she said. "I'm so glad I had this chance to meet you and hear your stories. I learned so much. And you were such a great father."

"No, I wasn't. I was just enjoying myself, doing what anyone would do."

She pursed her lips impatiently and gave her head a quick little shake. "Stop that. You were a fantastic dad. Exactly as I knew you would be."

He peered at her. "What are you talking about?"

57

"There were so many people praying for you," she said. "You have no idea. People here and people in the world. Praying that you would find the strength and courage and love to be a good husband, a good father, a good man. I was one of them. I prayed for you every day for years and years and years, and my prayer was answered. You *were* wonderful. Just the way I always imagined you would be."

Dan stared. "Who *are* you?"

There were tears gathering in her eyes, and her voice had grown thick with emotion. "My name is Amy," she said. "It means beloved."

Something was stirring in the back of Dan's mind, but he couldn't grasp it. "I don't understand," he said.

"You will." She quickly brushed her tears away. "Please don't try to follow me. You can't go where I'm going. Not yet."

"Amy, I don't—"

"Just know that I love you," she said. "I've always loved you, Daddy. Always."

She kissed him lightly on the cheek and slipped away into the gathering dusk.

He stood there, astonished and confused, as her soft footfalls faded and the forest grew completely still. Finally, long after she was gone, he nodded his head slowly. It had finally begun to make sense.

"Oh, Amy," he said. "Oh, sweetheart. I'm so very sorry."

Buddy looked up at him and whined softly.

7

As a child, ashamed, stares at the ground and cannot speak, but hears and knows himself for what he is, sorrowing in the knowledge, so stood I.

—Dante Alighieri, *Purgatorio*

He did not cook dinner that night. He didn't even have the heart to put up the tent. Instead, he dragged the sleeping bag out of his pack and sat at the edge of the clearing, watching the stars come out one by one as the sky darkened. There were fireflies in the forest; they floated silently through the dim trees, blinking softly. There was no wind.

But the tranquility of his surroundings did nothing to calm the seething turmoil in Dan's mind. Memories assaulted him—there was no other way to describe their force and intensity. The easy flow of reminiscence he'd shared with Amy all day had been nothing compared with this. It was memory raw and bleeding, scoured of all justifications and ambiguities, stripped of all the mind's efforts to soften, forget, and excuse. And it was not remotely pleasant.

THEY WERE SITTING in his car, and it was raining—a hard rain that beat down and drummed relentlessly on the roof. He didn't look at the woman beside him, and she didn't look at him. They both stared out at the water that poured down the windshield in thick streams, as if it held some answer for them.

Her name was Melissa. She was twenty-four, blonde, energetic, and a little on the plump side. They had met months before at an office party, and Dan had found her carefree enthusiasm a welcome change from the tension and tedium he'd been feeling at home. But she was not carefree this afternoon, and neither was he.

"Are you sure?" he demanded, turning to her.

"No, I'm not. But I'm a month overdue, and I thought you ought to know. Normally I'm very regular."

"And you're sure it was me?"

She looked at him, shock and hurt on her face. "What do you think?"

He leaned back in the seat, sighed deeply, and stared forward again. This was definitely not fun anymore. He was working hard to suppress the rising panic and irritation he was feeling.

"All right, then," he said finally. "What do you want to do?"

"I don't know what to do," she said miserably. "I just thought you should know. Don't be angry. I'm scared, and I don't know who else to talk to."

"I'm not angry, Melissa," he said, although that was a lie. In his mind he was already blaming her. He'd assumed she was using birth control, like all the other women he'd hooked up with over the past few years. Why in hell hadn't she said something? "I know this is scary for you, and I want to help if I can. But there's only so much I can do."

She said nothing. The silence settled over them again.

It was a far cry from the wild, panting episode that had taken place the last time they'd been in this car together.

"I'm married, remember?"

"You never let that stop you before," she said sullenly. And he had to admit, she was right. It hadn't stopped him with Melissa, or a dozen before her. He searched desperately for something to say, but the words that came out of his mouth next sounded vile even in his own ears: weak, cowardly, and despicable.

"I have money," he began. "If you need any help with, you know, taking care of this situation . . . I could—"

She turned to face him, horror and loathing in her eyes.

"You mean an abortion," she said. "You think I want your money? To kill my baby?"

"Melissa, I—"

But she already had the door open and was scrambling out of the car. "I should have known it would be like this."

"It's raining, Melissa. Get back in the car. At least let me drive you home."

"I'll walk, thanks." She was already soaked. "You can go home to your wife."

She slammed the door and walked off into the downpour. He watched her go, feeling guilty, scared, and desperate himself. But what was he going to do? Follow her down the street?

He sat for several minutes, then started the car and drove off. He didn't drive home; instead, he spent the next few hours driving aimlessly along the streets of the neighborhood.

Even in his customary state of self-delusion, he had to admit that it wasn't hard to figure out how he had gotten

61

to this point in his life. He'd been playing this game for a long time, and his luck had finally run out.

It had begun years ago, when he was an awkward, bookish, and solitary kid who didn't have much luck making friends with boys his own age. Girls had always seemed more sympathetic and attentive, and he'd come to depend on that attention, working hard to be charming and likable, and gravitating toward girls who were as shy, self-conscious, and hungry for kindness as he was. And although there was a certain amount of fumbling sex involved, the real goal was always an emotional one.

He would feel all the excitement and happiness of starting a new romance, the warm glow of feeling valued and treasured, and finally the tragic drama of the breakup. There was always a breakup—sooner or later one of them would get bored or exhausted, or someone else would come along. It was a kind of emotional joyriding: exciting but temporary, and highly addictive.

In his own mind, at least, he was a nice guy. A thoughtful guy. A guy who knew all the right things to say, who understood and respected women. And what was the harm, anyway? Both parties got what they wanted.

In some corner of his heart, he could recognize those rationalizations for what they were. He knew that what he was doing was not at all thoughtful or understanding but selfish, monstrous, cruel, and pathological. But he never let that stop him, and none of the young women ever told him to stop either.

Anna had been the one girl in all his high school dalliances who'd been different. She was steadier, more seri-

62

ous, and seemingly aware of some quality in him that he was unable to see himself. They dated on and off several times, and in the end Dan decided she was his best shot at becoming a healthier, more dependable man.

And so they were married. Not in the Church, of course; he'd left all that behind to pursue his career as an adolescent Romeo. Still, he had stood before the judge with Anna, promising to be true to her for the rest of his life, and for eight years he had managed to keep that promise—in the strictest sense of the word, at least. In reality, he was still acting like a single man, constantly flirting and responding to flirtation.

And in the sexually liberated world of the 1970s, there was a great deal of flirtation going on, especially in the professional milieu where Dan was starting to make a name for himself. Suddenly there were admiring women everywhere, all wanting to know him better and not particularly caring that he was married; for some, it even seemed to add to the attraction. And they were openly, bluntly, and avidly interested in sex.

To a man with Dan's desperate appetite for attention, it was like heroin. Finally, he fell. And he kept falling, again and again. He became a popular figure, a man about town—sensitive, polite, and charismatic, a supporter of all the correct causes and a possessor of all the correct opinions—but in a small corner of his soul he despised what he had become. He'd been cheating on his wife for almost three years now, and things had gotten only more frantic and difficult to control. This time, he realized he might have painted himself into a corner that he couldn't escape.

He finally arrived at the house, two hours after Anna had gotten home from her own job and made the usual excuses for his lateness. But he was distracted and evasive during dinner, and she eventually gave up trying to engage him in conversation. He stole occasional glimpses across the table at her, watched her picking at her food. She looked . . . so sad. He felt ashamed and angry with himself.

Mostly, though, what he felt was fear: the fear that he would be caught, unmasked, and exposed for the fraud that he was and had always been. It made him feel small, petty, and dirty.

The fear didn't go away. In fact, through the nights and days that followed, it grew and festered, feeding his self-loathing and poisoning his time at home and at the office. During their evenings together, Anna responded with sadness, worry, and a concern for him that eventually faded into resigned detachment. But even in the throes of his panic, he noticed that she didn't show any particular surprise at his behavior.

Like the coward he was, he didn't try to contact Melissa. Finally, though, after several anxious weeks, he got a phone call from her at his office.

"It's good to hear from you," he said with feigned heartiness. "How have you been?"

"I've been better," she said. Her voice was flat and cool. "I just called to tell you that you don't have to worry about . . . what we talked about before. It was a false alarm."

An intense, gratifying wave of relief swept over him. It was like being released from prison. His heart sped up, and he began breathing normally—realizing only then how

64

abnormally his body had been functioning since that day in the rain.

"That's great news, Melissa," he said. "But how are you feeling? Are you all right?"

"I'm fine. Like I said, you don't have to worry anymore. Okay? It was a false alarm."

A shadow of unease stirred in one corner of his mind.

"False alarm? What does that mean?"

"It means you don't have to worry anymore." Again, that unnerving flatness in her voice. "There's no problem. I made a mistake."

"Well, all right. All right. Well, I'm sorry if I acted like a jerk before, but I'm sure you're as relieved as I am."

"There's one other thing," she added. "Please don't call me or try to get in touch with me ever again. I thought you were a kind person, but now I know that you aren't. You aren't really a very nice person at all, Dan. You use people. You're really smooth in the way you go about it, but that's what you do. And I don't ever want to see or hear from you again."

She hung up before he could say a word. In any other circumstance he might have felt hurt, misunderstood, or even regretful about the end of the affair—but he was too relieved to give it much thought. He had dodged the bullet. Disaster was no longer staring him in the face. Life was good again, and now it was time to patch things up at home.

He finished the day's work with enthusiasm, made dinner reservations at Anna's favorite restaurant, stopped at the florist shop for roses, and hurried home through the rush hour traffic. This will never happen again, he told himself. I'm never going to let this happen again. Filled with good intentions and warm feelings, he pulled into the driveway and practically bounded into the house.

The dog was there to welcome him, tail wagging furiously. But his wife was not. Instead, there was a hand-written note on the kitchen table.

Dear Dan,

I don't think you realize how very much I love you. You are breaking my heart. You've become so cold and distant, so preoccupied and worried. I feel completely locked out of your life, and I know that you've been lying to me about a lot of things.

When we got married, I promised to be with you forever, and I've tried to keep that promise. But I'm starting to think that I can't do it anymore.

I've gone to stay with my mom for a while because I want you to have some time to think about this. I really want to believe that there's still hope for us. I really want to believe that you can be the man I thought you were. But I can't live like this anymore, Dan. I'm sorry, but I can't. You're trying to live two lives, and you need to decide which one you really want.

Please don't call me right now. You really need to decide whether you want a life with me in it, or one without me.

Anna

He stared at the note. A wave of nausea and panic swept over him. He couldn't breathe, and he was certain he was about to throw up.

Oh no.

That was the only thought in his head. *Oh no. Oh no. Oh no. Oh no . . .*

8

If we take what is often vaguely called "a more spiritual attitude to life," we find that we are postulating
some large and lazy cosmic benevolence which ensures
that, no matter how we behave, it will all somehow or
other come out right in the long run. But Christianity says, "No. What you do and what you are matters, and matters intensely. It matters now and it matters eternally; it matters to you, and it matters so much
to God that it was for Him literally a matter of life and
death."

—Dorothy Sayers, *The Meaning of Purgatory*

Dan couldn't remember falling asleep, but he obviously
had. He woke up in his sleeping bag—stiff, chilled, and
damp from the morning dew. Sunlight was sweeping
down strong and dazzling through the trees and into the
clearing. There were birds singing, and he could smell
. . . coffee?

It was. He sat up at once and looked around. Rafe was
sitting on a log several yards away, sipping from a large
steaming mug that read *Give Thanks in All Circumstances*.
Buddy, that fickle dog, was lying happily at his feet.

"Good morning, sunshine," said the angel. "You must
have had a bad night. No offense, man, but you look like
hell."

"No offense taken," Dan groaned. "Yes, it was a bad night, and hell is exactly what I feel like. Give me a minute, will you?"

He struggled out of the bag, stumbled off into the woods to relieve himself, and returned feeling slightly less sluggish. Rafe held out a second mug.

"Try this," he said. "It's one of my favorites, a Guatemalan dark roast from the mountains above Antigua. I figured you might need something better than freeze-dried this morning."

"You figured right, friend," said Dan, accepting the mug and inhaling the deep, rich aroma. "Thanks!"

"All thanks to God, who made the humble coffee bean," said the angel, raising his own mug in a sort of toast.

"Amen to that."

They sat side by side on the log for several minutes, enjoying the fragrant brew and listening to the soft sounds of the forest as it came awake around them. Rafe pointed to the far edge of the clearing, where a doe and two fawns grazed among the tall grass, stepping delicately in and out of the shadows.

"All she wanted was someone who would listen to her," said Dan. "I realize that now."

"Just so I'm sure . . . who are you talking about, exactly?"

"Melissa. Don't pretend you don't know, Mister Dark Roast Guatemalan Coffee."

"Not pretending," said the angel. "Just making certain we're clear."

Dan stared down at the mug in his hands. "She didn't want my advice or my money, or for me to do anything," he said. "She just wanted me to listen, because there was nobody else she could go to. And all I saw was a problem to be solved. My problem, not hers. All I wanted was to make the problem go away." He looked up. "And the problem's name was Amy, wasn't it?"

Rafe nodded somberly. "I'm afraid so."

"So what happened? All this time, I've been telling myself that the pregnancy was just in Melissa's imagination, just a panic over a late period, but it was obviously more than that. Give it to me straight, Rafe. Did she have an abortion?"

The angel shook his head. "It was a miscarriage," he said. "Very sad, and very hard on Melissa. It haunted her for a long, long time. She even named the little child."

"Amy. She said it means beloved."

"And she is beloved, Dan," said the angel with a gentle smile.

"So, all of what happened yesterday—meeting her and hiking with her—that was part of that penitential suffering I'm supposed to be doing here?"

Rafe shot him an impatient glance. "If that's how you want to look at it," he said. "But you could also consider that Amy has waited years for the chance to see you, talk with you, and listen as you spoke about your life. She loves you because you're her father. And her love is perfectly pure, without the least bit of self-interest or complication. She never lived long enough to acquire any of that. You were her hero."

"Some hero," said Dan in disgust. "The only thought I ever gave to her—ever—was when I wanted her to disappear. It doesn't matter that Melissa didn't abort her. The truth is, in that moment I wanted her to."

The angel shrugged. "She loved you anyway. That's what pure love can be, Dan. In your worst hour, the hour when Amy was born into eternal life, she knew instantly what you were. More important, she also knew what you could become, and she made you her personal project. All this time, she's been storming the gates of Heaven on your behalf."

"So, I owe her my life," Dan said. "Don't I?"

"Yup. You really do."

He shook his head slowly. "This is going to sound really ungrateful, but I don't know that I can bear the weight of that love. I don't deserve it. I can't repay it."

Rafe stared at him solemnly for several seconds, saying nothing. Dan dropped his gaze and looked off to the edge of the clearing, where the doe and her fawn were still nibbling at the grass.

"And Melissa? What became of her?"

The angel shook his head slowly. "Sorry, Dan," he said. "That's not my story to tell. Someday you'll learn all those things, but this isn't the day or the place, and I'm not the one you should ask. I can only tell you that things didn't get better for her. That's the simple truth." He finished his coffee and stood up. "Time for me to be going. And time for you to break camp and get back on the trail. You've got a lot of ground to cover."

Dan nodded and rose. He felt sick to his stomach.

"I don't know what to say," he mumbled, holding out the empty coffee mug. "Well, thanks for the coffee, anyway."

"Keep the mug," said Rafe. "Consider it a gift." He hitched his day pack, studying Dan's face. "It's all a gift.

Everything. You don't deserve it, and you can't repay it. You can only show some gratitude. Get used to that."

He turned and headed toward the trail. The dog whined softly but didn't try to follow. Dan looked down at him and bent to pat his head.

"Looks like it's just you and me again, Buddy," he said. "Let's get ourselves ready."

It didn't take him long to break camp, since he hadn't really unpacked the night before. It was the work of a few minutes to wash up, brush his teeth, and stuff the still-damp sleeping bag into the top of his pack.

He was just getting ready to leave when he heard a faint rhythmic drum of footfalls and looked up to see the first runners passing by.

There were six or seven of them, men and women, moving swiftly and gracefully as a herd of deer through the distant mist-skirted trees. They didn't stop or even slow down, although one smiled and gave him a friendly wave as they went by. Dan raised his own hand tentatively but then thought better of it. Who were those people, he wondered, and how could they move through this place with such supple confidence?

He watched, surprised and perplexed, until they passed out of sight and hearing. Then, shrugging his pack on— somehow it felt heavier than it had the day before—he, too, set out along the trail. Whoever the runners might be, they seemed certain of where they were going, so he decided it would be wise to follow them.

The woods that had felt so stately and contemplative the day before now seemed to wear a different aspect. There was an air of somber melancholy to the massive trees that surrounded him, and the constant twilight of the forest felt oppressive. He walked slowly, feeling weary, clumsy, and discouraged. There was a knot in his stomach, and a pain in his chest that he couldn't dislodge or wish away.

Lack of sleep, he told himself. But he knew that it was really the encounter with Amy and what she represented —the lowest and shabbiest moments of a low, shabby past —that had startled and unsettled him so profoundly. For the first time, he was beginning to wonder about what awaited him at the end of this journey and whether he would have the strength to face it when the time came.

Not punishment. He could handle that, because now he realized he deserved it—in fact, he was growing more and more certain of that fact by the moment. No, he could endure punishment. Even welcome it. What he couldn't bear was what he had seen in Amy's eyes and heard in her voice—the weight of that undeserved forgiveness, that undeserved love, that debt he could never, ever repay. It grew heavier with every step he took, until he felt as though it would crush him.

HE READ ANNA'S NOTE over and over again. Each time, it provoked a different response. Panic, anger, fear, sadness, despair—and finally, remorse.

She had known.

Over the last few years—perhaps even longer—he'd persuaded himself that, all in all, he was a pretty good fellow. A sensitive, caring guy, dispensing sexual and emotional healing to neglected housewives and frustrated bachelorettes. Even his dishonesty was a sort of compassion, he told himself; if Anna didn't know what was going on, she wouldn't ever be hurt by it.

But he hadn't been nearly as clever as he'd thought he was, had he? Anna *had* known. She may have known all along, in fact, and she must have been carrying that pain silently for a long time.

Suddenly the truth was staring him in the face, and it wasn't pretty. This wasn't one of those insipid romantic comedies in which the beautiful characters have great fun with new and exciting sexual partners without anybody getting hurt, and he wasn't some amiable chap having a little harmless fun. He was an adulterer, a liar, a phony, and a cheat. He'd been using women as if they were characters in his own private movie—not as fellow human beings whose hearts could really break, whose lives could really be ruined. He'd trampled on his wedding vows as if they were so much trash and wounded the one person who had ever truly loved him.

He spent the evening sitting in the empty living room, staring out the front window and thinking about all the things he had spoiled. He wanted to call Anna, to apologize, to promise her that everything would be different. But he knew better than that. She would see his promises as another lie, and she would be right. He was not a man but an overgrown, selfish child who could not be trusted to keep any promise, and she was right to ask him to stay away.

When he finally went to bed, his sleep was fitful, his dreams unpleasant, and morning was no better. Work brought some relief, since he was able to lose himself in the sheer volume of briefs and documents waiting on his desk, but all afternoon he pondered the bleak evening that waited for him. He thought about going out for a few drinks or a movie—but that seemed even more pathetic. Instead, he drove home, took a long run with the dog, and came back to ponder the situation he'd created for himself.

For years he'd been living in a fantasy world, staving off reality with regular doses of fake romance. But reality had been waiting for him all along, and in all that time it had been accumulating interest. He was going to have to deal with the consequences of his actions—and even that would not magically free him from the self-loathing that was clawing at him now.

He had to admit that there was a sort of poetic justice in it. There he was—the man who couldn't bear to be alone, who couldn't even be certain of his own existence unless he could see himself in the admiring faces of pretty women—sitting in an empty house, contemplating the ruins of his life.

What am I going to do? he wondered. But no matter how many times he asked the question, there was no answer.

Finally, on the third day, he did something he had not done since childhood, something he'd sworn he would never do again. He started to pray.

In his misery, he'd started remembering fragments and pieces of sermons he thought he'd slept through as a kid, stories and prayers the sisters had made him memorize in elementary school. He remembered music echoing in the high vaulted spaces and the feeling of peace he had known, however briefly, in those days. It didn't seem as pointless or as laughable now as it had when he was sixteen.

He was still not entirely sure that there really was a God —a God who cared enough to listen to prayers, anyway

—but to his own surprise he found himself down on his knees on the living room carpet, pushing the Sunday *Times* out of the way and wondering how to say what was welling up in his heart.

"Help me," he said. "Help me, God. There's something wrong with me. Something is broken. And I don't think I can fix it by myself."

He knew it wasn't a very good prayer. In fact, it was kind of halfhearted, because at some level he wasn't entirely sure he even wanted it answered. What he really wanted was for the whole mess simply to disappear so he could start feeling good about himself again. The last thing he wanted was more pain.

And that's when he heard someone say, "Face the pain, son. For once in your life, take it like a man. Nobody can help you until you stop running away."

Was it God Almighty or his own feverish imagination? Whoever it was, it sounded a lot like his old drill sergeant back at Fort Benning, and it spoke a message he really, really hadn't wanted to hear. Which, strangely enough, made it more believable.

By the time he got up from the floor he felt wrung out and wobbly, but for the first time in years he also felt at peace—the kind of peace that comes from knowing what you have to do and being resolved to do it. He had his marching orders now, and he knew if he just followed them he'd be all right.

He took a long walk to clear his head and get his thoughts in order. Somehow the world looked entirely different to him now. The people seemed friendlier, the colors seemed brighter, the sunlight felt warmer. And when he got back to the house, the first thing he did was to pick up the phone. His wife answered on the second ring.

"It's me, Anna," he said. "Before I say anything else, I just want you to know that I love you, and I'm so very sorry for what I've been putting you through. Can we get together and talk?"

To his great relief, she said yes.

9

Our souls demand Purgatory, don't they? Would it not break the heart if God said to us, "It is true, my son, that your breath smells and your rags drip with mud and slime, but we are charitable here and no one will upbraid you with these things, nor draw away from you. Enter into the joy." Should we not reply, "With submission, sir, and if there is no objection, I'd rather be cleaned first." "It may hurt, you know." "Even so, sir."

—C. S. Lewis, *Letters to Malcolm*

The forest was vast and unchanging. Day after day, Dan followed the trail without a sight of open sky. Each morning he rose in gloom and shadow, broke camp, and trudged in silence through the endless dusk of dense forest, pitching camp only when it was impossible to see his way forward. Each day the memories assailed him—especially at night, when his sleep was fitful and dream haunted despite his weariness—and each day he felt slower and more discouraged.

Something in his heart—a massive logjam of denial, forgetfulness, and concealment—had been shaken loose by that day with Amy and the truth about himself that it had revealed. It was as though a great backwater of stale, stagnant water was pouring through his memory:

a lifetime's accumulation of self-indulgence, cowardice, and small-mindedness. Every betrayal and transgression, every casual cruelty and thoughtless word, was there in unmistakable, inescapable detail.

And there were so many . . . so many. More than he could ever have imagined. Every time he thought he'd come to the end of it, another dismal crowd of them would show up, waiting to be recognized, acknowledged, and added to the list.

It did no good to remind himself that these were, by and large, the shoddy everyday sins of every man's life. Or to tell himself that he was no great sinner compared with some people he could mention, or to comfort himself that he had made up for any of it through good deeds or charitable donations, or even to remind himself that he had already asked for forgiveness and—thank God!—it had been granted. The flood of memories was relentless, and there was nothing he could do to turn away from it.

Here is what you were. Here is what he forgave, and it was no small thing.

Surveying the damage he had left behind him in his seventy-seven years, he was deeply and profoundly ashamed. There was so much of it, and some of it was sickeningly vile. But the greater quantity—great heaps and piles of it —was simply infantile. Trite and asinine. Stupid.

There were no more visits from Rafe. Occasionally he saw more of the mysterious runners passing through the most distant trees; some were solitary and others in small groups, but none came as close as the ones he'd seen that first morning. Sometimes he wondered if they were even real. They passed silently, effortlessly, always in the same direction, following what had to be a different way through the forest. He envied them their speed, their confident grace, but was no longer tempted to call out.

The journey did have its minor consolations. For one thing, he never seemed to have to worry about his food or water supply—no matter how often he dipped into the pack for a drink, a snack, or a meal, it was always well stocked. For another, Buddy was the perfect canine companion, never running off after squirrels or deer, as he so often had done in his earthly existence.

Eventually Dan stopped keeping track of how long he had been traveling through the dim, needle-carpeted wood, pursued by memories of his worst and darkest moments. It had certainly been more than a few days—for all he knew, it might have been several weeks. He awoke in misery, walked in misery, and fell asleep miserable and exhausted. Eventually the unceasing stream of memories no longer even had the power to appall him. It had grown mind-numbingly repetitious, predictable, and tiresome.

How could I ever have thought of sin as something exciting? he wondered. *In the end, it was all so pedestrian, so stupid, so . . . boring.*

Finally, late one afternoon as he shambled along lost in thought—how painfully appropriate that phrase sounded now!—he began to notice a brightening of the air ahead of him. He'd grown so accustomed to the gloom of the forest that the light seemed strangely, unnaturally intense. Thick, warm, and honey-gold. It wasn't evenly diffused either; instead, it seemed to be coming from a distinct area to the right of the trail.

The radiance grew stronger and more defined as he quickened his pace, and before long he realized that it had to be coming from a clearing of some kind—a large clearing, and not all that far ahead. With every step he took, his surroundings grew clearer, sharper, and more detailed. Through the trees he began to catch glimpses of blue sky and sunlit foliage, and finally the forest opened out before him like a pair of welcoming arms to disclose a beautiful, sun-drenched lake.

It was a small forest lake, nothing more—but after so many days and miles trudging through shadow, he found his heart filling with gratitude and simple, uncomplicated happiness. The calm water reflected the deep blue sky with heaps of snow-white clouds. Hemlocks, maples, and oaks were filled with birdsong, and everywhere he saw clouds of colorful butterflies and squadrons of darting dragonflies—all brilliant and transfigured in the light. He raised his face and felt the sun's welcome warmth soaking into him like a healing, soothing salve.

"Oh my," he breathed, dazzled by the unaccustomed brilliance that surrounded him.

It was the perfect place to set up camp, and he wasted no time finding a pleasant spot between the evergreens and the shore. Within minutes, he'd put up his tent and hung his musty clothing and damp sleeping bag out to dry. Then, stopping only to shuck off his clothes, he ran straight for the water and plunged in with a loud, exuberant splash. Buddy's ancestors had been bred for swimming, and he needed no encouragement to follow.

The water was perfect: clear, cool, and clean. Dan swam underwater for several yards before surfacing and rolling over to float on his back. He blinked up happily at the sun, the sky, and the encircling trees, feeling the stiffness and weariness begin to leave his body. The sorrow and discouragement that had oppressed him during his endless journey through the forest seemed to fade as well, and he dared to wonder if he might finally have exhausted the long, dismal recapitulation of his sins and misdeeds.

On a sudden impulse, he swam back into the shallows. Standing in the knee-deep water, he grabbed handfuls of clean sand from the floor of the lake and rubbed them briskly over his body from head to toes, scrubbing his skin until it was red and tingling. Then, with another mighty splash, he dove and swam, dove and swam—over and over, welcoming the coolness of the water and the feelings of clarity and freshness that it brought him.

Afterward, he and Buddy stretched out in the sun, letting it dry and warm them and watching it move steadily toward evening. As the afternoon lengthened, the light grew thick and syrupy, illuminating the tiny insects that played in the air above the lake so that they glowed against the dark trees like dancing stars.

This is a good place, Dan told himself as a flock of swans circled the lake and landed on the water with a series of loud machine-gun slaps before coming to rest in perfect, placid silence. *I think it would be good to stay here awhile— just a day or two. I can wash out these clothes and rest a little, and maybe start putting things back into perspective.*

He leaned over to pat Buddy's damp head. "What do you think? Should we stick around here for a couple of days?"

Buddy's tail gave an answering thump—but that, of course, could have meant anything. Dan got up and made dinner, and when it was done he and the dog returned to the shore and resumed their quiet reverie. Memories continued to drift back into his consciousness, but this time they were different. There was sweetness in them, and healing, and Dan was glad to return to them.

HE AND ANNA WERE SITTING on the sandy beach below the high bluffs of Afton, watching the Saint Croix River roll past on its way to the Mississippi. Their blanket was shaded by overhanging maples, but across the river in Wisconsin the shore glowed warm and radiant in the afternoon sunlight.

He had decided to have this discussion not at the house or in a restaurant but here at the state park—one of Anna's favorite spots and the place where he had asked her to marry him so many years before. He'd packed a picnic lunch, picked her up at her mother's place, and driven here in a jumble of fear, remorse, and excitement. In some ways, it felt as though he were proposing to her all over again—except that this time he wasn't nearly as confident that she would accept.

Anna looked at him with what he wanted to interpret as a guarded hopefulness.

"All right, Dan," she said. "Here we are. I guess the question is, where should we go from here?"

She was a patient woman, but he could see from that look that she was nearing the end of her patience. He knew—he knew to the bottom of his heart—that he had finally learned his lesson and found the will to change the way he'd been living his life. But after so many failed attempts and so many broken promises, he wasn't sure he could convince his wife that this time would be different —that now he possessed the moral strength to turn good intentions into reality.

He took a deep breath.

"This isn't easy, so forgive me if I stumble a bit," he said. "First, Anna, I need to tell you that you are absolutely the best thing that ever happened to me in my whole life—beautiful and loving, patient and kind, without a doubt the most wonderful wife a man could ask for. I plan to remind you of that every day for the rest of my life, but it still won't be enough."

She waited, and he could see that she was still unconvinced. She'd heard pretty words from him before, and didn't seem inclined to let them sway her now.

"But there's no hiding the fact that I haven't loved you in the way that you deserve to be loved," he added. "I've been selfish and insensitive and cruel, and I've dishonored the vows I made at our wedding. I've never treated you with enough respect or affection. I've acted as though you were the least important thing I have—instead of a treasure that I should cherish, protect, and honor, every moment of my life. It's not just that I've been a bad husband—I haven't really been a husband at all, because I've never learned how to love you the way you ought to be loved. To tell the truth, I don't think I've learned how to love anyone."

Ever the consoler, she reached a hand toward him. "Dan . . ."

"No, Anna. You know it's true. Even when I seemed to be thoughtful and kind, I've been acting like a character in a book or a movie, watching myself and congratulating myself. It's always been about *my* feelings, *my* needs, *my* self-esteem."

He looked at her bleakly. "There's something in me that's broken. I think maybe it never worked right to begin with."

83

She pursed her lips and stared down at her lap for several seconds before speaking, very quietly. "So, is that it then? Are we done?"

"No, no, no. That's not what I'm trying to say at all." This time he was the one who reached out, grasping both of her hands with his own. "I'm not just trying to flatter you when I tell you how precious you are to me. What I'm trying to say is that I understand that if I lose you, I'll lose everything. I've been spending a lot of time thinking about this over the last few days, and I realize that this isn't something I can fix with a few promises and good intentions. I have to change deep inside. I have to become an entirely different man."

Anna looked up at him. Her face was somber, but he felt a slight squeeze from her hands.

"I'm listening," she said. "Go on."

"I've also realized that it's not enough just to say I'm going to change. I need to start doing lots of things differently, concrete things. I need to start now and never turn back. And I need you to help me with this, because I can't do it alone."

She looked intently at him. "What kind of things are you talking about, Daniel?"

"First, I have to change the people I spend time with. From now on, there will be no single friends—especially women—and no married friends who act as though they're single. And I'll be coming straight home every night after work. There'll be no after-work socializing, no evenings out, unless we go together as a couple. You're the most important person in my life, and you're the person I'm going to spend all my time with."

She nodded. "All right. That would be a nice change."

"Then, when the time is right, when I've shown both of us that I can do these things . . . I think we need to talk about having children."

Anna stared at him in astonishment. "Really?"

"Really."

For the first time, he saw the first tentative twitch of a smile. "Okay, who are you, and what have you done with my husband?"

"You've got it backward," he said. "I'm your husband. That other guy was just somebody you used to date. He always said he wasn't ready for kids, but I think what he really meant is that he wasn't ready to grow up."

She shook her head. "Having children shouldn't be a means to some other end, Dan—even if it's a good end. It isn't something you do as a favor to your wife or because you're trying to fix your marriage."

"I get that," he said. "I really do. But I've decided that this is something I really want. I'm not afraid of it anymore."

She stared across the river, saying nothing. Although her silence made him nervous, he knew better than to disturb it.

"This is a pretty ambitious plan," she said finally. "Are you sure you can actually do this?"

"Not by myself, no. That's why I'm asking you to help me. I'm going to need you to hold me accountable for keeping these promises and not let me get away with anything." He paused, uncertain now, but took the plunge anyway. "And there's something else. Honestly, Anna, I think I'm going to need more help than even you can provide. I want us to start going to church together."

Shocked, she turned to look at him. "Church? You're kidding, right?"

"Anna, something's been happening to me. I'm not exactly sure what it is, and I don't even feel very comfortable talking about it. But I've spent a lot of time alone lately, and some things have become clear to me. One of them is that there really is a God who loves me, who loves both of us and wants to help us stay together. I thought I'd stopped believing in him, but it turns out that I haven't."

"And this makes you think you need to go to church."

"That's part of it, yes. I want to learn how to love, Anna, and I'm pretty sure that this is where I need to start. I want to surround myself with people who will help me be a better man, a better husband—and a better father—instead of people who don't really care about any of those things." His head was starting to ache, and his voice was getting wobbly with emotion and embarrassment. How ironic that this, of all things, was turning out to be the hardest part of his speech. "I'll do it alone if I have to, but I'd much rather do it with you."

She nodded slowly, regarding him with an appraising stare that he wasn't sure how to interpret.

"All right," she said finally. "I have to give you credit for determination. I'm willing to try."

THE SUN WAS ALREADY going down, leaving a gentle peach-colored blush in the western sky, and the first few stars were coming out. Dan leaned back and sighed; it had all been so long ago, and yet it felt so fresh in his mind. But that, after all, was the beginning. The point

86

where his life and everything in it had taken a sudden jolting turn into undiscovered territory.

By all rights, it should never have happened, he thought, watching as a generous slice of moon rose bright and clear over the trees. *I didn't deserve any of it. Oh Lord, it would have served me right if you'd left me sitting in the wreckage of my life, but you were merciful instead. You gave me a new life, and you gave me back my self-respect. Thank you from the bottom of my heart.*

Buddy sat up straight and listened attentively, whining softly. Faintly, Dan could hear the distant, high yowls of coyotes across the lake, greeting the moon with their strange, evocative, melancholy voices. It was an oddly comforting sound.

"Come on, Budster," he said. "Time for bed."

They spent two days at the lake, doing very little. Dan washed and air-dried his clothes, but most of the time he and Buddy wandered the shore, swam, sat around the campsite, and took long, lazy naps. Dan's memories were as sharp as ever, but now they revolved around Anna and those years of their miraculously reinvigorated marriage: the arrival of Brendan, Sara, and Paul, the thousands of celebrations, adventures, heartbreaks, and farewells that made up the story of their life together.

On the morning of the third day, he decided it was time to resume their journey. The forest was still there, waiting with all its shadowy depths, but Dan felt a new confidence as he and Buddy returned to the trail, a rising sense that he was prepared for whatever might come to him next. One day passed, and another. Dan spent a great deal of time praying and pondering, but the woods held only coolness and quiet now, and he was content.

Gradually, he began to detect a change in the sounds around them. The rushing whisper of wind through the high treetops, rising and falling like a constant refrain, was now joined by a deeper, stronger note. It was almost a physical vibration, a low throbbing in the atmosphere that grew steadily more insistent, drowning all other sounds, until he realized it had to be the thunder of an unseen waterfall.

Even so, he and Buddy hiked for another hour—through ever-increasing noise and a penetrating mist that crept through the trees and soaked everything around them—before the forest parted and they found themselves standing at the edge of a deep canyon beside the heart-stopping majesty of an enormous cataract.

The waterfall was an all-out assault on the senses, and it was magnificent. Several hundred feet above them, a titanic river was pouring through a chasm of slick black rock, leaping out into space and shaking the ground far below with the force of its impact. After the dim light of the forest, the blue sky and white water were almost blindingly bright. Clouds of spray and mist were constantly churning up from the bottom, and the sound was deafening.

He felt his heart expanding at the beauty and grandeur of it all, and tears came to his eyes.

"I had forgotten," he said. "You were with me all this time. Even here. Thank you."

IO

I believe—I daily find it proved—that we can get nothing in this world worth keeping, not so much as a principle or a conviction, except out of purifying flame, or through strengthening peril.

—Charlotte Brontë, *Shirley*

He stood in wonderment for a long time, reveling in the majesty of the scene. Eventually, though, he turned his attention to a few practicalities. Beautiful as it was, this waterfall presented him with a major challenge: the river was wide and fast, and although he could see that the forest resumed on the far side of the canyon, there was no way to get there. There were discernible paths to his left and his right, and he would have to choose one. Upstream or downstream?

"Any ideas, Buddy?" he asked the dog. As usual, all he got in reply was an eager look and an unhelpful tail wag.

"All right, then. I choose upstream."

It wasn't an easy path. Even well back from the river the rocks were slick with spray and moss, and the ascent was dauntingly steep. On his left, the forest pressed against him, lush with undergrowth thanks to the open sun and abundant moisture; on the other side, just a few yards away, the river rushed past in a dizzying display of power, the falls thundering in the background. Dan threw himself into the climb with a fierce intensity, reveling in the chance to get some strenuous exercise.

He had to admit that it felt good to be climbing. Buddy, soaked to the skin, led the way up the rocky bank toward the lip of the falls, looking happily backward now and then to make sure Dan was following. Great white-headed bald eagles dipped and circled in the sky overhead. Every so often, one would dive into the water and emerge with a flapping silver fish in its talons.

By the time Dan and Buddy reached the top—and it took nearly an hour—Dan had learned to appreciate the cool spray but was more than ready for a rest. He stopped and turned to survey the scene behind him, where the river churned and foamed as it made its way downstream—a silvery blue snake coiling away between dark cliffs. In the distance, beyond a lush green forest broken by outcroppings of rust-red stones, an immense body of glimmering, sparkling water spread itself across the horizon, vast and beguiling as an ocean.

"Thank you, God," said Dan. "And not just for the scenery. Thank you for giving me a challenge to help me escape from my head for a while. If you'll just guide me, I promise to follow. Right now, that's my only desire."

He turned his attention back upstream, where the view and the noise were almost as dramatic. Here the mighty river flowed through tall crags of smooth basaltic rock, rushing through a maze of huge, water-smoothed boulders before launching itself into the abyss below. Cliffs rose straight up out of the water on both banks for at least a hundred feet. Dan could see a narrow trail on his side that led diagonally up the face of the rock. Apparently, his climb wasn't quite finished yet.

Letting Buddy take the lead, he proceeded contentedly up the path and after a few minutes of careful climbing arrived at the top of the cliff. Here the trail leveled out almost immediately, moving into the trees again and following the river at a close but respectful distance as the gorge grew wider and shallower.

They made their way along its rim, and Dan was enjoying it all. This seemed much more cheerful than most of the walking he'd done in the past week or more—the surroundings were calm, bright, and relatively quiet—and he was able to settle quickly into his usual hiking rhythm.

Still, the question remained: Was he heading in the right direction? The view from the top of the falls hadn't told him much; he'd discovered that this river flowed into a large body of water, but he hadn't seen so much as a glimpse of the great mountain range that he'd been aiming for since his arrival. Was the river an obstacle he would eventually have to cross, or was it a highway that could lead him to the mountains?

Given its width and the swiftness of its current, the question was entirely academic for the moment. Besides, he could tell by the position of the sun that there weren't more than two hours of daylight left, so the first order of business would be to find a good campsite and get properly settled.

He found an appropriate spot a few miles farther upstream, where the canyon ended and the river tumbled happily along beside him through the middle of a wide floodplain, relatively flat, enclosed by tall, wooded hills and populated by low-growing willows, alders, and other shrubs. The soil was stony and sandy for the most part, so it would be an easy place for him to pitch the tent.

He chose a site that was far enough from the river to ensure a good night's sleep—free from the noise of the rapids and under the wide sky, with a fine view across the plain. After his long journey in the shadowy evergreen forest, it felt wonderful to be out in the open again. He even spied a hint of snowy white peeking over the forested hills across the river and suspected it might be the summit of those distant mountains he was searching for.

He made camp quickly, setting up the tent and hanging his waterfall-soaked sleeping bag and clothing over the branches of a waist-high spruce to dry out while Buddy nosed around in search of interesting smells. Dan went down to the river, stripped off his clothes, and bathed in the clear, icy water. It was breathtakingly cold; it cleared his mind and made him feel less raw around the edges.

Reinvigorated, renewed, and suddenly hungry, he set up his camp stove on a flat boulder and heated up a batch of spicy chili from one of the packets in his gear. Buddy wandered over to sit with him—more for the sake of companionship, it seemed, than from any desire to mooch a snack. He still didn't show any appetite, but Dan offered him a taste anyway, and he graciously accepted it. As for Dan, he was content to sit in the open and enjoy a hot meal, listening to the sound of the river and watching the shadows lengthen across the ground.

Evening came gently. The sun went down in a soft glow of gold, rose, and lilac; the moon rose bright and sharp over the hills, casting its silver radiance over the valley and the glittering river that ran through it. In the small trees around them, birds softly readied themselves for sleep, and a quiet peace settled over everything.

It had been days since Dan's memories had contained anything he needed to feel shame or disgust about, and for a moment he found himself wondering hopefully if he might have put all that unpleasantness behind him once and for all. He had a strong suspicion that Purgatory wasn't finished with him yet, but the memories that came to him this evening were gentle and comforting.

THE PARK WAS FILLED with laughter, the shouts of children at play, and the easy talk of adults who had nothing to prove and no one to impress. The aroma of smoke and grilled meat wafted through the air, and Dan was contentedly sipping from a bottle of beer. In this moment, everything around him was colorful, bright, and happy.

It was a church picnic, of all things. And here he was—a husband among husbands, a parent among parents—his own children romping with the other kids, his wife chatting eagerly with the other wives, and he himself having a splendid time.

Who would ever have expected any of this? Not Dan. Not in a thousand years.

A warm breeze rippled through the leaves overhead, and he watched his younger son scrunch his face and toss a beanbag unsuccessfully at the waiting target. He felt a smooth, cool hand on his arm and glanced over to see his wife, smiling into his eyes with a look of calm, contented love.

"This is the best idea you ever had," she said.

"What is?"

"Joining this church. I feel as though we've found a home and a family here. And I'm starting to think that God is not at all the guy I thought he was."

He knew what she meant. Christianity certainly looked a lot different from the inside than it had when the two of them were on the outside looking in.

True to his promise, he'd searched with Anna for a church where they could both feel comfortable. What they eventually found wasn't a Catholic parish—that was a step Dan wasn't sure he'd ever be able to take—but a pleasant evangelical fellowship just a few blocks from their house, with a young pastor and a vibrant social life. Somewhat to their surprise, they discovered they actually liked it—and it almost immediately began to change them.

During the early years of their marriage, they had spent very little time talking or even thinking about God. Now they suddenly found themselves closing doors on entire areas of their lives and opening others whose existence they had never expected. The big, sprawling church became their second home; they started attending weekly Bible classes, immersing themselves in study, joining in all manner of groups and activities. They learned how to pray together, how to ask God for help, how to weather together the inevitable storms that arose during the years it took Dan to clean up the mess he'd made of their life together.

Slowly but steadily, their marriage began to blossom. Anna learned how to trust him again, and he learned how to be the kind of man who deserved a wife's trust. It wasn't long before their children began arriving, which to his immense surprise proved to be an overpowering, indescribable blessing. It wasn't all perfect all the time, because neither of them was perfect—but it was turning out to be a good, sweet, wholesome life. The kind of life he couldn't have even imagined for himself only a few years before.

And as Anna had pointed out, they had begun to see God himself differently—as a person, not an intellectual concept or an impassive cosmic force. A Someone rather than a Something. Someone who offered welcome, forgiveness, and help to anyone who had the courage to accept it, and who loved human beings enough to become one of them, to live among them and die at their hands, in order to save them from themselves. Dan had known the stories, had heard and learned them as a child. But now he was starting to understand what they meant.

He turned to Anna and kissed her. Church picnic or no church picnic, it was a good, long kiss. He had never been happier in his life.

SOMEWHERE IN THE FOREST behind him Dan heard a barred owl calling. Another, farther away, answered.

"This is good, Lord," he said. "Whatever happens, don't let me ever forget moments like this. Don't let my worries and fears keep me from seeing all the beauty, all the mercy you have placed in front of me."

Then, after praying for his wife and for their children, he closed his eyes at last with a deep sense of gratitude and peace.

Dan awoke feeling refreshed and discovered that the morning was already well advanced; the tent was bright and warm from the heat of the risen sun, and birdsong was coming from all directions. He and Buddy emerged under a deep blue sky speckled with tiny cotton puffs of cloud and set about their morning business. Soon coffee was steaming in his mug and apple cinnamon oatmeal was steaming in his bowl, and he settled back to bask in the sunlight and enjoy a leisurely breakfast.

"Good morning, God," he said with a smile. "Thanks for this lovely day, for this good food and the company of this fine dog."

Buddy gave a low growl. Startled, Dan glanced at the dog, then followed his intense gaze across the river, where an immense bear was splashing in the shallows.

There's nothing to worry about, he reminded himself. *No danger, no harm. Just enjoy the bear and the fact that he's here.*

He could tell from its huge size, flat face, and large hump on its back that it was a grizzly, and this was as close as he'd ever been to one. As far as he could tell, it had to be at least five feet high on all fours, and he guessed its weight at easily a thousand pounds. It didn't seem particularly interested in them, which was perfectly all right with Dan. He sipped his coffee and watched until the massive beast finally grew bored and ambled off toward the far hills.

"I guess it's time for us to get moving too," he told Buddy.

It was the work of a very few minutes to clean the dishes, take down the tent, and break camp. Soon they were back on their journey upstream, keeping the river in sight—or at least within hearing—as they made their way through the scrubby vegetation. There was no broad path here as there had been in the woods; what they followed was a faint game trail, likely made by deer and other creatures that followed the river.

It looked as though the floodplain over which they traveled was spreading out into something wider; the hills on either side seemed to be growing more distant, and the land had a more spacious, open feel. The weather was fine—a blue sky marked with curls of high, wind-blown cloud—and once again Dan was reminded of how glad he was to have left the gloom and shadow of the forest behind. A large flock of birds wheeled overhead and sped off to the west, too high to be identified. Others sang their morning songs from nearby bushes and trees, and Dan spotted the unmistakable flash of a brilliant red cardinal.

He stopped at midday for a rest and a snack lunch, watching Buddy sniff at the rocks along the riverbank and enjoying the antics of a pair of otters frolicking in the water, their graceful bodies wet and gleaming, their whiskered faces amusingly cheerful.

Suddenly his thoughts were interrupted by the sound of voices.

Across the river, more brightly clad runners were going by, laughing and chattering as they went. They were heading upstream, too, but didn't seem to be even slightly slowed down by the rocks and brush around them. Maybe the trail was better on that side, he thought.

"Hey, over there!" he yelled. "How's it going?"

"Great!" said the leader of the group, waving cheerfully. In fact, all the members of the little group—at least a dozen in all—waved and smiled at him. But they didn't stop, or even so much as slow down. "Have a great hike!" called the leader, and in a few minutes they were out of sight and hearing again.

Not for the first time, Dan felt an intense pang of longing for his wife and children, remembering the times they'd enjoyed places and moments like this and thinking of the many hikes they'd done together when they were all much younger. Even with a dog to talk to, this journey was sometimes a lonely business.

It would be nice to have a little company, he thought. *Once in a while, anyway.* Sighing, he shrugged his pack into a more comfortable position and kept walking.

After several more hours of upstream travel, he noticed that the vegetation around them was beginning to change again. Scattered groves of birch and aspen appeared, leaves fluttering merrily in the slightest breeze, and their numbers gradually multiplied until he and Buddy were once again making their way through a forest. Unlike the tall, silent evergreens that had shadowed their earlier journey, these woods were filled with light, sound, and constant motion. Birds darted from branch to branch, squirrels scolded from their high lookouts, and chipmunks scurried across the forest floor with chirps of annoyance.

Dan found himself humming a simple, lively melody and was surprised to realize that it was a scrap of Saint Francis of Assisi's "Canticle of the Sun." *Now where did that come from?* he wondered. A good tune, he had to admit, with just the right rhythm for a brisk walk. He even dredged up a few of the words and started singing them out loud:

> All creatures of our God and King,
> Lift up your voice and with us sing!
> Alleluia! Alleluia!
> Thou burning sun with golden beam,
> Thou silver moon with softer gleam,
> Oh, praise him! Oh, praise him!
> Alleluia! Alleluia! Alleluia!

Maybe it was the remembered hymn, or just the joy of singing, but he found himself reliving another set of strong memories. These, too, carried more healing than regret. In the main, they were reminders of the kindness and mercy he'd been shown—by Anna, of course, and by Amy. But also, and most unexpectedly, by his Creator. God's graciousness had been, and still was, an amazing and priceless gift. He felt as though the brief innocence of his childhood had been restored to him—battered and scuffed, to be sure, but still recognizably his.

It's a very untidy outfit you're hooking up with, but
it's the only thing that will be around till the end.

—Walker Percy, to a friend becoming Catholic

It was late morning, so there was no Mass going on in
this dusty, somewhat shabby downtown church. A few
elderly men and women from the surrounding neighborhood were scattered among the pews, quietly praying or
dozing. A soft clatter and scuffle of broom and dustpan
issued from one of the transepts, where an unassuming
custodian went about his work. Even the smallest sounds
echoed through the vast twilight space.

This was the first time Dan had entered a Catholic
church in many years, and it felt both familiar and strange.
Years before, when he and Anna had joined the evangelical fellowship near their home, everything had seemed
simpler and less intimidating. But lately he had been feeling a growing desire to return to the faith of his childhood, and today he had finally decided to take the first
tentative step.

Quietly, he approached the custodian in the transept—
a working man in his fifties or sixties, gray as his nonde-
script coveralls—who stopped to lean on his broom and
peered at him questioningly.

"Is there a priest I can talk to?" Dan asked.

That was all it took. Within minutes, he was being ushered through a side door to the rectory that adjoined the church. The priest, a surprisingly young man who called himself Father Nick, invited him in for coffee and conversation. Even though it was the middle of a working day and Dan had a deskload of unfinished work waiting for him at the office, he avidly accepted.

"I'm one of those lapsed Catholics they talk about," he said once they'd made their introductions.

"I'm familiar with the species," said Father Nick, and they both smiled.

"Okay, then," Dan said. "It's taken me a long time to get back here, Father, and I honestly don't know what's been keeping me away. Pride, maybe. Awkwardness. The fact that I've been pretty happy where I was. Or maybe the fear that I wouldn't really be welcomed back."

"Really?" asked the priest, raising a skeptical eyebrow. "Well, then—in case you still have any lingering doubts, welcome back, Daniel."

Dan grinned sheepishly. "Thanks, Father. I appreciate that."

"I don't mean to pry, but may I ask how long it's been?"

"Since I was sixteen. That would be well more than thirty years, I'm afraid."

The priest nodded. "A lot has happened in that time. For the Church, as I'm sure you know. And also, I imagine, for you. Why don't you tell me a little about yourself?"

"It's kind of a long story, Father."

"Then you're a lucky man, because today I happen to have a good deal of time."

So Dan began, and before long the whole story came

tumbling out, as though he'd been waiting years for just such an invitation. He went all the way back to the very beginning—describing how he'd grown up in what had looked at the time like a securely Catholic family in a securely Catholic neighborhood, attending the parish school, serving at Mass, singing in the choir. Confession on Saturday afternoon, church on Sunday morning.

The rhythms and rules of midcentury Catholicism, with its feasts and festivals, statues and ceremonies, prayers and devotions, had been a snug and comforting envelope to grow up in. There were even times when young Daniel could sense the gleams of an immense, resplendent world hidden behind the day-to-day business of classroom and playground: a realm crowded with saints and angels, redolent of incense, singing, and bells.

"Don't get me wrong," he added quickly. "I was no saint. Like most boys my age, I tried to get around the rules whenever I could—and I had my share of run-ins with my teachers, especially those nuns. But despite all that, I still had this strong feeling of safety and reassurance because of the Church and everything she represented. Which was good, because things at home weren't feeling very safe or reassuring at all."

By the time Dan entered his teens, cracks had already become apparent in his parents' perfect marriage, and with bewildering swiftness the Geary home became a place of apprehension and anxiety. He and his brothers and sisters walked in constant worry that they would say or do something to set off a new round of shouting. They grew silent and anxious and no longer invited friends to come home with them after school.

Dan's ordeal had been especially difficult. As time went

on, he'd become the target of his father's growing anger and frustration, and their relationship descended swiftly into a desperate spiral of passive rebellion, ridicule, beatings, and threats.

By some cruel coincidence, Catholicism seemed to be going through her own domestic crisis just as the tensions in the Geary household reached their peak. When Dan turned to the Church for help, direction, and relief, she had little to offer. The solid, comforting world she had represented only a short time before now seemed weak and faint, guttering like a spent candle. When Dan's parents finally divorced, they also left the Church. And so did their children.

"So . . . how did all of that make you feel—the fighting, the divorce, the lack of attention or interest from your parish?" asked Father Nick.

"At first, all I could feel was relief. When my mom kicked my dad out of the house, that was the end of the shouting, the fighting, and the beatings. And since Mom was busy working at her job and learning how to be single again, we kids pretty much were free to do whatever we wanted to do. No rules, no curfew, no restrictions to speak of."

"And God? What about him?"

Dan sighed. "Look, to be honest, I was relieved not to have him looking over my shoulder anymore. I was tired of commandments and rules, Father. And frankly, I was tired of the Church. The way I saw it, she'd failed me when I needed her the most, and now she seemed useless and irrelevant. If she wasn't interested in me, then I wasn't interested in her. I was more interested in girls. A lot more."

"I see your point," Father Nick said drily. "There you were, suddenly free and unsupervised, a world of romance and excitement spread out at your feet. And all you had to do was turn your back on God."

Dan felt himself growing annoyed.

"Really, it was a little more than that, Father. My family had just disintegrated. My parents had pretty much announced that they were bored with parenthood, with their children, and with each other. All I really wanted was to feel loved, valued, and important to someone. And at the time, an admiring girl or two seemed a lot more appealing than some invisible, distant God whose very existence I was beginning to doubt."

The priest sipped his coffee and said nothing. But the penetrating look he gave Dan spoke volumes.

"Well, I know better now," Dan added lamely. "But I'm a slow learner, and when I finally learned my lesson, it wasn't a very pleasant one."

So he told that story too. And the young priest listened intently, nodding his head from time to time but otherwise betraying no sign of what he was thinking.

"So that's how it ended," Dan said at last. "Once my wife agreed to give me another chance, I found myself back where I'd started—trying to find some version of myself that was truthful and decent and worth salvaging. And somehow that all led me back to God, and to the church."

"But not to this Church, apparently."

"Well, no. Not this Church."

Father Nick studied him for a few more seconds, silently but not unkindly.

"More coffee?" he asked at last.

"That would be great, Father. Thanks." He gave his mug to the priest, who disappeared into the kitchen and returned with it a few moments later. "Am I boring you yet?" Dan asked.

"Not at all," said Father Nick. "I'm finding this very interesting. Please, continue."

"Well, as I said before, I wanted to fix things between me and God, but I couldn't quite bring myself to go back to Catholicism, whatever the reason. It had never been part of Anna's upbringing, and I thought it might be simpler for us to start fresh, with something that was new to us both."

"Sounds reasonable," said Father Nick, leaning back in his chair. "At least you chose something that was recognizably Christian."

"It was more than recognizably Christian, Father. Believe me. I actually learned things there that I should have been taught as a Catholic. Anyway, that's how we started. I realize now that I was mainly thinking about how religion could help me fix what was wrong with my life—that getting up on Sunday morning and going to church would help me be a better husband, a better man. I can't pretend that it didn't help, either, because it did. But I learned pretty quickly that there was a lot more to being a better man than going to church on Sundays. A lot."

The priest gave a quiet chuckle. "Well, well," he said, "imagine that. Let's back up a little, if we can," he added, holding up a hand. "Indulge my curiosity for a few minutes. I'm interested in these things you've been learning that you didn't learn as a Catholic. What kind of things are we talking about?"

Dan shook his head. "Really, Father, I didn't come here to complain."

"Come on, Dan, give it to me straight. Believe me, I can take it."

"Well, most of the things had to do with the Bible. A lot of the criticisms people make about Catholicism are unfair, but they're right about one thing. For all the time I spent in the Church as a kid, I was pretty much a scriptural illiterate when I joined up with those evangelicals. Those guys take the word of God seriously."

"Okay," said the priest, nodding. "Point taken. We still have a long way to go in that department, I'll grant you. Although we're better than we used to be."

"And they taught me a lot about relating to Jesus straight-up and one-on-one, as if he's really a friend and companion. When I was a Catholic kid, I felt as though he was too important and too busy to spend time listening to my problems or answer my questions. If you wanted to get a message to him, you had to go through Our Lady or the saints or somebody else in the chain of command. Those evangelicals don't waste time dealing with intermediaries. They go straight to the top."

Father Nick sighed.

"So what about the Holy Eucharist?" he asked. "You know, where this same Jesus offers you his flesh and blood so that he can literally live within you and transform you from the inside? What about the Sacrament of Reconciliation, where you confess your sins directly to Our Lord and receive his forgiveness from him directly? That sounds like going straight to the top to me."

"But how many people even go to confession anymore,

and how many people who line up for Communion even think about those things?" Dan asked. "I certainly didn't. These evangelicals, Father, they take their faith seriously. They're not just kind and welcoming—they're enthusiastic about their faith. They act as if they really believe, down to the core of their hearts, the things they claim to believe. It permeates everything they say and do, inside the church and out in the world. When you're surrounded by that kind of simple, confident decency, it's hard not to start feeling that way yourself."

"Fair enough, although I think you'll find that there are both groups—the passionate and the lukewarm—in any group of believers. Regardless of denomination."

"The point I'm trying to make is that I can't help but be grateful to those people," Dan said. "I think God worked through their attention and encouragement to heal my life and my marriage and to teach me a different way of experiencing him—one that's been more personal, more friendly than what I knew as a kid."

"You're right to be grateful. Good for them. And yet . . . here you are."

"Yeah. Here I am." Dan laughed with embarrassment.

"Why do you suppose that is?"

Dan looked down at his hands.

"I'm not exactly sure," he admitted. "The Church just keeps . . . calling me."

There was no other way to describe it, and it still baffled him. Why, after so many contented years in the evangelical world, was he feeling this steady pull back to the Catholic Church? It wasn't nostalgia; he was well aware that the self-confident Catholic culture he'd known as a child was gone. It was something else—as if he had missed something important along the way. Something deep and strong that was waiting for him, gleaming like a treasure among the ruins of this ancient, humbled citadel.

It was something mysterious but not at all elusive. In fact, it was all around him now, palpable and distinct, as though the air itself were threaded with invisible conduits of divine grace and presence that could not be replaced by the warmest fellowship, the most inspired preaching, or the most enthusiastic worship services. He found himself longing to encounter God again—not just intellectually or emotionally but in the literal, physical sense that he'd experienced only in the Eucharist, where bread and wine became the actual Body and Blood of Christ.

Dan gestured helplessly. "I don't know what else to say."

Father Nick set down his coffee mug and got to his feet.

"Come with me," he said. "I have something to show you."

Silently, they walked back into the church and stood together just inside the door. Dan's eyes were drawn irresistibly upward into the shadowy vault where painted, gilt stars glinted against a deep blue painted sky, then to the high altar with its needle-peaked reredos and exuberant frescoes of saints and angels rejoicing around the celestial throne. He looked questioningly at Father Nick and saw that the priest's gaze was locked on the massive crucifix above the altar.

It was a traditional depiction of the crucified Jesus, the kind of intense, realistic portrayal that one didn't often see these days, and it struck Dan to the heart. For the first time in years, he gazed upon his Savior in all the ghastly, bloodied horror of his suffering and death, and all Dan's carefully worded pieties melted away.

This is what I did for you, Dan, it said. *This is how much I love you. Do not flinch or turn away. I did not flinch. I did not turn away. Because this is how much I love you.*

Dan stood for a long time, staring up at that haunted, heartbreaking sculpture.

"This is part of the journey too," the priest said. "If you really want a relationship with Jesus, then you have no choice but to accept him on his own terms. You can't pick and choose all the happy things—all the graces and blessings and forgiveness—and then just turn your back on the terrible price he paid so you could have them. If you really want to embrace him, you have to embrace this as well."

Dan nodded in understanding. It had been here all the time, waiting for him to return. Waiting for him to notice and finally understand. The cross was more than a piece of melodramatic artwork—it was a reminder of what it had cost for him to have that all-important personal relationship with Jesus, who had paid for it with his life.

What, then, was he, Dan Geary, willing to pay?

"I have an idea," the priest said gently. "You've already confessed to a great many things this morning. Why don't we go over to that confessional and make it official?"

Dan stared at him, confused.

"You may have thought you left the Church, Daniel, but the Church has never left you," Father Nick continued. "You're still very much a Catholic, and this sacrament—the sacrament of confession—is for you. Right here and right now."

And so—not without a good deal of prompting—Dan

stumbled through the half-remembered prayers, recited the sad list of his sins again, and bowed his head as the words of absolution were spoken over him.

"Your sins are forgiven," said the priest when it was over. "Go in peace."

"Thank you, Father," he said, rising from the kneeler.

"And Daniel . . ."

"Yes?"

"Welcome home."

Slowly and thoughtfully, Dan walked out of the church into the gray and crowded downtown streets. The day was overcast and windy; car horns blared, and there was a muddy smell wafting up from the unseen Mississippi. But he was impervious to it all. He felt as though a great darkness had been lifted from him, as though his eyes and hands and mouth were filled with light. He was luminous. Everything around him was luminous.

12

In the evening of life, we shall be judged on love.

—Saint John of the Cross

This forest of light, with its pale, slender trees and whispering leaves, buoyed Dan's spirits as the day passed and they continued their journey upstream. Overhead, the sky was streaked with swirls of delicate cirrus clouds, like powdered chalk on a bright blue chalkboard.

Now more than ever it was obvious that the trail had been leading them gently upward all day. They had gained altitude; the air felt cooler and drier, and a few of the trees were beginning to sport yellow leaves that shimmered like coins in the breeze. This was good hiking weather, and he was in no hurry to stop.

Another hour of pleasant walking brought them to a small clearing that seemed to have been made for camping. The ground was firm and dry, and several fallen trees lined the perimeter of the space, providing sturdy trunks for sitting. With a grunt of relief, Dan eased his pack down against one of them and began setting up the tent while Buddy made a quick inspection of the site.

Dan quickly completed arrangements for the night and set a pot of water on the camp stove. He was rummaging through his pack for something to heat up when Buddy gave a series of sharp, unexpected barks. Listening, Dan realized that more runners were coming their way—he could make out the thump of their feet on the ground and the sound of joyful, rhythmic singing. It wasn't English, he realized. And this time they were on his side of the river, coming directly toward the campsite.

The sound grew steadily louder for several minutes, and suddenly a small group of men and women burst into the clearing. Surprised to see Dan and Buddy, they stopped abruptly and stared wide-eyed at them, smiling and slightly out of breath. There were seven of them, dressed in bright, loose-fitting clothes and completely barefoot.

"Hello!" said Dan, getting to his feet.

"Good afternoon!" said the first man who had entered the clearing. He had a deep, beautifully accented voice, and his complexion, like that of all his companions, was a rich, gleaming ebony. "Please forgive our intrusion."

"There's no intrusion," said Dan. "I'm really glad to meet you! I haven't talked to any other travelers since I've been here." He held out his hand. "My name is Dan."

"And my name is Jonas," said the man, clasping his hand warmly. "I am pleased to meet you as well, Dan. And these," he added, sweeping his arm around to gather the others close, "are my friends: Maurice, Josephine, Martin, Elias, Victoire, and Thea."

"Welcome," said Dan. "You must be tired. Would you care to sit and rest a bit? I can offer you a drink, and perhaps some food."

Still smiling broadly, Jonas shook his head. "You are very kind, and a little water would be very nice, thank you. Still, I am afraid we cannot stay long. We are on our way to Heaven, and we hope to be there by nightfall."

Dan couldn't conceal his surprise.

"Nightfall?" he asked. "Really?"

"Oh yes!" Jonas and all his friends nodded their heads vigorously. "As you can see, we are not carrying any supplies. Not even so much as a change of clothes. We are bound for Zion, brother, and we cannot tarry along the way."

The smallest and youngest of the women piped up, "But it is very good of you to be so generous, all the same." Thea, he thought it was.

"I must say, I admire your optimism," said Dan, pulling two full water bottles from the pack and handing them around. "My journey seems to be a much slower one."

"That is all right, sir," said Thea, smiling at him. "We may not all travel at the same speed, but sooner or later we all arrive at the place where we belong."

"Well, I haven't seen anyone who is traveling as slowly as I am," Dan persisted. "You must be very fit, to be able to run so well, so swiftly, and for so long."

"I don't know about that," said Jonas, taking a deep drink from one of the bottles and handing it to the man beside him. "All I know is that I just want to be there so very much. To meet my Jesus. I have waited so long, and now I am almost there. Also, I have these kind friends who have come out from there to meet me and to bring me home. With such help, what man would not run like the swiftest deer?"

"It is our great pleasure to be with you, Jonas my brother," said the man called Maurice.

"I'm confused," said Dan. "You can come and go? How is that possible?"

"It is possible because we wanted it so," said Maurice. "If it were not for Jonas, we six would not be here. He was our neighbor and our teacher. It was he who first told us about Jesus and who shared the good story about how much God loves us and how much he did for us. It was he who lived such a life that it made us want to imitate him, and who has prayed for us constantly, all the way to Heaven."

"Yes!" added one of the women. "We have been waiting for this moment for many years, and now we are finally able to show brother Jonas our love and our thanks by sharing these last few miles of his journey. We owe him so much."

"No, no," said Jonas with a self-deprecating smile. "I did nothing exceptional. It is only that these are very gracious people. I am fortunate to have such good friends."

"Yes, you are," said Dan appreciatively, and a little enviously. "Very fortunate."

"But now, as I said, we must take our leave of you." He handed the bottles back to Dan. "We still have many miles to go, and I must confess that I am growing impatient. Thank you, Dan, for your hospitality. It was a pleasure to meet you. We pray that we will see you in Heaven very soon!"

"Yes!" cried the others. "Thank you, Dan!"

And then, as quickly as they had arrived, the seven of them melted into the forest and were gone. The rhythm of their footsteps and their laughter lingered for a few more minutes and then faded away.

Dan stood there, his heart lifted by their display of eagerness, elation, and unguarded obvious love. It had never occurred to him that a journey through Purgatory could be as cheery and sociable as a church picnic. Even his most optimistic expectations about this place had involved lonely trials, solitary remorse, and private struggles without benefit of friends or witnesses.

Considering his temperament and the kind of life he'd led, maybe this was just the way it was for him, he thought. *That watchman in the night, alone on the city wall. A very dramatic image but very depressing in practice.*

But now he'd seen that there could be a different way —and he couldn't help feeling more than a little regret that there had been no exuberant friends waiting to meet *him* at the trailhead. Where were the people *he* had led to Christ, by word or by example? Where were his Thea, his Maurice, his Josephine?

They probably didn't exist.

It was more than just sad. In fact, the more he thought about it, the more deeply troubling it seemed. For all his religiosity, all the changes he'd made to his life, and all those years he'd spent trying to make up for the carelessness and depravity of his youth, was there a single person who was in Heaven—or even on the way to Heaven— because he'd known Dan, met him, or talked with him? Apparently not.

Even his own children, once they were grown, seemed to have gone the way of the world—sleeping in on Sundays and smiling condescendingly at their parents' quaint piety. Dan thought he'd been doing a good job of raising thoughtful young Christians, but his efforts hadn't been nearly as effective as the opinions they'd absorbed in school, at work, and through the news, entertainment, and social media. Watching them drift steadily away had been a profoundly sad experience. He was convinced that somehow he had failed them.

So, if his conversion had been of no use to anyone but

himself, had it really been much more than a personal self-improvement program, with a sprinkling of religion added for flavor? The rock-bottom truth was that he had been given a treasure, a second chance at life, and he'd done very little with it. He'd been surrounded by friends, coworkers, and even family members who desperately needed what he'd been given, but instead of sharing it he had kept it to himself.

Why? he wondered. *Was I afraid? Embarrassed? Or was it something else?*

These were thorny questions, and he pondered them, turning them over in his mind as he cooked and ate his dinner, rinsed the dishes, and sat down with Buddy to watch the sun go down. Once again, his thoughts had awakened a host of the vivid, powerful memories that seemed to be the bone and sinews of this Purgatory experience. This time they were not memories of the ugly, stupid things he had done but recollections of the good he had *failed* to do—the many missed opportunities to give hope, demonstrate love, or share faith.

This round of memories—and there were hundreds of them—came as a tremendous, distressing shock. So many of them were relatively recent—encounters and incidents from a time when he thought he'd gotten his life in order and become a decent, moral person. He was stunned by the sheer number of times he'd ignored the sorrow and desperation around him, and ashamed that he'd never felt particularly uncomfortable about any of it.

The lesson was clear. Although he had started out on his road back to the Church with eager enthusiasm, wanting to spread light and joy wherever he went, that exhilaration had quickly been dulled, tamped down, and worn away.

Somewhere along the way, through weariness, force of habit, or inattention, he'd lost the better part of his passion for God and his compassion for the people around him.

It wasn't as though he hadn't been warned either.

THE CONFESSIONAL WAS DIM, warm, and evocative of his childhood, smelling faintly of incense, furniture polish, and the last occupant's aftershave. Kneeling, Dan crossed himself, spoke the familiar words "Bless me, Father, for I have sinned . . . ," and launched into a brief account of his most recent lapses and misdeeds. The ones he could remember, anyway—and even those weren't particularly memorable.

Suddenly he stopped himself. "Father Nick?"

He could hear his parish priest lean closer to the screen that was supposed to keep them anonymous from each other. "Yes?"

"Don't you get tired of hearing me confess the same boring things every few weeks?"

The priest gave a dry chuckle. "My feelings are irrelevant. You're not confessing to me; you're confessing to God. And what makes you think your sins are boring?"

"It's just the same stuff every time. Small potatoes. I snapped at my wife, I used bad language at work, I had uncharitable thoughts. It's all so . . . trivial."

"What makes you think so? Do you think it's trivial to Our Lord?"

"I can't imagine why it wouldn't be. After all, he's got an entire universe to run, and there's a lot of evil out there. Big evil. I've done some really bad things, but I confessed them a long time ago, and I don't do them anymore. Why should God care about the f-bomb I dropped at the office, or what I said about the guy who cut me off in traffic yesterday?"

"Maybe because he cares about you?"

"Yes, but—"

"Yes, but nothing. When you talk about 'big evil' I assume you mean the front-page stuff—adultery, murder, drug dealing, racism, that sort of thing. And if you're not doing any of those things, good for you. But that means only that you've gotten the easy part out of the way."

"Easy? Believe me, Father, there was nothing easy about it."

"What I mean is that those big-ticket sins are easy to spot, easy to recognize for what they are and start rooting them out. Isn't it much more difficult to see the evil in a harsh word, a nurtured grievance, or a festering envy? A kindness you didn't take time for, a word of pardon you were too angry to speak? Yet each of these things can cause great damage, both to you and to the people around you. And each of them also wounds the heart of God. You understand this, right?"

Dan squirmed uncomfortably on the kneeler. "Yes, Father."

"Good. Because this is not a joking matter. Just as a little stream carves its path into a mountain, these small things can eventually carve deep channels through which your future thoughts and actions will flow, until one day you look into the mirror and see a cold, loveless, self-absorbed man. A man you never intended to become."

Dan grimaced. He understood this all too well.

"If you think that this life of faith is simply about avoiding sin and being a moderately good person, you are seriously mistaken," the priest continued. "Avoiding sin is only the beginning. The object, my friend, is to become holy. To become a saint. To follow the path of excellence. And that isn't something that happens by accident. It takes determination, dedication, and courage. It's not for the fainthearted. Or the halfhearted.

"Each day you must strive to love more deeply and selflessly than you did the day before. That is a struggle that never ends, and you're going to need all the help you can get. So I'd strongly suggest that you come back here often to ask for and to receive the forgiveness of God. And don't worry about boring me. I can handle it."

IT HAD BEEN GOOD ADVICE; he couldn't deny that. But like most advice, it was easy to forget in the hustle and flow of daily life. And that is pretty much what had happened.

Somehow, at least, he'd avoided becoming that cold, loveless man in the mirror. Things hadn't gotten nearly that bad; he'd made generous donations to charity and volunteered his time to the local homeless shelter and soup kitchen. But anyone could have done that. All the while, there had been people in his path who needed more than the checks he wrote or the stew he ladled out.

They'd needed his time, his attention, his love, his forgiveness and mercy. More than anything, they'd needed to know Jesus—and he couldn't remember speaking that name to anyone who wasn't already among his circle of church friends. As far as anyone else was concerned, he might have been a particularly amiable atheist.

What did that say about his love for God? If you truly loved someone, wouldn't you want to talk about that person all the time? If someone had saved your life, wouldn't you want to share that story with somebody who was in the same danger? Wouldn't you make loving him, thanking him, talking about him the very center of your existence? In his brief conversation with Jonas, he'd known in minutes exactly what was most important in that good man's life. Could anyone have said the same about him?

The sad truth, he realized, was that he had settled for far less than what God had wanted for him. He was a son and an heir, a beloved child. He was supposed to "have life and have it more abundantly," to recklessly expand the horizon of his love and his trust, to leave the warm shallows and head out into the deep. Instead, he had accomplished the bare minimum—he'd kept his nose clean and stayed out of trouble, and that was pretty much it.

Sitting there with Buddy in the fading light of sunset, he found himself slipping from simple regret and sorrow into something deeper and more disturbing. *Do I really love God*, he wondered, *or am I just afraid of him?* And suddenly he was reliving, in excruciating detail, a brief but troubling conversation he'd had with his wife many years before.

ANNA LOOKED UP from her reading and stared across the room at him thoughtfully for several minutes. It was early morning, the time when they typically sat together over coffee to study, pray, and prepare for the day ahead. He'd just delivered what he thought had been a particularly clever observation on a passage of Scripture they'd been reading together, but his wife didn't seem very impressed.

"What?" he said. "What is it?"

"I was just wondering how you really feel about God," she said. "Sometimes when you talk, it sounds as if you don't like him very much. I hear respect, gratitude, and admiration, for sure, but I don't think I've ever heard a lot of love or even affection. And I wonder why that is?"

Dan was at a loss for words. He wanted to tell her what a silly notion that was. How could she ever have come up with such an idea? Wasn't *he* the one who had been responsible for all this praying and churching and other godly things?

It had been years since that Easter Vigil Mass when she and the children had been received into the Church. It had been one of the best moments in their shared life, and sometimes he was still amazed by how thoroughly Anna had embraced the faith. Like many converts, she'd taken to it more quickly and more enthusiastically than he himself had, and she was not afraid to challenge him —usually with bull's-eye effectiveness—about his own commitment to the Gospel.

Which she had just done again, in her quiet, incisive way. Something about her observation—the way she looked at him when she made it, the answering twinge of discomfort he felt in his own mind—stopped him from making the automatic denial that was on his lips.

"That's a very good question," he said instead. "I honestly don't think I can answer it until I've given it some thought."

And he did give it some thought. For a while, anyway. But it was an uncomfortable subject, and in the end he decided that there really wasn't much to be gained by brooding endlessly over it. Yes, there were times when he felt as though he feared and resented God. Yes, there were times when he felt like a pawn in some cosmic game. Yes, there were times when he felt as though every other

Christian he knew was more beloved, more blessed, more favored than he was.

But feelings weren't facts, and he wasn't going to slide back into his old way of life just because he wasn't getting regular pats on the back from God. If this was simply the way it was going to be for him, then he might as well suck it up and get on with his life. If there were any deeper ramifications to be dealt with, he'd deal with them at some later date.

BUT HE HADN'T dealt with them, had he? And now here he was at last, in a place where they could no longer be deferred.

If the challenge was to love and trust God and love the people around him—really love them—then he hadn't done such a great job. Quite the opposite, in fact. He may have been pretty good at being friendly and sociable, but the horizon of his love had been pitifully, woefully small.

And if I don't truly love God, I've got no business in Heaven, he told himself. *By all rights, I shouldn't even be in Purgatory.*

This dark train of thought chugged slowly through his brain as he turned in for the night. All the dreams of his fitful sleep were filled with self-reproach. He woke to a cold gray day and took to the trail as soon as he could get packed and ready, but he was only vaguely aware of the terrain through which he and Buddy now traveled.

All day he pushed onward despite the weariness and discomfort, as if he could overcome through sheer force of will the inner turmoil he was feeling. The next day was no different—and neither were the days that followed. The path before them grew steeper and craggier, the river more filled with unfordable rapids. The clear skies he'd enjoyed since his arrival were now interrupted by episodes of rain, cold, and wind.

He became obsessed with the idea that he was approaching some crucial truth he'd been avoiding for a very long time—something deep and dark that lay at the root of all the false turnings he'd taken in his life, all the bad choices he'd made. He could feel it out there, lurking at the edge of his awareness, maddeningly close but just out of reach.

Whatever it was, he was certain that he had to find it, yank it up, and stare it in the face, because unless he could do something about this halfhearted faith, this refusal to love and trust God fully, he would never feel worthy of Heaven. In that place of utter light and clarity, every eye in the universe would be turned on him, and they would see not a friend but a fraud.

It was in that frame of mind, haggard and exhausted with self-doubt, that he finally reached the top of a rock-clogged pass between two dark, jagged peaks and found himself standing before it at last: the goal toward which he had been straining since his arrival in Purgatory.

It was heartbreakingly beautiful. Ahead lay a wide basin of deep green grass, sprinkled with a rainbow of wildflowers and dotted with clear blue lakes. And towering above it all, soaring into the sapphire sky, was the great snowy bulk of the mountain range—distant no longer but filling his entire field of view. Rank upon rank the peaks and summits stood: a shining wall of white battlements streaked with outcroppings of silvery rock, and he knew with absolute certainty that this, finally, was the gate of Heaven.

The wind at his back seemed to be pushing him forward, and the trail ahead looked clear and welcoming. He longed to climb those mountains and to reach what awaited him there. It was a desire so intense that it ached in him like a physical wound. But now—just as strong and just as painful—he also felt the desolating conviction that he had no right to set foot in that place.

He fought back tears. Somewhere ahead was his home. He knew that. But he was an exile, and he was afraid to go home. He had not earned a place there, and now he began to wonder if he ever would.

"No," he said, shaking his head. "Not yet."

Miserably, he tore himself away from the sight, turned from the pass, and retraced his steps down the loose, clattering rocks. Buddy stayed behind at first, barking and whining anxiously, then raced down the slope to confront him in silent reproach.

"Sorry, pal," he said. "I can't go there yet. I just can't."

The dog stared at him sadly for several seconds, then walked slowly past him, up the slope of broken scree and over the rim, finally passing out of sight.

Can't blame him, he thought. *He was here to guide me, and I wouldn't listen.*

What the heck is wrong with me?

Resignedly, he retraced his steps and made his sad way down the mountain—fighting the urge to turn around, run after Buddy, and climb together up that luminous height. He had no clear idea where he should go now or what he should do. All this time he'd had a goal for which to strive, but he'd just turned his back on it. In its absence, any path—even no path at all—was as good as any other.

13

We cannot begin to know ourselves until we can see the real reasons why we do the things we do.

—Thomas Merton

He wandered for days, leaving the river and letting the landscape itself guide him. Gradually he descended from the highlands, passing through forests and valleys into lower, warmer, and drier regions. Eventually, he found himself trudging through sun-blasted scrub and chaparral into a burned and dusty place: a labyrinth of eroded rock spires and crumbling, rust-streaked hills that looked like ancient piles of ash.

It was a place that perfectly matched his state of mind: severe, unappealing, devoid of beauty or adornment. He plodded along for the better part of a day, marinating in the bitterness of his thoughts. Finally, exhausted, he sat on a sun-warmed rock to take a drink, rest his feet, and gather his wits.

"This is not where I expected to find you, my friend."

He looked up. He'd been so absorbed in his thoughts that he hadn't even noticed Rafe's arrival. The angel was back in his ranger's uniform again and looked as though he'd been on the trail all day. There was even sweat on his forehead.

"Oh, it's you," Dan said. "Finally. I wondered what had become of you."

Rafe shook his head mournfully. "Honestly, Dan, you disappoint me."

"Join the club. I disappoint myself too. I'm sure I disappoint God. Apparently, I've even disappointed my dog."

"Pouting doesn't particularly become you, Dan. I doubt that you'll find it very useful either."

"Thanks for the advice," Dan muttered sullenly. "What exactly do you want from me?"

"Well, since you ask, what I exactly want is for you to be happy and joyful for all eternity," Rafe said gently. "That's the truth, friend. And not just because it's my job. Cantankerous and prickly as you sometimes are, I actually like you. Mind if I have a seat?"

Dan shrugged. "Suit yourself."

The angel sat beside him. Neither of them said anything for several minutes. Finally, Dan couldn't take the silence any longer.

"I'm sorry I snapped at you, Rafe," he said. "I don't mean to be ungrateful."

"No problem," said the angel. "I get that a lot."

Dan eyed him thoughtfully. "Looks to me as though you've been having a tough day too. Can I offer you something to drink? I've got water, though it's probably kind of warm by now."

"Actually, I think I may have something a little better." Grinning, Rafe reached into his own pack and pulled out what looked for all the world like two long-necked bottles of beer: brown, cold, and wet with condensation. "How about one of these?"

Dan's eyes went wide. "Are you kidding? Heck, yes."

He reached for one of the bottles. It *was* a beer—a nice cold IPA, in fact, with a label he didn't recognize. "Thanks, Rafe. This is very gracious of you."

They clinked bottles, and each took a long, grateful swallow. The brew was fresh and crisp, mildly bitter with a delicate hint of pine. "Wow," said Dan. "Beer in Purgatory. Who'd have thought it?"

"Think of it as a peace offering," said the angel.

"I have to give you credit. When you do peace offerings, you do them well."

"I thought it was time you had a little enjoyment. When I saw you sitting on this rock just now, I couldn't help remembering how happy you were on that day when you first arrived—how glad you were to be here, how eager you were to be on this journey. And now look at you, standing in your own way just when you're about to reach the finish line. What's up with that?"

"Good question," Dan conceded. "Very good question. To be honest, I'm not entirely sure. I trekked all the way to the foot of those mountains—I was right there —and I just couldn't make myself go any farther."

"Well, then, you might want to give some thought to whatever it is that's holding you back or weighing you down."

Dan laughed bitterly.

"Seems to me I haven't been giving thought to much else. Ever since that day with Amy, all I've been able to think about are my sins and shortcomings, and they're making me feel worse, not better. I'm starting to wonder if *somebody* hasn't made some kind of clerical error about me. I may not be heavenly material, Rafe."

"Okay." The angel nodded slowly. "Okay. That's not

a bad starting point. But as I've been trying to tell you, you're not remembering all these things in order to beat yourself up over them. You're simply facing reality. You're being set free from a false picture of yourself, and it would be a mistake to replace that picture with another one that's equally false." He fiddled with the label on his beer bottle. "Tell me, Dan, why do you want to go to Heaven?"

Dan made a face. "Shouldn't that be obvious?"

"It's not, actually. Have you ever asked yourself why you'd rather be there than somewhere else? Is it because Heaven is where all the good people go? Because it's where you've always assumed you belonged? Because you can't think of anything else to do or anywhere else to go? Come on, give me a reason."

Dan looked at him bleakly. "I give up. I know you're trying to make a point, so make it."

"All right, I will. There's only one reason anyone would want to be in Heaven, and that's because he loves God fiercely and passionately and wants to be with him more than anything else. Really, Dan, that's the only difference between Heaven and Hell. One is for people who want to be with God; the other is for people who would prefer not to be. So why would you want to be with God if you don't particularly like him? If you don't particularly love him? If you don't particularly trust him?"

Dan sighed. *This again*.

"I suppose it's because I feel I haven't lived up to his expectations," he said. "I was a fairly rotten person for a long time, and now I've started to realize that I also ended up being a pretty mediocre Christian. Now I'm feeling guilty and ashamed and embarrassed, and I guess I'm angry at God for putting me in this no-win position. Even when I'm not being awful, I'm still not good enough."

"Angry?" Rafe shook his head. "That's an interesting reaction. I warned you not to overthink things, because this is where it gets you. You realize it makes no sense to blame God for your own shortcomings."

"I know it makes no sense. I'm the one I should be angry at. I'm just telling you how I feel. And how I feel is . . . inadequate."

"Oh, trust me, I get that. You're not the first person I've had this conversation with. Frankly, if you could make it through this place without realizing that in one way or another you've failed to measure up, there really *would* be something wrong with you."

"But what about all these people I see running along the trails without a care in the world? I talked to one of them a few days ago, and he seemed pretty self-confident."

"Confident, yes." Rafe nodded. "But not self-confident. There are people for whom Purgatory is a fairly easy journey. But that's not because they've lived perfect lives—nobody does that—or because they're somehow unaware of their imperfections. It's because they're convinced that God loves them in spite of those things, that he loves them passionately, fiercely, and can't wait to see them."

"I'd love to have that same conviction," Dan said. "But right now I don't."

"Oh, but you do. That's what I'm trying to tell you. It's there, inside you. If it weren't, you wouldn't be here to begin with."

"I don't think so."

"You're more complicated than you realize, Dan. Deep down, you've never forgotten the old story. You know that God is not far away and distant, that he knows you personally and loves you better than you could love yourself. Enough to make you perfectly free. Enough to give his life in exchange for yours. He took a bullet for you, man. That's what Jesus is all about: God loving you so much that he can't wait to see you and welcome you home. You never lost any of that, no matter what you think."

"I know all this," Dan said. "But it's all up here, in my head. In my heart, I'm still . . ."

"Afraid?"

Dan looked up and stared at the angel for several seconds. Finally, he nodded. "Okay. Afraid. Maybe."

"And what exactly are you afraid of?"

"I'm not sure. I suppose I have this idea that if I get to Heaven—"

"*When* you get to Heaven," Rafe corrected.

"*When* I get to Heaven, then—I have this idea that I'll be standing there with all these people around me, and all these angels, and God himself, all staring at me and knowing everything about me that I know about myself. And all of them . . . I don't know . . . either horrified at how badly I've lived or snickering at how ridiculous I am."

The angel sighed with exasperation.

"Dan, look at me. I know all those things about you already. Do I seem horrified or amused?"

Dan smiled ruefully. "Okay, not horrified. But you do sometimes seem more than a little amused."

"You're not alone in this, my friend. To some extent, almost everybody who comes through this place has the same struggle, and some of them have much more formidable obstacles than yours. Somehow, in the face of all reassurance and encouragement, they carry a little nagging fear that their sins really haven't been forgiven and that God doesn't really love them. He may love other people, but not them. Or they believe that he somehow wouldn't love them if he really knew them."

Rafe paused and took a healthy swallow from his beer.

"The problem—well, one of the problems—is that in the world people are lied to all their lives. Persistently, in ways subtle and ways explicit. You're told that you're not lovable, that you have no inherent dignity and are no better than the lowest animal. You've heard it from other people, from the books you've read, and from the endless, poisonous chatter that passes for sophisticated conversation. But it all comes from one source.

"Let me tell you a story. You've heard it before, but let me tell you how it was from my point of view. I was there to witness it, and I played my own part in it.

"Long, long ago, before any of the universe came to be, we angels were created to be servants and messengers of God—purely spiritual beings, more enlightened and more powerful than anything you could imagine. We flashed through the heavens like sparks in a fire, entirely outside the categories of time and space. We were like the unspoken thoughts of the Almighty.

"But along with all these other powers and abilities, we were given the same dangerous gift that was given to you: the freedom to think our own thoughts, to choose our own paths, to say either 'I will' or 'I will not.' And however incomprehensible this may sound to you, even a being of soaring intellect who can see and understand perfectly the consequences of his actions and decisions can decide to say, 'I will not.'"

"Ah," said Dan, nodding. "I get this. We're talking about Satan here."

"Exactly. Except that wasn't his name then. He was the brightest, the strongest, the most beautiful among us."

He sighed. "And he was my friend. I admired him and loved him; so did we all. But intelligence, strength, and beauty are no sure defense against pride. It's quite the reverse, actually—we're all inclined to regard our talents and abilities, not as undeserved gratuitous gifts, but as virtues that we somehow acquired for ourselves and for which we should be praised and flattered.

"My friend became proud. His pride grew steadily more powerful and hungry until it devoured his reason and extinguished his love. He found it unbearable to be surrounded by so many inferior beings, unbearable to serve even the One who had created and loved him. And in the end, as you know, his pride taught him how to hate. He turned against God, broke the bonds of our fellowship, and took a third of us with him into the darkness."

Though he had indeed heard the story before, Dan found himself following it intently. But now he interrupted.

"Hold on a second," he said. "I've always wondered about this. If angels exist outside of time and space, Satan must have known from the start how it would all turn out. Even before he rebelled, he had to have known he would be defeated, would lose everything. Why make such a disastrous choice when you have absolutely no hope of success?"

"Exactly! It was precisely *because* he had no hope. It's the death of hope—the conviction that nothing is really of any use, that there is no way out, no light at the end of the tunnel—that gives birth to the most destructive forms of madness. He decided that if he could not rule the universe, he could at least make it as miserable a place as possible. Hate and despair drove him, and they drive him still. He has *become* hate. He has *become* despair, and there is nothing left of the friend I loved."

"But you still love him," said Dan, wonderingly. "Don't you?"

"Of course I do. And I love and grieve for the countless others who listened to him and followed him into Hell. God loves and grieves for them too, because loving is his nature. But they made their choice in full knowledge of its consequences, and for them there is no going back. There never will be."

"A sad story."

Rafe nodded slowly, staring down at his hands.

"Yes, it is. The only reason I tell it is to remind you that Satan hates you and every other human being—personally —with a deep and abiding hate. There was not a single day in your seventy-seven years on earth when he was not doing his best to destroy you. He is the smoothest, most seductive, most accomplished of liars; he knows exactly which buttons to push, which tactics to employ, and how to blend truth and deceit most skillfully to obliterate hope and strangle love. It is his only weapon, and he has made the most of it."

He looked up and stared intently, unsettlingly into Dan's eyes.

"By the grace of God, you were able to fight your way clear of Satan's poison during your life, but you couldn't help absorbing some of it along the way: the suspicion that God can't be trusted, that he doesn't really love you . . . that no one really loves you, in fact, and that you are as Satan was: a solitary, despised creature who thinks the only way to assert his tattered dignity is by shaking an angry fist at Heaven. Very Promethean, Dan, very Byronic. But it's all a lie. The dignity you actually possess is so very, very much more profound than any of that."

Suddenly, to Dan's amazement, the angel reached out a hand and firmly gripped his shoulder.

"Listen to me," he said. "You have something I can never have. For all my gifts and powers, I am only a servant of God. That is what I was made for, what I always have been and always will be, and I am honored to serve him. But you, Dan, were meant for something much higher and infinitely brighter—to be his friend, his adopted son, his brother. Why in the world would you refuse such an overwhelming joy?"

Dan squirmed a little. "I don't know," he said. "Perhaps because I don't deserve it."

"Of course you don't deserve it! Nobody deserves it. It's not a merit badge; it's a gift. And yes, you're free to reject it. But don't assume that rejecting it—even if you're doing it out of some misguided notion of unworthiness—makes you nobler or more principled than anyone else. It just makes you an ingrate with shockingly bad manners."

Dan laughed nervously. "Gosh, Rafe. Why don't you come right out and tell me what you really think instead of sugarcoating everything?"

"Sorry to be so harsh about it, but there it is." The angel removed his hand and raised his gaze to the low volcanic hills around them. They were being transformed in the light of late afternoon, glowing softly, striped with pastel shades of pink, lavender, orange, and yellow, and Rafe spent several long seconds contemplating them. "This isn't the place I would have chosen for you, Dan, but it does have a certain strange beauty. Another beer?"

Dan nodded gratefully. "That would be an excellent thing."

Rafe rummaged around in the pack, brought out two more bottles, and handed one of them to Dan. Friends again, they clinked the bottles together.

"The next one's on me," said Dan.

"They're all on you, friend. I'm putting them on your tab."

They laughed easily and sat beside each other, not bothering to say anything. A magpie, concealed somewhere among the ashy mounds, called out plaintively. A breeze had sprung up at the waning of the day, and they enjoyed its coolness.

"Just a tip, Dan," said Rafe finally. "If you're interested in learning how to trust God more, try asking him for something once in a while and see what happens."

"Why would I do that?"

"Why would you *not* do that? Do it because it pleases him to be asked."

"All right," Dan said. "I'll try."

"And you're still making this a lot harder than it needs to be. It would have been a lot easier for you if you'd simply shown a little trust and followed Buddy up that mountain. I'm just saying."

"I get that." He took a thoughtful swallow and looked around. "I have to admit, I do miss that dog. This is a lonely place."

"Try to remember that you're never alone, even here. I know it's not always easy to keep that in mind. But Jesus is with you always, even when you can't see him or feel him. And remember what Amy told you: there are multitudes of people—men, women, and angels, on earth and in Heaven—who are thinking of you, praying for you, cheering you on. Clouds of them. Take some strength and some courage from that."

Multitudes of people? Dan pursed his lips. Even at the best of times, he'd always had trouble wrapping his mind around that idea—people offering up prayers for complete strangers—and in the self-disgust and weariness of the last few days it had seemed even less likely. But now, as he began to relax in the afternoon quiet, things were starting to come into focus again. He wasn't ready to retrace his steps to the mountains, and he still had no idea where he was going. But now he knew that he wouldn't be wandering aimlessly anymore. And that he had not been forgotten.

"All right," he said haltingly, "I may be getting close to something important now, to understand what my problem here might be. Honestly, I think I'll be okay now. If I can just have a little more time to work it out."

Rafe smiled. "Take all the time you need, Dan. There's no deadline here." He stood up, recovered the empty bottles, and shouldered his pack. "It's time for me to go, and we may not see each other again. At least not in this place. You've chosen your own path now."

"Yes, I have. There's something I need to do here."

The angel nodded solemnly.

"I know. You have to find your father."

14

I saw most certainly that just as our contrariness brings us pain, shame, and sorrow here on earth, so, on the contrary, grace brings us solace, honour, and bliss in heaven—and to such an extent that when we come up and receive the sweet reward which grace has created for us, then we shall thank and bless our Lord, rejoicing without end that we ever suffered sorrow.

—Julian of Norwich, *Revelations of Divine Love*

How did he know that? Dan wondered. *Almost before I knew it myself.*

What he knew was that over the course of their conversation, what had been a vague, nagging urge at the back of his mind had solidified into a sharp and definite conviction. Throughout this journey, he had been ignoring—or avoiding—the most powerful and troubling influence in his life, the man who had shaped so many of his attitudes, so much of his behavior. His father.

He was here, somewhere in this vast unpeopled place. Dan knew it now, knew it with absolute certainty. And whatever it cost, he needed to find him.

Somehow, he thought. *Talk about a needle in a haystack.*

An hour had passed since Rafe had shouldered his pack and set off to whatever angelic business was waiting for him, and Dan was still sitting on the same rock. The daylight was fading quickly now. He listened to the soft sounds of life stirring around him as the cool of evening began to settle over the unpromising terrain of the badlands.

Rafe was right about this place, he thought, watching the sky deepen into shades of orange, rose, and violet—colors that mirrored themselves in the crumbling maze of hills, spires, and ravines that surrounded him. This spot had its own kind of beauty. All the same, it was no place to linger. As the shadows gathered and lengthened around him, he felt the familiar ache of the evening blues coming on. He missed Anna. He missed the dog. He even missed Rafe.

Where were those well-meaning souls the angel mentioned, the ones who were thinking of him, praying for him, wishing him well? Where was God? Try as he might, he couldn't feel their presence. It was one thing to talk about such things, perhaps even to accept them intellectually, but even now it didn't seem particularly real. With a pang of guilt, he realized that he hadn't even remembered to pray lately. Not since the day when he'd turned back at the foot of that mountain.

Well, that was nobody's fault but his own, and it was easily fixed. Maybe he should do a little less talking *about* God and a little more talking *to* him.

"Here I am, Jesus," he began, and the name still felt more than a little strange coming out of his mouth. "Here I am, starting a journey I didn't ever expect to take and don't even know how to begin. All I can say is that I know I don't know you or love you or trust you nearly as much as I could, and I know that I can't fix that by myself. All I can do is ask you to help me. Show me where to go, and I'll go there. Show me what to do, and I'll do it."

He didn't feel particularly hungry and saw no reason to put up the tent; all in all, sleeping under the stars sounded like an appealing idea. He washed the dust and sweat from his face and hands, then wrapped himself in a blanket and lay down against his pack to watch the light finish fading from the sky. A thin arc of moon rose over the ghostly hills. One by one the stars appeared, until they filled the heavens in a great shining river of light.

Coyotes yipped and howled nearby, sounding for all the world like a pack of squabbling twelve-year-olds, and an assembly of smaller creatures snuffled, chirped, and chuckled as they emerged to go about their nocturnal doings. It was all music to Dan, and before he even knew he was drowsy he was asleep.

Hours later, sometime in the darkness, he found himself starting to come awake. It was cold. His mouth was dry, and he felt as though he'd swum up out of a disturbingly sad dream, although he couldn't remember any of its details. He'd been moaning or trying to speak, and he must have wriggled out from under his blanket without knowing what he was doing.

Before he could fully awaken, he felt someone gently rearranging the blanket over him again, felt a hand smoothing his hair—and for some reason this didn't alarm or frighten him. Just the opposite—it filled him with a feeling of peace and grateful stillness. He heard a woman's voice, very gentle, very close, shushing him softly—a sound he had not heard since he was a child, a sound that had lain unremembered in the deepest parts of his mind —and crooning a melody that was barely a whisper as he returned to deep, peaceful sleep.

He awoke to find the sun shining warmly on him and the morning well advanced. He felt rested and strong, and his mind held the memory of a beautiful young woman who had sat beside him—had she really cradled his head in her lap? He remembered the stars shining through her hair, the sweetness of her voice, a sad smile, and the warmth of her hand on his forehead, but nothing more.

It had not been his mother. He was sure of that much. She'd discovered after the divorce that she had no need or love for God, and Dan felt certain—to his deep sorrow—that she would never be happy in any place that belonged to Him. He had loved her passionately, with all the devotion of a young boy for a beautiful mother, but he did not expect ever to see her again. Not here, anyway.

Perhaps his mysterious visitor had been the mother of Jesus, who had promised long ago that she would be Dan's mother too. Hadn't she? He struggled to sharpen and add details to the memory of that encounter but could not. It remained a mystery and a wonderment to him, and it filled him with quiet consolation as he went about the business of making a light breakfast and repacking.

"Thank you for this, Jesus," he prayed. "And thank you, gentle Lady, whoever you may be. Thanks to you both. Help me to trust this kindness. To trust all kindness."

That's another thing I never got right, but I think I'm starting to understand now, he thought. *For as long as I can remember, part of me has been cramped and blighted. I've never trusted kindness or love, mercy or forgiveness—only the things I thought I could grab or earn for myself. What a miserable, stunted way to live.*

"I'm sorry for that, Lord," he said aloud. "I missed so

much happiness, and so many chances to give happiness. Please help me to change that. Even now, when it feels like it's too late to make any difference, change me. I want that. I really do."

Lighter of heart than he had felt for some time, he shouldered the pack and headed downward, farther into the sunbaked labyrinth of the badlands. In the end, he'd simply have to trust that he wouldn't be led into any place he wasn't meant to go.

It was a long, dusty descent, winding endlessly through crumbling ravines of tawny ash and gravel where pale weeds and stunted shrubs struggled to survive. There was no wind, and the day grew oppressively hot; the only sign of life he could spot was an occasional vulture soaring far overhead, tilting skillfully to catch currents of rock-heated air. Dan took frequent sips of water, rested when-ever he came upon a scrap of shade, and wished he still had Buddy around to lighten the mood with his doggish enthusiasm.

As he made his careful way along, he began to think about how, in his struggle to understand his difficulties with God and the deformities in his faith, he had seized so unexpectedly and powerfully on the memory of his father. Even now, he found himself resisting the idea.

Isn't this really just a little too convenient, this pop psychology copout? he wondered. *It's such a cliché. If God is my Heav-enly Father, then my ideas about God are going to be shaped by my relationship with my dad. And if that relationship sucked, well . . .*

Still, Dan knew that what makes a cliché a cliché is that it usually has some kind of basis in truth. If there was really something he needed to do here, perhaps his turning back at the mountain was more than a failure of resolve, and this new journey was more than a delaying tactic.

When all was said and done, he couldn't deny that his relationship with his father had been stained and disfigured—for a time, at least—by violence, heartbreak, rage, and fear, any more than he could escape the longing he still felt, or the sad, forlorn wish that things could somehow have been different.

HE KNEW THE BLOW was coming as soon as he saw his father draw back his arm, but he didn't try to duck or hide; that would only have infuriated him even more. It was bad enough that he was crying like a baby, crying like a girl, crying like the sissy he was, so when the strike landed, he took it. The blow was open-handed, because his dad knew better than to use a fist, but it still split his lip and sent him reeling. His ears were ringing, and there were little sparks at the edge of his vision.

The second blow and the third, when they came, didn't seem to hurt as much; the first had spread a fog of confusion and shame over him that blotted out much of the physical pain. He was simply miserable, waiting like a whipped dog for the verbal assault that would follow. Because it always followed. If he was lucky, there would be no parting blow, and then it would be over.

He stood up straight again, tasting blood in his mouth, sniveling and hating himself for sniveling, hating the pathetic sounds he could hear himself making. Somehow this meaningless argument had escalated once again into something dangerous, and even though he should have seen the signs, he hadn't stopped himself in time to prevent it. This was the price you paid for not paying attention.

"You think you're really something, don't you?" his father snarled, panting. His face was red, and he was out of breath. "You think you're better than anybody else in this family, but you're nothing! You're useless! You're a useless, lying sneak, and you disgust me. Get out of my sight before I do something I'll be sorry for."

That was the signal for dismissal, and he knew he had to move quickly. His mother met him in the hall, her face a mask of irritation and concern. "Go and wash up," she said. "Don't let him see you. And Dan? I think it would be better for everyone if you found somewhere else to spend the night."

He went into the bathroom and washed the blood and the tears away, avoiding any eye contact with the pathetic face in the mirror. The face he, too, had come to hate. Quietly, he buttoned himself into a coat and went out into the autumn darkness to the house of a friend whose parents wouldn't ask too many questions. It wasn't the first time, and he knew it wouldn't be the last.

How, he wondered, had it come to this? He could still remember times not long past when his father had been a rollicking, cheerful dad, always singing as he worked around the house and in the yard, ready to take his young son on hikes through the woods, presiding over summer camping trips to the North Shore and standing proudly with his wife and children at Mass.

Pat Geary's childhood dream had been to be a fireman, and when he'd won his place on the city fire department roster, he was the proudest, happiest man in Saint Paul. He'd been Dan's hero in those days, and the boy had loved imagining his dad risking his life to save ladies, babies, and dogs from burning buildings. He was proud of his father, and life had been full of happiness.

But then something had happened. Whether it was sudden or had developed over a long time, whether there'd been trouble at work, trouble between his parents, or something else entirely, Dan had no way of knowing. It was a mystery—secret, strange, and terrifying—and in the way of most children, he'd assumed that it was his fault, that somehow he was the one responsible for the growing atmosphere of fear and anxiety that had settled over his family.

It certainly looked and sounded that way. As far as he could tell, all his father's growing frustration and anger seemed to be focused on him. Everything about Dan— the way he talked, the clothes he wore, the music he listened to—seemed to infuriate his dad, and the relationship between them had become poisonous and hateful.

Dan's instinctive response was to withdraw into sullen, furtive teenage resistance, which only made things worse. Soon, he really *was* lying and sneaking, and what had begun as a means of escaping punishment quickly turned into a habit of shabby, slinking dishonesty that seemed to validate his father's poor opinion of him.

But he was not nearly as good at lying as his father was at detecting it, and the punishments had only increased. Whatever was tormenting that man in other areas of his life, the two of them seemed locked in a spiral of ever-increasing animosity. The worst of it was that beneath Dan's hurt feelings and his resentment at the injustice of it all, part of him began to suspect that it was all true, that he really was what his father said he was.

Even his mother, who had tried to defend and protect him at first, seemed to have decided he wasn't worth the effort anymore. And he was inclined to agree.

In the tight-knit suburban community where they lived, it wasn't long before word began to get around that Dan's family was having "problems" and the Gearys were quietly but firmly placed in a kind of social quarantine. Friends no longer dropped by, invitations to their homes dried up, and Dan found other, less savory people to spend time with. He started skipping classes at school, his grades began to plummet, and he began the first of many needy, reckless relationships with needy, reckless girls.

And as for God, the Church, and all the supposed consolations of religious faith . . . well, they had ceased to interest him. The bland new Mass held no wonders for him, and its God seemed like a puffed-up version of his father: more kindly, perhaps, but even less approachable and even less trustworthy. Behind all that talk of love and mercy lurked an unpredictable, undependable Father who could still burn you to a crisp if he'd had a bad day. Dan had already lived that story, and he didn't find it particularly appealing.

As the weeks turned into months, his desperation and fear grew to the breaking point. He ran away from home twice—on the second attempt he hitchhiked as far as western Kansas before the police picked him up at a freeway on-ramp and held him for his parents. That only made matters worse, of course, and he began considering darker, more permanent ways to escape. There were pills, there were razors, and no one would miss him. Not for very long.

Finally, on a Wednesday in early spring, he emerged from school at the end of the sixth-hour class and found his mother waiting beside her car in the parking lot.

"Get in, Daniel," she said, sternly but not unkindly. "We're going for a ride."

"Okay." He slung his books into the backseat and climbed in, not without a measure of apprehension. "Where are we going?"

"It's just a ride. We need to talk. There are some things I need to say."

She didn't say any of the things he had hoped to hear from her—that she loved him still, that she didn't believe the things his father said about him, that she had confidence in him and faith in his goodness. Instead, as the car wound its way through one subdivision after another, past manicured lawns, beds of daffodils, and brilliant explosions of forsythia, she told him what he already knew: that the last year had been hard on her, on his brothers and sisters, on their entire family.

"And I know it's been hard on you too," she added, looking straight ahead as if concentrating very hard on her driving. "So, I think . . . well, I think we all need to take a vacation from this turmoil and conflict. Don't you?"

"Yes, ma'am."

"Good. That's good." She smiled a tight little smile. "I've asked your aunt and uncle if they'd let you come and stay with them in Hibbing for the summer, and they said they'd love to have you. You can work at the bakery, so you won't have to worry about being bored. And it's

146

pretty up there. Lots of woods and fresh air. It should be a nice getaway for you."

He nodded grimly. It could have been worse, he decided. It could have been reform school. He hated Hibbing and wasn't particularly fond of his mother's relatives—neither was she, for that matter—but since he'd been trying so frantically to leave home over the past few months, he could hardly complain.

"That's settled, then," his mother said with a satisfied nod. "It'll be good for you. It'll be good for all of us. We'll have time to work things out. You'll see."

Predictably, the summer was miserable. The rundown old Iron Range mining town was depressing—no wonder Bob Dylan had left as soon as he could. The work bored him to tears, and his relatives made no attempt to hide their resentment at having this shiftless delinquent nephew thrust upon them. To be fair, Dan had not done much to ingratiate himself with them either.

Somehow he managed to get through the summer without getting into serious trouble. At the end of August, when the tired old Greyhound wheezed into the Saint Paul bus terminal, there was one significant face missing from the welcoming committee on the platform.

"Your father isn't living with us anymore," explained his mother as she drove the children back home. And that was as much as she said about it. Later, his sister told him about the final shouting match, when their dad came home from a long night out to find his belongings piled on the front porch, the doors locked, the locks changed.

"So, tell us, Daniel," his mother asked brightly, "what was the best thing about your summer in Hibbing?"

The best thing? There wasn't one, unless maybe it was

147

this moment, right now. Maybe this news would make that whole sad ordeal worthwhile. But that isn't what he said. And in the end, it wasn't even true.

AS THE HOURS AND MILES slowly passed, the brittle badlands began to open out into a wider landscape of low, cream-colored cliffs and mesas. Dan found himself traveling on a wide shelf of pale stone high above a deep V-shaped canyon. He began to notice healthier trees and grasses among the stony crags, and far below him a bushy strip of green forest wound along what he assumed was the bed of a river or stream.

There was something else. The trail he was following had begun to look like an actual path, and he caught a faint but unmistakable scent of woodsmoke in the air.

Smoke could mean a campfire, and a campfire could mean another traveler like him—not a runner sprinting effortlessly through Purgatory but another hiker taking the long way, someone who might be able to help him on this new, self-imposed quest. He picked up his pace and began looking around for more signs of human activity.

They were not long in coming. He began to hear a distant rhythmic noise somewhere down the canyon, echoing off the stone walls. It sounded like someone hammering or cutting wood. After so much time alone, Dan found the clatter intrusive and unsettling, and he began to feel some misgivings about what he might be about to encounter. But the trail was wide and firm, and he pushed forward at a brisk pace.

After another mile, the shelf ended abruptly at the foot

of a towering outcropping of rock that thrust itself up like a squat battlement. At first, he thought he had reached the end of the trail and would have to retrace his steps, but a few moments of closer study revealed a series of broken ledges, like a rough stairway, that could be climbed without too much trouble. Carefully, he made his way up from one ledge to another, until he reached the rim of the outcropping.

Spread out below, as far as his eye could see, the rest of the canyon ran on—and it was like no other place he'd seen since he'd arrived in Purgatory. Cliffs and bluffs of pale volcanic tuff reared up on both sides of the forested valley floor, pocked with caves and overhangs where tiny human figures sat, stood, or moved aimlessly about. This was no overnight campsite but a human settlement—a city, almost—and it was vast.

Hundreds, maybe thousands, of people were down there, dressed in an array of colors and carrying on an assortment of activities that he couldn't identify from his high vantage point. A few scattered, lazy threads of woodsmoke rose into the air but not nearly as many as Dan would have expected. And although the place wasn't entirely silent, he couldn't detect any sound of voices— no shouts of children or adults at play or at work, none of the oceanic murmur of conversation one would expect from such a multitude. It was more than a little spooky.

"Man, oh man," he whispered. "What is this place?"

Looking closer, he saw to his relief that the path he'd been following resumed just below the ledge on which he stood. Carefully, he made his way down the face of the rock until he reached the trail. It was much wider on this side, marked with the prints of many feet, and it seemed to descend gently toward the floor of the canyon and the settlement that sprawled across it. Fascinated and curious, he headed quietly down the path, wondering what kind of welcome might be waiting at the bottom.

15

As for paradise, God has placed no doors there. Whoever wishes to enter, does so. All-merciful God stands
there with His arms open, waiting to receive us into
His glory. I also see, however, that the divine essence
is so pure and light-filled . . . that the soul that has
but the slightest imperfection would rather throw itself
into a thousand hells than appear thus before the divine
presence.

—Saint Catherine of Genoa,
Purgation and Purgatory

It took more than an hour for Dan to make his descent.
The canyon was deep, and its walls rose steadily around
him as he neared the bottom along a series of switchbacks,
and he went slowly for fear of dislodging any rocks or
gravel that might fall on the people below. Each turn
brought him closer to the quiet community nestled there,
and he could discern more of its details now.

As he'd suspected, there was a narrow stream running
through the middle of the gorge, punctuated every so
often by rude log bridges that allowed the inhabitants to
cross from one side to the other. He could see, too, that
some of the natural caves in the wall had been widened;
others had been fitted with rough stone walls, brush en-
closures, and awnings made from what he guessed had
once been camping tarps or ground cloths.

All in all, it didn't seem to be an unpleasant place. Whoever these people were, they'd chosen a good spot for their colony: well lighted and dry, sheltered from wind, rain, and prying eyes. If privacy was their main objective—and for whatever reason, it certainly seemed to be—they had achieved it.

Just the same, it seemed odd. Who did they think they were hiding from down here?

A few of the inhabitants had already spotted him as he grew closer—he saw their faces lifted toward him with vague interest, and there were one or two polite waves of greeting—but no one seemed alarmed, excited, or even more than mildly curious. He gave them a hesitant wave, and their answering nods were equally perfunctory. It didn't look particularly threatening, but it was obvious that no one was going to throw a party in his honor either.

The trail finally brought him to a ramshackle bridge across the stream, where a cluster of good-sized boulders had been scattered—presumably by some long-ago flood. Three of the smaller ones formed what seemed to be an informal office at the side of the path, in which a middle-aged fellow sat with a well-used spiral notebook on his lap and a pencil tucked behind his ear. He looked up as Dan approached.

"Welcome, brother!" he said with a smile, opening the notebook and retrieving the pencil. "Are you lost, or have you come to join our little community?"

"I'm not sure," said Dan. "What is this place?"

"This place?" The man appraised him with a long look. "Doesn't have a name, really. It's just where we wait. And you're welcome to wait with us if you like." He scratched his head absentmindedly and held his pencil poised over the grubby page. "May I have your name, please?"

Dan gave his name, and the man wrote it down carefully. "Nice to meet you, Daniel," he said. "My name is Ted."

"Nice to meet you, Ted. But if you don't mind my asking, why do you need to write down my name?"

"No reason." Ted snapped the notebook shut. "I try to keep track of everyone as they come and go. Sometimes people find it helpful, but mainly it's just something I do to stay out of trouble." He eyed Dan's pack. "I'm afraid you'll have to hike a few miles down the canyon to find a good spot to settle. Everything at this end is taken right now, and we don't get that many new vacancies. But there are some nice roomy sites down that way, if you don't mind the walk."

"That's all right," said Dan. "I'm not planning to stay long."

"A visitor? We don't get many visitors."

"Actually, I'm looking for someone."

Ted leaned back against the rock wall and beamed at him. "Good for you! Very good! Maybe I can help. What's the name of this person?"

"Pat Geary," said Dan. "Patrick. He's my father."

"Geary? Hmm. That sounds familiar." He reached behind the rock and brought up a whole stack of stained, tattered notebooks. Humming a little, he flipped through them and pulled out a pale blue ledger that was only five or six from the top. "Yes, I think I remember," he said, leafing through its smudged pages. "Ah! Here it is. Geary, Patrick. Looks like he's been here quite a while already. He's settled in at Third Turning—that's the third bend in the creek as you head downstream. Left-hand side, second level. Not so far from here, maybe an hour's walk."

Dan nodded. "Third bend, left-hand side, second level. Got it. Thanks, Ted."

"My pleasure. As I said, sometimes people find me useful, and that makes me happy." Ted stood and held out a grimy hand. "God bless you for coming, Daniel. We don't get many visitors here. Can I be of any other help to you?"

"No, thanks. I think I'm good." Dan peered down the canyon, hesitating, then looked up at Ted again. "Okay, there's one thing about all this that puzzles me, and maybe you can tell me. You said everyone here is waiting. What exactly are you waiting for?"

"To be called, of course," said Ted, as though he were explaining something very obvious to a particularly dense child. "We're waiting to hear that our time here is up. That we can move on."

"I'm confused," Dan stammered. "Haven't you already been called? Haven't you already been up there, in the mountains?"

The man nodded. "Oh yes. We've all been there. Every one of us has stood there at one time or another, looking up at that high place and realizing that we weren't ready yet. Some wandered off to other places, and for all I know they're still out there, roaming aimlessly in the wilderness. But most of us . . . well, we ended up here."

Dan shook his head. "Ted, you know there's nothing holding any of you in this place. Surely you realize that. You can move on any time you like."

"Really? Is that so?" Ted eyed him with an ironic smile

on his face. "Then let me ask *you* a question, Daniel. What are *you* doing here? You turned back too, didn't you? Why didn't you climb when you had the chance?"

"I'm not exactly sure," Dan admitted. "But I'm starting to think it's because I have unfinished business to take care of."

Ted nodded. "So do we all, one way or another. We all have unfinished business. But don't believe for a moment that we don't want to climb that mountain one of these days. We yearn for it every bit as much as you do, and it gets more painful the longer we're here."

He peered upward, toward the high rim of the canyon and the cloud-flecked sky so far above it. "Maybe more painful for some of us," he added. "I was a Methodist. This isn't at all what I was expecting."

"But . . . nobody ever leaves?"

Ted brightened. "Oh, no, no. Many leave, every day. Of course they do. Some days it's just a handful and some days it's quite a parade. Some change their minds and come back—a few don't even reach the rim of the canyon—but most leave and never return. I can't say what happens to them, but I like to think they find the strength they need to finish their journey. One of these days, God willing, I'll be one of them. That's a thought that encourages me."

Ted shrugged and put away his stack of notebooks. "Well, Godspeed and good luck to you, brother! Pray for me sometime when you can spare a moment, and I will pray for you."

"I will do that, Ted," said Dan. "I will. Thanks for your help." And he set off, following the stream as it gurgled over rocks and logs, and trying not to look too obvious as he studied the quiet village and the people who had made it their home.

They had certainly made a good job of it, he thought. What must have originally been intended as a temporary encampment had evolved over years—perhaps over centuries—into something much more permanent. Makeshift homes clustered along both banks of the stream and on every ledge of the creamy canyon walls and in the caves and alcoves, the whole connected by ladders and walkways. It seemed to go on forever.

Everywhere he encountered men, women, and a few children sitting, standing, or walking from place to place. Some smiled and nodded as he passed by, and a few even greeted him—the standard greeting here seemed to be, "Pray for me, brother." Nobody was at all unfriendly, but the preponderant atmosphere was subdued, restrained, and quiet. He felt as though he'd stumbled into some sprawling jerry-built monastery.

I guess I'm not the slowest traveler in Purgatory after all, he thought. *Some of these people look so discouraged, as if they're not even trying anymore.*

Almost automatically, he found himself saying a quick prayer.

Lord, have mercy on Ted and on all the souls down here— those of us who are walking and those of us who are waiting. Bring us all soon to the place where we are meant to be.

He'd been walking along the stream for a mile or more when the canyon began to take a gentle but unmistakable curve to the left. The light fell differently here—more of it was reflected from the overhanging cliffs than directly from the sun—and there was much more shade. This must be the first turning, he decided—that meant there were two more to go.

This section of the canyon seemed less densely populated than the area near the bottom of the trail where he'd encountered Ted and his pile of notebooks. But there were still a great many people here, some gathered around their dwellings and others on the paths. They, too, carried an air of benevolent detachment and quietude. It was so strange to think that his father would choose to linger here. How could such a strong-willed, stubborn, restless man bear this all-pervading mood of passivity and patience?

Soon the canyon began to curve off to the right again, regaining its original direction and brightening noticeably in the process. As he hiked along, Dan noted that the number of inhabited caves and shelters had increased again. Apparently, these sunnier stretches were home to the more desirable neighborhoods. Here the stream ran deep and close to the foot of a sheer cliff on the right-hand side where he was walking, and someone had thrown up another makeshift bridge to the opposite bank. He crossed it, looking down into the clear current of the stream, where small fish darted in the shadows.

Not far ahead was another sharp turn to the left and another shady stretch of canyon. *Third turning*, he thought. *This must be the place*. Since he was already on the left-hand side of the stream, he began scanning the series of ledges and alcoves just above him for signs of his father. But it wasn't long before he realized he was going to have to ask for directions.

Just a few yards away, at the side of the path, he spied a woman sitting on a large rock in the sun. She seemed to be waiting for someone, and at Dan's approach she jumped up with a soft cry of happiness, then tried to hide her disappointment with a kindly, if tentative, smile.

"Oh, hello!" she said.

She was a small, birdlike woman with short, dark hair and a round, pleasant face that radiated friendliness. She was dressed in a blue skirt, an immaculate white blouse, and a pair of shoes that were much too stylish for hiking, and had taken obvious pains with her hair. It was as though she were about to leave for a dinner date, not sitting on a rock at the bottom of a desert canyon. Dan wondered how anyone could be so well coiffed and well dressed in such a place.

"I'm sorry," she said. "I thought you were . . . somebody else."

"I'm looking for Pat Geary," he said, feeling suddenly awkward. "I was told that he's staying somewhere near here."

"He is!" Her smile grew brighter. "You've come to visit Patrick, then?" she asked wonderingly, as though this were a great thing.

"I have. He's my father. I'm Dan Geary."

"Oh my. How wonderful!" She came to him and took his hand. Hers was warm, dry, and soft. "I'm very glad to meet you, Dan. My name is Rose. Your dad and I have been neighbors for a long time. I can take you to his place. It's just up there." She pointed to the ledge above, where a series of shallow alcoves had been carved into the face of the cliff. "Come, follow me."

She led him—very nimbly under the circumstances, Dan noticed—up a dozen hand-carved steps and along the narrow ledge to a neatly kept hollow in the rock.

He peered into the shallow cave, but there wasn't much to see: a few blankets, and some clothing that had been neatly folded and laid aside on the ground. Of his father, there was no trace.

"He's not here," Dan said.

"Yes, it certainly looks that way."

"Oh well." He couldn't hide the disappointment he felt. "I guess maybe I should keep moving, then."

She patted his arm reassuringly. "Don't worry. This isn't unusual. Patrick is always up and about—always doing things, talking to people, staying busy. It's just his way. But the day is late, and he may be back soon. And I'm sure he'd want you to stay as long as you like. Just settle in and make yourself comfortable. Can I bring you anything, or do anything for you?"

"No thanks. I'll just sit down for a while and rest, I guess." He shook her hand again. "Thank you very much, Rose. It's been nice to meet you. You've been a great help."

"Not as much help as I would have liked," she said. Then, hesitantly, she looked up and held him with her eyes. "Pray for me, please. If it's not too much trouble."

"Of course." They exchanged smiles again, and he watched her return the way she had come, back down to her sunny spot, still wearing that sweet smile, as though meeting him had been the high point of her day.

He shrugged out of his pack and sat down at the entrance to the alcove to wait. *This is ironic*, he thought. *Now I'm just like everybody else here. Waiting.* As he'd casually promised, he made a quick prayer for the kind little woman who'd helped him, knowing that if he didn't do it immediately, he would probably forget.

His father's chosen spot might have been somewhat short on amenities, but it provided a useful perch from which to watch the neighbors and enjoy the soft arrival of evening. All around, as the shadows lengthened and the milk-white cliffs began to glow with reflected light from above, he could discern the sounds of individual voices as the residents of Third Turning prayed and bade each other good evening.

His own mind, unfortunately, returned to memories of his family and the chaos that had overtaken them after his parents' divorce. The chaos had been the worst surprise of all—that, contrary to all his expectations and despite all his fervent wishing, his father's departure from their home hadn't really solved anything. In fact, it had made everything much, much worse.

DAN SAT ALONE in the kitchen of his mother's house, staring dully at the piles of papers, photographs, and letters that lay scattered across the table in front of him. It was night and he was alone, and the place was so quiet that he could hear the ticking of the clock in the next room. His mother was dead.

There had been no funeral—she hadn't been to church for decades, except to attend other people's weddings and funerals, and had traded her Catholicism for a do-it-yourself patchwork of reincarnation, séances, and piles of self-affirmation books. Her friends had held an awkward and profoundly sad "celebration of life" party at a nearby restaurant, but that had ended hours ago, and everyone was gone now.

He was numb. He had no idea what he was feeling or even what he was supposed to feel. His mother, the heroine and sweetheart of his childhood, was dead. And here he sat, at the table in this house where she had spent the last decades of her life, doing his last duty as the family attorney: sorting through piles of paper and trying to make sense of what she had left behind. It was not an insignificant task—she'd been a highly successful businesswoman, admired and respected throughout the city at the peak of her career—but he found it a sad, depressing task nevertheless.

As he leafed through the morass of bank statements, tax returns, notes, and cards, he came upon a thick manila envelope and opened it to find a series of yellowed photographs from his parents' wedding. There they were, the two of them—his mother and father. Not the bitter, battle-hardened enemies of those last terrible years but a pair of attractive kids—Mom in her fluffy white chiffon dress and her bright 1950s lipstick, Dad in his gallant fire department uniform. Both of them bright eyed, eager, and very obviously in love with each other.

They had been his heroes. His beautiful mother, his dashing, handsome father. But how terribly wrong it had all gone, and how quickly it had happened . . .

He leaned back in his chair and studied the pictures sadly. For the first time he saw them, not as his parents, but as a pair of youngsters who had started their life together with all the best intentions and had somehow gotten lost in the forest—never knowing how much grief and pain was about to sweep over them, over their children, over their children's children. Sorrow upon sorrow, spreading outward like ripples across the surface of a moonlit pond, poisoning the lives of descendants they would never even meet.

What happened to these two young people? he wondered. What happened to that love, that certainty, that eager expectation? It couldn't have disappeared overnight. Surely there must have been some point along the dark, heartbroken road they walked together at which they could have stopped, retraced their steps, and started over. Did they ever notice the chance when it came, or were they too busy, too angry, too desperate to see it?

And what if I could have made a difference? he asked himself. *What if I had been helpful and encouraging, instead of adding to their troubles? Would they have had a better chance of making it work?* It was a mystery, all of it, and he would probably never know the answer. But it made him profoundly sad for them both. For them all.

At first, his parents' separation and eventual divorce had seemed like a godsend. For Dan, it meant an end to the beatings, the humiliating tirades, the constant fear of saying or doing something that would bring rage and pain down on his head. And since his mother would be busy meeting the demands of her growing business, supporting her children, and coping with a blossoming social life, he and his siblings would be free to choose their own friends, keep their own hours, and follow their own proclivities.

Now, looking back, he could clearly see the threads and cracks of impending disaster already present in the early days following the divorce, but he hadn't noticed them at the time. Focused so intently on his own misery, he didn't realize until much later that everyone around him—father, mother, sisters, and brothers—had emerged from that dark time of rancorous infighting with deep emotional and spiritual damage. And the worst possible treatment for that damage was to be suddenly handed a life without boundaries or accountability or supervision —worse yet, a life without meaning or purpose or faith.

His own fall into depravity, adultery, and self-loathing had been only the first rumblings of a storm that eventually engulfed them all. The list of painful snares and sorrows they'd endured—the drugs and alcohol, the casual sex, the abusive relationships and failed marriages, the quasi-religious cults, the nervous breakdowns and attempted suicides—was as familiar as it was disheartening, and even now there was no end in sight. Like some uncontrollable, malevolent machine, the family legacy of misery kept finding new victims in each generation.

He stared at the wedding photographs until his eyes began to blur, thinking about his parents and their blighted marriage, thinking inevitably about Anna and his own all-too-recent rescue from disaster. In the end, he thought, there were no villains here. Only people who had followed the wrong dreams and lost their way, never realizing the damage they were doing in the process.

16

Man . . . can certainly hate God and be hateful to God, but he cannot change into its opposite the eternal love of God, which triumphs even in his hate.

—Karl Barth, *Church Dogmatics*

Dan didn't remember falling asleep, but sometime in the middle of the night he found himself dreaming once again—*Was it a dream?*—of the beautiful, queenly woman who'd soothed his sleep during the previous night. She was there, in the shallow alcove of his father's camp, sitting quietly on a low ledge beside him, and with a sad smile she reached out gently to brush the sweaty hair from his forehead. There were tears in her eyes, he noticed. Had they been there before?

"Courage, Daniel," she said softly. "Have courage. All will be well. You, too, are a beloved son. Have courage, and do not falter."

The next thing he knew, dawn was brightening the narrow band of sky above the canyon. His quiet visitor was gone—if she had ever really been more than a product of his needy imagination to begin with—and his father had not yet returned. He was alone again in this village of patient, fainthearted souls, amid the quiet sounds of the morning.

He stood up and stretched. On the path below, a small group of people—three men and four women—sat together on a waist-high ledge of rock, enjoying the sunlight and chatting quietly among themselves, their voices soft and musical. He immediately recognized Rose; she was sitting where he had first seen her the previous day, stitching a torn sleeve on a shirt that was too large to have been her own.

"Good morning, Rose!" he called.

She looked up from her work and smiled brightly. "Good morning, Dan! You prayed for me last night, didn't you?"

"Well, yes, I did," he said, taken aback. "I told you I would."

"Thank you! I could tell! I think I'm feeling a little more . . . intrepid today."

He felt puzzled and a little embarrassed by the intensity of her gratitude. "It was my pleasure," he said.

Rose turned to the others. "This is Daniel—Patrick's boy, come to pay him a visit. Dan, meet my neighbors: Maria, Robert, Shirley, Daoud, Anthony, and Felicia." One by one, they nodded, waved, and smiled as their names were mentioned.

"It's good to meet you, Daniel," said Shirley, a young, motherly redhead whose kind smile was a mirror image of Rose's.

"But Patrick isn't here," said the man called Daoud. "He's almost never here anymore, I'm afraid."

"That's our Patrick. Always up and doing things," Rose added. "But you already know that. Pat's not a man who can sit still for very long. He's always going off by himself —sometimes for a few hours, sometimes for a day or a week. One of these days he won't come back at all, and we will all be so happy for him. Won't we?"

Her companions nodded enthusiastically.

"He's very brave," said Shirley. "It makes us feel brave just to be around him."

Dan nodded politely, amused and a little mystified by these admiring descriptions of his father. Pat had obviously made quite an impression in these parts.

"Pardon me," he said, "but I just woke up and I need to wash . . ."

The man called Anthony stood and pointed to the left. "Down there a quarter mile and over that bushy ridge," he said. "Just follow the path. You'll find it."

"Thanks. It was nice to meet you all. I'm sure we'll see each other again soon."

He pulled a towel and a bar of soap from his pack and ambled off down the creek, and by the time he returned a half hour later, they had all dispersed. He sat down, opened his pack, and enjoyed the heat of the sun-warmed rock as he ate a salted peanut granola bar. But it wasn't long before he grew restless again, and soon he was wandering up and down the canyon observing the place and its inhabitants.

All told, he spent three days there, hanging around his father's old bivouac, exploring the vast settlement in hope of finding him in some other neighborhood, holding sporadic conversations with anyone who seemed open to a chat. He noticed two things almost immediately.

First, no one ever seemed to be eating or drinking, and whenever he tried to share his rations, the offer was politely declined. "Most of us are fasting from food during our time here," a lanky fellow finally explained. "It's our way to show sorrow for our sins and to ask for the strength we need to move on."

Second, almost every encounter ended with a shy request for his prayers. It seemed to be more than a conversational convention too; these people seemed to hunger for prayer with an intensity that fascinated him. After the first dozen requests, he began carrying a notepad and pencil with him so he could keep track of all their names.

All the while, though, he found himself growing increasingly impatient with his surroundings. He could understand how some people might find this canyon snug and comforting, but the whole setup was getting on his nerves. It all seemed unnatural and faintly oppressive. He was feeling the call of those high mountains again, stronger than ever, and he wanted to start moving once more.

Each night, he dreamed the same dream, and each morning he found himself feeling comforted, stronger, and more resolute. Finally, he awoke at dawn on the morning of the fourth day and walked out onto the ledge. As always, Rose was sitting on her usual rock in the sun, busy with another bit of mending.

"Good morning, Dan," she said as he returned from his morning trip over the ridge to wash and say his prayers. "From the look of you, I'd guess that Patrick still hasn't returned."

"No, he hasn't." He sat down across from her and smiled sadly.

"Ah. I'm sorry. You know that you're very welcome to wait here as long as you like. Very welcome."

Dan made a face. "You're very kind, Rose. But I'm not particularly good at waiting."

"Well, you're definitely your father's son," she said

with a laugh. "Maybe it would be best if you tried to find him on your own, then."

Dan nodded. "I'm beginning to think the same thing. Do you have any idea where I should look?"

"My guess is that he's gone up above. Climbed up to the rim of the canyon. When he does that, he's usually gone for a long time."

Dan found himself frowning. If his father had left the canyon, wouldn't the fellow back at the entrance—Ted, the man with all the notebooks—have noticed?

"I'm confused," he said. "I thought there was just the one way in and out of this place."

"Heavens, no! There are all kinds of trails," said Rose. "None of them is as easy as the one that brought you here, but your father wouldn't have gone that way. You'll find a likely one just over there." She pointed to a narrow break in the canyon wall a half-mile distant, on the opposite bank. "I can't guarantee that's where he went, but it's the one he seems to use the most."

Dan brightened. "Maybe I'll try that one, then. If nothing else, a little adventuring will give me something to do with my time." He peered up at the cliff, then turned back to her. "Listen, Rose, I have an idea. Why don't you come with me? We can look for him together, and I'll bet you could use a little change of scene."

She shook her head, and this time her smile was sad.

"I can't do that, Dan. Marcus might come, you see. It would be just like him to arrive while I'm away. I've been waiting for so long, and I can't bear the thought that I might miss him."

"Marcus?" He looked closely at her. She wasn't weeping, but he could see that the corners of her eyes were damp. "Who is he? Your husband?"

Rose nodded. "When we were both still in the world, I promised I would wait for him. But it's been such a long time, and I'm worried that something might have happened."

Dan wasn't certain how to respond. *How long is a long time when you're in Purgatory?* His own experiences with time had been confusing enough; he wasn't really sure if he had been here for weeks or months. And who knew how much time had passed in the world he had left, or what had become of the people he had known?

"I see. Waiting for someone you love must make the time pass even more slowly. But I'm sure your husband will be along one of these days."

Rose waved off his words with a flutter of her hands. "Don't mind me. My worries are nothing special. Lots of other people here are waiting for loved ones. Lots of people worry."

But Dan couldn't help wondering how true that was. He missed his own wife a great deal, but he'd never really been worried about Anna or considered waiting around for her to join him. This had been *his* journey of recollection and repentance, not hers. He'd assumed that she had her own trail to walk—probably a much shorter one—and that they'd see each other again when both of their journeys were done.

There's something else going on here, he thought.

"I'm afraid I don't understand," he said. "Why would you worry?"

"Because sometimes I think . . . sometimes . . . that he may not be coming at all. And I couldn't bear that. I can't imagine Heaven without him."

"Oh." He nodded somberly, realizing what she meant. "I'm sorry to hear that, Rose. It must be very, very hard for you."

"Marcus is a good man. Really, he is. A kind man. Always gentle and sweet with me, and always honest and fair and generous to other people. A very upright, moral, decent man. But . . ." She fell silent, her face a mask of misery.

"But he doesn't believe?"

She shook her head ruefully. "Oh, he believes, Daniel. God is very real to him—real enough to hate. To him, God is a tyrant and a bully, the enemy of all human freedom and happiness, the cause of all injustice and superstition and oppression. He hates God so deeply that he can't bear to hear his name mentioned."

"I see," said Dan, who had known a great many such people. For a time, he'd even been one of them. "Obviously, you don't share those feelings, so how . . ."

"How could two people fall in love if they had such different ideas about such an important thing? Well, it happens. It happens all the time."

"What I meant was, how did it happen for you?"

"We met in college, which is probably what you'd expect. Marcus was a teaching assistant in one of my history classes. He was terribly romantic and handsome— kind and sweet and very gentlemanly—and he swept me completely off my feet. He has so many wonderful qualities, and our religious differences didn't seem that much of a problem. At the time, I suppose God wasn't very important to me either."

"But that changed later on?"

"Yes, it did. Things happen in life, you know. Tragedies, disappointments, challenges. And you find yourself thinking differently. The strange thing is that Marcus and I experienced the same things, but we changed in opposite ways. Everything I saw as a blessing he saw as an insult, and the more I learned to love God the more passionately Marcus learned to hate him."

Dan nodded. "I can't imagine how painful that must have been for you."

There were actual tears in her eyes now, but she brushed them impatiently aside. "He never stopped loving me, Dan. I firmly believe that. He never mocked my love for God, though he could be pretty unpleasant about other Christians, and when I started going to church he never tried to stop me or make me give up my faith."

"But he never joined you? Never honestly considered that you might be right and he might be wrong?"

She shook her head. "Marcus was a very strong-minded man. He had his own principles. I thought that eventually his love for me would lead him to love my Lord too. But that never happened, and after a while I suppose I stopped trying to persuade him."

"And now you're afraid it's too late for him."

She nodded. "But he's a good man, Dan! You'd feel the same way if you could meet him. I pray for him all the time, and I can't think that God would condemn such a decent man to an eternity of punishment. And if Marcus can't go to Heaven, I don't think I want to go either."

Well, well, Dan thought. *It sounds as if Marcus isn't the only strong-minded person in this marriage.*

But he understood what she was saying. A lot of people

172

—himself included from time to time—seemed to think of Heaven as some kind of vacation resort designed to their personal taste. The kind of place you might even decide to walk away from if you didn't care for the furnishings, the menu, or the guest list. He'd known several otherwise intelligent people who assured him that they had no interest in a Heaven where their dogs or cats weren't welcome too.

But a beloved spouse, on the other hand . . .

Still, if the whole point of Heaven was nothing more and nothing less than the pure and constant joy of being with God, it was hard to imagine that Rose's husband was going to be happy there. Or that Rose was really going to be happy either, if she had to share eternal life with someone who was miserable all the time.

"I think . . . ," he began, then stopped himself. What *did* he think, really? This was a time for thoughtful, careful words—not for easy platitudes or false comfort on the one hand, and not for rigid formulas that would rob her of hope on the other. In the end, given all he'd experienced, there was only one proper response, and that was the truthful, humble one.

Don't pretend that you know what God is thinking, he told himself.

Rose was still looking at him, waiting for him to finish.

"I think you're right not to give up on Marcus," he said finally. "I've been doing a lot of thinking lately about my mother. Your husband sounds a little like her, and I'm beginning to wonder if I haven't been exactly fair with her. I know nothing meaningful about the state of her soul, the state of her heart. I'm starting to think that the

173

best course of action is to keep hoping, to trust in God's wisdom and his mercy, and not pretend I know what he thinks or what he's going to do. I think it's really important that you're praying for Marcus. I think I'm going to start praying for my mom."

"I'm glad," said Rose. "I think you should do that, Daniel."

"Still, I think you'd also feel a lot better if you left this place and got back on the trail."

She shook her head, sadly but firmly. "I'm sorry, but I can't. Not yet."

"All right, then. I understand." He squinted up at the wide crack in the cliff that she'd pointed out to him earlier. "I guess I might as well see if I can find out where my dad has gotten himself off to."

He climbed quickly to the alcove to gather up his gear and hoisted the pack to his shoulders. Its familiar weight and the pull of the straps felt comfortable and right, like the touch of an old companion. He made his way back down the steps to her and put a hand on her shoulder.

"Goodbye, Rose," he said. "If I don't find him up there, would you let him know I'm looking for him?"

She took his hand in her own. "Of course. I'll keep an eye out, and if I see him, I'll tell him. You be careful up there, Daniel. That's not an easy climb."

"I will." He hesitated, but only for an instant. "I want to thank you for your kindness. And I'm truly sorry if I made you upset with all my questions."

"Don't worry about that," she said. "I'm not upset."

He glanced back at his pack. "Can I offer you anything else before I go?"

She shook her head. "I don't need anything. But if you have a moment or two to spare, pray for me, will you? For courage?"

"Yes, of course," he said. "I'll pray for Marcus too, and I'll pray that you find each other again. Goodbye. I hope to see you again soon."

"Me too," she said. "God bless you!"

17

There is no point, you see, at which God says, "Your term's up," or "All things considered I think that will do now," or "I have received a great many prayers and offerings on your behalf, so I'll let you off the rest." Nobody comes to release the soul. It is its own judge, and when it feels that it is clean . . . it simply gets up and goes.

—Dorothy Sayers, "The Meaning of Purgatory"

Courage, he thought as he headed toward the cleft in the canyon wall. That was the word the woman in his dream had spoken, and it was what Rose was asking for. *Courage*. Is that what it all came down to? Were all his scruples and self-doubts, all the passivity and fatalism on display in this cream-colored canyon, simply a failure of nerve? In the end, wasn't faith really a matter of courage—courage to take the risk, accept the gift, trust the giver?

At some level, Rose seemed to understand that too. Courage was what she needed—the courage to accept God's mercy and to trust in his love, to surrender the idea that she could blackmail him by refusing to budge until he gave her the Heaven she had already picked out for herself.

Dan could sympathize; he was struggling with the same

dilemma. Hard as it may have been for him to admit and apologize for the stupid and evil things he'd done in his own life, he was finding it much, much harder to accept that he had been really and truly forgiven and that something more wonderful than he could imagine on his own was waiting for him.

When you got down to it, he thought, accepting forgiveness—really accepting it—meant putting yourself completely at the mercy of someone you had shamefully betrayed and deeply hurt, trusting that the forgiveness you were offered was genuine and not some kind of trap. Eyes closed, you had to force yourself to fall backward into those waiting arms, the arms you had bruised and gouged, trusting that they would really catch you.

The skeptics have it backwards, he thought. *Faith isn't a crutch for people who aren't brave enough to face reality. It takes no courage at all to play it safe, refuse to risk, sneer from the sidelines. That's the coward's game. Believing, now—that takes guts.*

Lost in thought, he made his way downstream to a spot facing the opening Rose had pointed out. There was no bridge across the stream in this part of the main canyon, but someone had taken the trouble to arrange a few dozen good-sized rocks in the water. With the help of his hiking stick, he found it a simple matter to pick his way from one rock to the next until he reached the other bank, where a modest trail led up from the water to the cliff.

He could see now that the opening was more than a simple crack in the wall. It was a narrow, shadowy slot canyon, perhaps seven or eight feet across, that seemed to extend deep into the cliff. Exactly how deep was anyone's guess; he couldn't see more than a few hundred feet ahead, where the passageway curved off to the right. If it was anything like the other slot canyons he'd known, it probably meandered all over the place, and in wet weather it very likely carried a good deal of rainwater down to the main canyon too.

Fortunately, at the moment its floor was dry and sandy, and dimpled with the prints of a good many feet. He was relieved to see those footprints, because it meant plenty of others had been here before him, but it still wasn't at all clear how this passage was going to lead him up to the rim of the canyon.

No sense dawdling, he thought, stepping into the shadowy pathway. It was cool and dry here, lit only by a thin strip of blue sky far above, and every noise Dan made as he walked seemed to create a wave of little echoes. He thought about whistling, shouting, or singing, just to test the acoustics, but the atmosphere of the place seemed to discourage such shenanigans. It was a bit like being in church.

He turned around only once, looking back at the bright light of the main canyon that blazed in at him through the entrance, thinking of the throng of long-suffering souls he was leaving behind. In that moment he realized he would not be back this way again, and he was glad of it.

Bless them all, my Jesus, he prayed. *Bless Ted and Rose and all of them. Grant them the courage they're yearning for.*

The trail ahead was level and clear of obstructions, and it felt good to lengthen his stride and do some real walking for the first time in days. The soft light made it easier for him to appreciate the subtle stripes and bands of color in the rock: striations of beige, cream, café au lait, and ocher that swirled around and above him and put him in mind of a giant caramel layer cake. The penitents in the main canyon may have put all thoughts of eating and drinking behind them, but Dan was cut from different cloth. The idea of a caramel layer cake sounded pretty good to him.

Chuckling to himself as he strode up along the passage, he tried to put his wandering thoughts into some kind of order and focus on the task at hand. In particular, he needed to think about his father. Why did he feel so absolutely certain that it was his mission to find Pat? What was he supposed to do after that, and what was any of it supposed to prove?

All he knew was that this was something he had to accomplish. And having a job to do, however baffling it might be, suited him a lot better than sitting on a ledge in the canyon like a customer at the DMV, waiting with thousands of other baffled souls for someone to call his number.

The slot canyon wound its way through the rock, following whatever path the rain and streams had carved into the mountainside over endless ages. Far above, Dan could hear the soft voices of birds nesting in its upper reaches, but there seemed to be no animals or plants here at the bottom. The passage was scoured clean and he made good time, striding along and enjoying the colors and curves in the walls on either side.

Then suddenly he came to a stop.

"What the heck?" he said aloud, and the sound of his voice echoed around him.

The way ahead was blocked by a massive rockfall: stones and pebbles and gigantic boulders all piled helter-skelter for hundreds of feet. Here there was finally some vegetation—enough soil and moisture had accumulated in the cracks and crevices between the rocks to support a thriving community of sedges, mosses, and small, stunted trees. It was lovely in its way, like a vertical garden, but from here on he was going to have to climb if he wanted to reach the rim.

Fortunately, the rockfall didn't mean he was going to have to blaze his own trail. The more closely he looked at it, the more it seemed to be as much a stairway as an obstacle. The footprints on the canyon floor converged on a spot at the right edge of the piled heap, where its gradient was relatively gentle; sure enough, a well-traveled path snaked its way up through the tumbled stones. There were plenty of handholds, and all a climber had to do was avoid twisting an ankle or slipping on a damp patch.

"All right, then," he said as he began to climb.

This wasn't quite the carefree stroll he'd been having through the sandy passageway below, and it wasn't long before he broke into a sweat, grateful that at least he was still in the relative coolness of the slot canyon. In full sunlight, this would have been more than a little uncomfortable.

He spent the next hour climbing slowly and carefully, leaning into the slope and choosing each step before taking it. Every so often, he would come upon a flat rock or an upthrust boulder whose smooth, moss-free surfaces showed that previous climbers had wisely stopped to rest there, and he gladly followed their example. He could see that the rockfall was growing steadily more precipitous as he made his way upward; the vegetation was less abundant, and the smaller rocks were not as steady as they'd been at the bottom. On the brighter side, he could see that he was nearing the lip of the cliff and that only a few minutes of strenuous work remained before he would reach it.

It felt satisfying, actually. He hadn't done this kind of climbing since his Army days, and it was a relief to be able to enjoy the physical exertion without worrying that a hidden sniper had him in his sights. It had been a long time since Dan had given much thought to his four-year stint in the military, though it had been a major turning point for him. It had paid for his college education, taught him some useful lessons about life, and unexpectedly created the first tiny opening in the massive wall between him and his father.

His parents' separation and divorce had been not just an emotional and spiritual disaster for the family but a financial one as well. As a teen, Dan had never realized how thin the ice was under their feet until it suddenly gave way. Overnight, the Gearys had fallen from the upwardly striving middle class to the struggling, one-paycheck-from-catastrophe class. Despite his mother's desperate hard work and his father's sporadic child support payments, they found themselves buying groceries with food stamps, missing house payments, and wearing hand-me-downs from the neighbors.

Higher education after high school was no longer an expected option for any of the Geary children. Instead, they were instructed to go out and find jobs, for which they had no experience or training. After trying his luck as a busboy, janitor, and dishwasher, Dan had decided that his only escape was to enlist in the Army, which was glad to take him, remake him, and teach him how to handle responsibility like a grown-up. When his four years were up, the GI Bill provided him with funds for a college education—and the Army had provided him with enough experience to profit from what he learned there.

But the least expected consequence of his enlistment had been the postcard he received during his second month of basic training. Years later, he still remembered every detail of that card. On one side was a photo of a typical Minnesota summer scene: a clear blue lake surrounded by spruce and pine. On the reverse was a brief message: "Well done, Daniel! I'm proud of you.—Dad."

When he read that short note, he had to sit down on his bunk and spend several minutes getting his emotions under control. It wasn't a reconciliation, or even the start of a reconciliation—he was still too immature, too full of anger and pain for that—but it was something. And it had surprised him to realize how the most perfunctory expression of his father's approval could affect him so deeply.

The last few feet of the climb were the hardest. The massive pile of stones ended well below the lip of the cliff, and the remaining distance was nearly vertical. Someone had hacked rough handholds and footholds into the soft stone, and it looked as though there were still people using this pathway, but it was no place for carelessness or speed, especially for someone carrying a fully loaded pack. Gingerly, he chose each step and tested each handhold before committing himself completely, gradually hauling himself upward until he finally stood at the top.

If he'd expected to find his father standing or sitting nearby (and in some small corner of his mind, that's exactly what he'd been expecting), he was quickly disappointed. Instead, he found himself on a perfectly flat expanse of pale stone exactly like the walls of the canyon he'd just left. The stone pavement stretched around him on every side, interrupted only by the immense chasm behind him and the smaller cracks spreading out from it like the limbs of a tree.

Far, far ahead he could make out a range of low, tawny humps that looked as though they might be sand dunes. Beyond those, however, he saw—with a quickening of his heart and a sudden flush of yearning—the great looming massif of the mountain from which he had turned away so many days and weeks ago, rising like a cool white pyramid against the cobalt sky.

I'm more than ready now, he thought. *When I reach that mountain this time, there won't be any turning back.*

But that moment lay far ahead of him, he knew. He still had a job to finish, and a good many miles and days of hard slogging afterward just to recover the ground he'd lost. It was already hot on this griddle of stone; the sun was nearly overhead, and there was little shade to be had. Looking around, he decided that his father must have headed toward that mountain and those dunes. There simply wasn't anywhere else to go.

That verdict was confirmed when he saw that someone—perhaps many someones—had marked out a faint westward trail along the ground, using modest stacks of flat stones set at widely spaced intervals. He could see dozens of the little cairns, and there might be hundreds, for all he knew, all of them leading toward the dunes and mountains in the distance as if to say, *Yes. This way. Don't give up. It can be done.*

That was a helpful thing, he thought. Considering the time and distance involved, laying down this faint highway of stones had to have been a huge job. Whoever had done this, it was a thoughtful, kindly gesture. Gratefully, he hitched up his pack and started walking across the flat, treeless pavement, glad that at least his water bottles were full and he'd had a decent night's sleep.

The trek toward the dunes was every bit as uncomfortable as he'd expected, but not nearly as tedious. Gradually the arid landscape around him began to reveal small details he hadn't noticed before: tiny green plants growing in the cracks of the stone; small, bright lizards that scurried from rock to rock; and a faint breeze from the far peaks that wasn't strong enough to cool his brow but carried the faint heart-lifting scent of fresh snow and pines.

He found himself giving thanks even for this minimalist, alien setting, increasingly sure that it held a blessing for him if only he had the courage to find and accept it. The very sameness of his surroundings gave him the freedom to think about the meeting that lay ahead and to unravel, if he could, its significance, its necessity, its seeming inevitability. He still couldn't see why this excursion was so important, but he knew that it was.

It wasn't as though he and his father hadn't been on good terms by the time the old man had died. Surprisingly, they'd even learned how to enjoy each other's company from time to time—thanks to Anna's insistent urging, the slow passage of the years, and whatever it is in the human memory that softens and dulls the ache of old injuries. He could still remember vividly the night when their fifteen-year silence toward each other had finally been broken.

It was the evening before his sister Shannon's wedding. Her tiny house had been crowded with friends and family members who'd gathered for an informal celebration to congratulate the bride. Every room was stuffed with wine-sipping, snack-munching relatives, and among them were Dan's father and his shy, uncomfortable young wife. Dan had known they'd be there, and the knowledge had made him skittish with anxiety for days.

ANNA POINTED ACROSS THE ROOM toward the kitchen door, through which Dan could see his dad holding forth among the guests—still handsome (the silver in his hair had only made him better looking), still unfailingly larger than life, still able to enthrall everyone around him with the sheer exuberance of his personality.

"Tonight's the night, Daniel," said Anna, holding one hand over her swelling pregnancy, "and this is the place. I don't care what you say or how you say it, but before we leave this house I want to see the two of you talking to each other. I know this is hard for you, sweetheart, but it's not up for discussion. I will not allow my children to grow up not knowing their grandfather."

There was no getting around the utter awkwardness of the situation. Years ago, at their own wedding, Dan had pointedly left his father off the guest list, supposedly for the sake of his mother's feelings—she'd still been alive at the time and had been escorted by a male friend of her own. But in retrospect the gesture now seemed shabby, vengeful, and cruel, even to Dan; he was ashamed and embarrassed at its pettiness.

In any case, a lot of time had passed since then, and a great many things had changed. His mother's death had forced Dan to see his parents as real people, flawed but understandable, and to acknowledge that he really had no idea what had been going on in their home during his childhood. Meanwhile, his own descent into darkness—

and the unexpected, undeserved mercy he'd been shown —had taught him a little humility. Perhaps it was time he started showing some mercy of his own.

"All right," he said to his wife. "Come with me, then. I'll introduce you, and you can give me some moral support."

"That sounds good to me," she said, though it was obvious that she saw this stratagem for what it was. "Let's go."

Unsure what to say or how to say it, he led her across the room and into the kitchen, where his father was winding up another story to the amusement and admiration of his listeners.

"Hi, Dad," he said.

What happened then was utterly astonishing to Dan. His father stopped in midsentence and stared for a second, then stepped forward and enveloped him in a wide, warm, and painfully enthusiastic embrace. "Daniel!" he cried, in that rich baritone voice that had not faded with the years. "I can't tell you how wonderful it is to see you, son!"

It was no performance either. The man actually had tears in his eyes, and he was gripping Dan by the shoulders as though he were afraid to let him go. In spite of himself—despite every reservation and suspicion, every carefully nursed grievance—Dan felt his own eyes filling with unbidden tears. Pat Geary was a force of nature; his rage had been a storm impossible to withstand, and his contrition was just as overpowering.

"It's good to see you too," Dan said, stepping back. "I . . . this is my wife, Anna. She's wanted to meet you for years. Anna, this is . . . my dad."

"Anna." Pat spoke her name like a prayer. He held a hand gently out to her, and she took it. "I'm so pleased to know you. This is my wife, Cindy. She's been wanting to meet both of you for a very long time."

The shy, sweet-faced woman beside him took Dan's hand in both of hers, and her smile was filled with light. "God bless you for this," she said quietly. She turned to Anna and kissed her cheek. "Both of you." And in that moment, it was as though the rest of the people in the room had disappeared, and the four of them were standing in a brief, bright bubble of happiness.

"It's been too long," said Dan.

"Yes, it has," said his father. "Much too long. I'm sorry, son."

"So am I, Dad."

And that was that. They spent a long time chatting about fairly pedestrian matters and, as it is with such occasions, were gradually drawn away to other conversations with other friends and relatives. Still, at the end of the evening, as everyone was struggling into coats and scarves for their journeys back to their various homes and hotel rooms, Pat sought out his son again and treated him to another of those prodigious hugs.

"I can't tell you how glad I am," he said in Dan's ear. "I love you, son."

Dan was finding it hard to speak, but he managed a choked response. "I love you too, Dad."

18

Remember pain, sorrow, suffering are but the kiss of Jesus—a sign that you have come so close to Him that He can kiss you.

—Saint Teresa of Calcutta

Dan stopped to give himself a drink of water and study his situation. The sun was beginning to settle toward the west, but there was plenty of daylight left, and it was shining straight into his eyes. The endless stone surface on which he was walking reflected that merciless glare and heat upward, and there was no relief or shade anywhere nearby. His legs were weary, but it was ludicrous to think of sitting down. Even the faint morning breeze had died away. This place was like a broiler.

Squinting, he used his hat to mop the sweat from his forehead and peered ahead, but as far as he could tell, he hadn't made any appreciable progress. The mountains and dunes seemed as far away as they'd been when he started. *It might have been smarter to do this hike at night,* he thought. That's probably what everyone else who'd climbed out of the canyon—including his father—would have done.

"Okay, God," he said aloud. "It looks as if I've gotten myself into another tight spot. But I'm pretty sure this is where you want me to be and that this is the way my dad went. So if you'd please just help me get through this with a cheerful heart, I'd be very grateful. And I'll also try not to do any more stupid things."

He took a good long drink out of the bottle, tucked it back into the pack, and continued his walk into the afternoon sun, following the little piles of stones that led off toward the horizon. He'd detected a subtle pattern or rhythm in their arrangement: spaced out in groups of ten, each separated from the next by a larger cairn. *Like beads on a very big rosary*, he noted with a smile. Inevitably, his thoughts turned once again to his father and to the change in their relationship that had followed that brief reunion in his sister's kitchen.

Their reconciliation hadn't been an immediate thing by any means; there'd been far too much sorrow and too much bitterness for that. But a beginning had been made, and over the following months and years they had gradually learned to understand and forgive each other.

The mutual confessions, apologies, and words of forgiveness that needed to be spoken were eventually spoken, and they were every bit as clumsy and difficult as one would have expected. No amount of reconciliation could enable Dan to unravel the mystery behind those awful years. The story behind his father's terrifying anger and the collapse and ruin of his parents' marriage remained forever closed to him. In the end, he realized that there was no need for him to delve deeper. Sometimes you simply decided to forgive even those things you didn't understand.

Fortunately, the two of them found a great many other, more pleasant topics to explore together. During long, relaxed conversations, they shared stories about all the things that had happened to each of them during the years when they'd been avoiding each other. Dan told of his law practice, his marriage, his love for Anna, and their growing family. His father spoke about how he'd used his own experience as a firefighter to start a successful Florida safety consultancy business, and talked feelingly about the love and guidance he'd gotten from his own wife.

Finally, once the most superficial details had been disposed of, they reached down to their most private and least praiseworthy moments, and that's when the truly remarkable thing occurred. In a fit of honesty, Dan shared the story of his descent into darkness and self-loathing and admitted that only the gift of God's grace had saved him from himself—only to discover that his father had a strangely similar tale to tell.

He, too, had come to a place where he could see what a mess he'd made of his life. And thanks to Cindy, he too had found his way back to God. There were individual differences in the details of each man's conversion, of course, but these particulars didn't diminish the wonder of this unexpected link they'd discovered between them. And from that time forward they had a new way of relating to each other, and a shared vocabulary to discuss the things that meant the most to them.

As the relationship continued to unfold, it brought unexpected pleasures in its wake: intergenerational family vacations, frequent phone calls and visits, and all the other normal trappings of a life Dan had never thought he would experience. His children grew up knowing and enjoying their grandfather, and he himself had a father once again—one very different from the volatile and tormented man who had long haunted his dreams and darkened his memories. A part of his heart that had been held as tight and stiff as a clenched fist quietly began to relax and heal.

But love does not ripen without pain. All joys eventually bear their crop of heartbreak, and this joy was no exception.

IT WAS EVENING in Bradenton, one of those tropical December evenings: a flock of seabirds flying black against the mango-colored sky, palm fronds rustling in a warm wind coming down from Tampa Bay, couples murmuring to each other as they strolled the Riverwalk, the river murmuring back. Dan, Anna, and their three children were down from Minnesota, visiting Pat and Cindy and enjoying a break from the winter cold.

This was Pat's birthday, and everyone was excited about the dinner that Cindy had planned for them all at Mattison's. She and Anna had spent the day shopping, and Dan was sunburned and relaxed from exploring, walking, and swimming at the beach with the kids and their grandpa. They'd dropped Pat off at the house a few hours earlier to rest up from the excitement of the day, and now they were gathered here at the river, hungry and eager, waiting for him to arrive and pretend to be surprised by his "surprise" party.

But the wait seemed particularly long, and as the light began to fade and the wind began to cool, Anna and Cindy began glancing furtively at their watches. The kids sensed their elders' growing unease and started getting fidgety. Little Paul tugged at Anna's hand and asked if they could have dinner soon.

"I sure hope everything's all right with Dad," Dan said.

"Not to worry," said Cindy brightly. "He probably just took a nap and forgot to set the alarm. I'll call home and see what's keeping him."

She went into the restaurant to find a phone while Dan and Anna herded their restive children to the edge of the boardwalk and pretended to help them search for manatees. After all, it was the Manatee River, he told them.

It was several minutes before Cindy returned. "There's no answer at the house, so he's probably on his way," she said. "I let the hostess know we're running late, and they'll hold our table."

But by the time another fifteen minutes had passed without an appearance from his dad, Dan's disquiet got the better of him.

"Why don't you guys go in and get settled while I go and see what's keeping Dad?" he said. "It won't take long; the house isn't that far." He was getting a bad feeling. Whatever was going on, he didn't want Cindy to go back to that house alone.

The apprehension stayed with him during the five-minute drive to the bungalow where his father and stepmother lived, but when he arrived he saw to his relief that his dad's car was gone from the driveway. Irritated now, and huffing a little about the inconvenience of it all, he returned to the restaurant expecting to find a laughing and completely impenitent Pat sitting at table with the two women and three grandchildren.

But Pat wasn't there. And although he tried to keep the worry from his face and voice, Cindy and Anna knew immediately that there was a problem.

"Maybe it's nothing," said Anna. "I'll bet he misunderstood when we told him where we'd be. He's probably waiting for us at a different restaurant."

Cindy nodded. "That's always a possibility," she said. "He does have a few other favorites. Fortunately, they're all close by."

"Okay, but it's getting a little late," said Anna, glancing at the children. "Maybe we should save the festivities for tomorrow night. How would it be if I took these three desperadoes back to the house and made them some mac and cheese while you two see where Pat's gotten off to?"

Luckily, no one had ordered food yet. Anna had the children finish their sodas and steered them out the door while Dan settled the bill, acting more relaxed and cheerful than he felt. Within minutes, Anna had the kids all bundled into their other car. He and Cindy stood watching as they pulled out of the parking lot.

"All right, then," he said briskly, turning to her. "Let's go find out what that rascal has gotten himself up to."

"Yes, let's," said Cindy, who nodded and managed a smile. "I'll drive, since I know all your dad's hangouts. You can keep your eyes out for him or his car."

It was a long and frustrating search. As they checked each bar and restaurant, Dan could see that his stepmother was having more and more difficulty hiding her anxiety.

"This isn't the first time he's done this, is it?"

"No, it isn't."

He could hear a faint tremble of rising uncertainty in her voice, and immediately regretted having said anything. "Don't worry," he told her. "I'm sure he just got confused from all the excitement of the day. We'll find him."

"Help us find him, Jesus," Cindy prayed. "Keep him safe, and please help us find him."

"Amen," said Dan.

They did find him—after three unsuccessful searches of

restaurant parking lots—alone in his car beside a beach-front seafood shack that looked as though it had been closed for the season. He was sitting upright, looking perfectly unruffled, staring out at the multicolored lights across the bay as though he had seen something out there and was trying to make sense of it. Intensely re-lieved, Dan and Cindy got out of the car and walked over.

"Hey, Dad," said Dan as casually as he could. "Whatcha doing?"

His father hadn't looked up at their approach, and even now it took him several seconds to break his gaze away from the harbor lights and look at Dan—as though he were rising slowly and unwillingly from some great depth.

"I . . . I was remembering. I thought . . ." And sud-denly the dreamy, uncertain quality of his voice sharp-ened and hardened, became the voice Dan remembered from a long time ago. "Who are you?" he asked suspi-ciously.

"It's me, Dad. It's Dan."

His father nodded, looking past him. "And that woman?"

"I'm Cindy," said Cindy, with a gentle sadness that made Dan's heart ache for her. "Your wife."

"I don't trust that woman," Pat said to his son. "Why did you bring her?"

"Because it's your birthday, and we love you," said Dan. "Happy birthday, Dad. Let's go home."

"Home." The word sounded flat in his voice. Like something dead.

"Yes, home," said Dan. "Can I drive? You can ride next to me, and we'll talk."

Surprisingly, his father offered no argument but un-buckled his seatbelt and got out of the car. Dan got in quickly, before Pat could change his mind, and waited for him to come around to the other side.

"I'll follow you," he told Cindy, who was standing beside the car trying to blink away her tears. "It's going to be fine. We've got him. Let's just take it nice and slow."

As it turned out, there was no talking on the way back. Dan tried, clumsily, to start up a conversation, but his father simply stared out the window sadly, like a condemned man headed for prison, and said nothing.

The house was quiet when they arrived. Anna had fed the children and put them to bed in the guest room. Waving off any idea of having supper, the old man allowed his wife to lead him away to bed, leaving Dan and Anna sitting in the living room, staring sadly at each other and speaking in whispers. He couldn't find a way to explain what was happening—"Alzheimer's" or "dementia" seemed terribly inadequate words for such a sudden and catastrophic collapse of personality—especially a personality as robust as his father's.

In the morning, strangely, everything seemed almost normal. Pat was in a subdued but cheerful mood when he came down for breakfast; he chatted amiably with his grandchildren as they ate on the veranda and watched the hummingbirds at the feeder, and he didn't seem to remember anything about the previous evening. But now that Dan was looking for clues to his father's unusual behavior, he could see a few small signs that he hadn't noticed before: a momentary vagueness, a slight tremor in the hands, a hitch in the walk.

In the afternoon, Cindy walked with Dan and Anna in the garden while Pat and the children took naps. "It comes and goes," she said. "Usually he's perfectly normal, the way he's always been. But every once in a while, when he's especially tired or stressed out, he gets like he was last night. He doesn't know me, he doesn't recognize any of our friends, and he gets scared."

They were already making regular visits to a gerontologist, she added, and were getting good advice from that quarter, but last night's episode had convinced her that he shouldn't be driving anymore. She was dreading the prospect of having that conversation. Eventually he was probably going to need some kind of institutional care, although she was hoping to delay that option as long as possible.

"I'm so sorry," said Anna. "This must be terrible for you."

"It's getting a little worse each time, and I can't pretend that it doesn't hurt," Cindy admitted. "I really don't feel unsafe or frightened, but it makes me sad when he doesn't know me—after all the years we've been together and all we've been for each other."

"Is there anything we can do?" Dan asked.

She shook her head. "I don't think so. For now, maybe we could pull back a little on all the activities and just make sure he gets a lot of rest. He's good when he can settle into a regular routine. But please, please, don't leave yet. Enjoy the rest of your visit. He really loves having you here. We both do. Please don't let any of this chase you away."

"Of course not," said Anna. "It will be lovely."

And so it went. The rest of their stay was uneventful—deliberately so. As they gathered around the loaded car on that last morning to say their goodbyes, there were smiles, tears, and hugs all around. Dan could see that his father was holding himself back, as though fearful of saying or doing something inappropriate, and there was an unfamiliar sadness in his eyes.

He knows, Dan thought. *Oh, Dad . . . That must be terrible. To know.*

"Goodbye, Dad," he said with false cheerfulness. "You take care of yourself."

Which meant (in Geary-speak), *I love you.*

His father nodded. "Goodbye, son. Drive safely."

Which meant, *I love you too.*

19

Though none go with me, still I will follow;
No turning back, no turning back.

    —S. Sundar Singh, "No Turning Back"

The sun was not going down yet—in fact, it was shining almost directly into Dan's eyes now—but it had lost a good deal of its heat, and the breeze from the mountains had returned to lend him a little relief. Each rock pile in the trail ahead stood out sharply now, accentuated by its own little shadow, beckoning him onward.

By now there was no denying that he was ready for a break. His feet were sore from walking on stone all day, his thighs ached from that climb out of the canyon, and the pack was starting to chafe his shoulders. Since this featureless plain offered no spot that was better or worse than any other, he shrugged out of the pack, propped it upright, and sat down in the meager shadow it cast. If nothing else, he could at least face away from the sun for a while.

A good long drink of water and a quick wipe of his face and neck with a soaked neckerchief made him substantially more comfortable. He rummaged deeper into one of the side pockets, found a packet of trail mix, and munched it contentedly. The rest was welcome after walking for so many miles; he took the time to enjoy it, and when he eventually rose to his feet again he studied the landscape around him with a renewed appreciation for its severe but indisputable beauty.

All around him the creamy stone extended to the sapphire sky, drawing a perfectly straight line of horizon that was broken in only one quadrant. There the great tawny sand dunes—much closer now—lay folded and watchful in the westering light like a resting lion. Beyond them the distant mountains thrust themselves toward the sky —and that high central peak, its lower slopes dark with forest and its snowy summit glowing with light, was impossible to ignore. He felt the pull of those far heights growing ever stronger, a yearning that was like an ache in his heart.

"Let there be no turning back this time, Jesus," he said. "No turning back. This time, help me to go the distance."

That brief prayer reminded him suddenly of the people he'd met back in the canyon and all the names he'd scribbled down during their conversations. He pulled the little notepad out of his pocket and spoke each one, slowly and lovingly, praying strength, comfort, and courage for each of them.

Then, shouldering his pack once more, he pointed himself toward the mountains and resumed his walk.

DAN AND ANNA HAD TRIED to stay in touch with Cindy by phone during the weeks and months that followed the Florida trip, commiserating with her at each new phase in Pat's gradual withdrawal, each new step she had taken to stave off the inevitable, as his episodes of panic and suspicion grew more frequent and his behavior more worrisome.

Finally, the day arrived when she'd reluctantly had him admitted to a nearby nursing home that specialized in dementia care. Over the course of the year that followed, she'd shared the stories of her daily visits to Pat, who had developed several physical problems that left him steadily weaker and less responsive, until he eventually lapsed into unconsciousness. From that point on, they'd known it was only a matter of time before he died. When the call came, Dan had been deeply saddened but not surprised.

The funeral was held in Florida, since that was where Pat and Cindy had spent the last few decades of their life together, and it was well attended by friends and neighbors that Dan had never met. They all spoke well and highly of his father, gathering around Cindy in a protective circle of compassion and kindness that Dan found touching.

Most of his own brothers and sisters had come too. They were a somber, shell-shocked group, uncertain how to relate to each other, to Cindy, or to their father's Florida friends, struggling to make sense of the sobering event that had brought them together. "Prickly as porcupines, that's how we are," Dan said to Anna. "And just as hard to hug."

Before the service began, the funeral home had set aside a brief family-only viewing period. One by one, Dan and his siblings filed up to the coffin to "say goodbye" to the body from which their father had already departed. His sisters wept quietly, his brothers stood staring grimly, and all returned to their seats. Dan, for his part, was just sad

—not at his father's death, but at how small and gaunt Pat looked in the coffin, stretched out on that satin lining. He had loomed so large, for better and for worse, both in life and in Dan's imagination. But in this box, he was meek, powerless, and pitiful. A toothless lion.

The funeral itself was more encouraging. The pastor, to his credit, didn't waste any of his sermon recounting stories about what a great fellow Pat had been; instead, he spoke of the mercy that had found Pat in the middle of his life, and how it was available to anyone, no matter how far from the light that person might consider himself to be. *Amen to that*, Dan thought.

When it was all over, the family gathered at a nearby restaurant before dispersing to their scattered hotels. Predictably, it was a subdued meal.

"Now we're orphans," said Shannon dejectedly.

Dan didn't feel like an orphan. To his surprise, he found himself strangely comforted by the solemnity of the service, the unpretentious decency of the people he had met, and the knowledge that his father's perplexing and sometimes tormented life was now making way for something much better. Even if theirs had not been a perfect goodbye, he was grateful that it was still much better—so very much better—than it might have been.

A SUDDEN WAYWARD BREEZE brought him out of his reverie, sweeping a curl of sand past his feet with a faint, dry whisper. He was still walking westward toward the dunes, following the line of stones, as the sun eased itself down behind the mountains and spread a warm peach-colored glow across the sky. The air was rapidly cooling, and Dan decided he would keep walking as long as he could; it was so much more comfortable than trying to hike in the desert sun.

And the desert itself was beginning to soften its face; he noticed more vegetation working its way up through the cracks in the stone—even a few small green bushes here and there. Perhaps if he walked through the night, he might reach a shady spot of some kind in which he could hole up during the hottest part of the coming day.

As he made his way across the plain, the sunset slowly faded from the sky and the stars came out, one by one, in the hundreds, thousands, and millions. The celestial lights were brilliant in the clear, dry desert air—great pulsing lamps of white, yellow, blue, and red scattered among luminous clouds of impossibly distant suns.

Even though there was no moon at the moment, the stars themselves gave more than enough light to walk by, and the pale stone beneath his feet reflected their radiance softly, glowing like snow on a winter night. So did the actual snow on that distant mountain range. The scene was sublime, beautiful, and utterly silent, and he found himself whispering a sudden prayer of gratitude.

How often I was surrounded by beauty like this and never let myself notice it, he thought. *How often I failed to thank you for the splendor through which I walked. But I thank you now —for this moment, and for all the moments when you showed yourself to me in loveliness and I paid you no mind.*

The path led onward, rock by rock, under the starry sky. He felt no fear—not of darkness, prowling animals, or his own dark, prowling thoughts—but only a sense of peace and a quiet eagerness to see and know what lay ahead. No matter what the coming day would bring, it was good to be traveling in the right direction again.

It was easier walking without the sun's heat, but the dunes and mountains were still far away, and Dan's progress seemed painfully slow. As far as he could remember, he'd made much better time—if you could call it that—when he'd fled away into the badlands after losing his nerve all those days ago. *I suppose it's easier to make good time when you're not going anywhere in particular*, he thought. *Once you have a goal, you're all the more impatient to reach it.*

He took several rest breaks during the night, watching the stars wheel silently overhead as he sipped from his water bottle and thought about the strange and roundabout journey he'd taken since his arrival in Purgatory. He was no longer particularly surprised that he'd ended up wandering without much real sense of purpose while travelers like Jonas seemed to have sped unerringly to the finish line.

At least he hadn't come to a complete stop like those timid souls who had settled in the canyon behind him . . . but that was an uncharitable thought, and he chided himself for entertaining it. *You don't know what their lives were like or what their struggles have been*, he told himself. *Don't forget that you lost your courage too. Just like them, you let fear overcome your desire. Don't judge them; pray for them.*

And so he did. All through that gentle night as he walked ever forward, he prayed—for Ted at the canyon entrance who had found his dad's address, for Rose who'd shown him the alcove where Pat had been living—and for her problematic husband Marcus, of course—and also for Maria, Daoud, Anthony, Robert, Shirley, Felicia, and all the other people he'd encountered in that strange open-air waiting room. He prayed for Anna, for their three grown children, for friends, neighbors, and business associates whose faces and names he could barely remember.

He was still praying, in fact, as the dawn brightened gently in the east and spread its pale lavender glow across the world, and as the sun thrust itself over the flat horizon, throwing its clear red light against the dunes and mountains.

They were much, much closer now, which cheered him, but it was discouraging to see that there still wasn't a great deal of vegetation around—certainly not enough to provide meaningful shade from the sun. He felt the first warm stirring of a dry wind at his back and knew that his first priority would be to find a place where he could hole up and sleep for the day.

But where in blazes was his father? Dan had walked all night and most of the previous day without encountering any sign of him, telling himself that it would be easy to spot him on this flat, featureless table of rock. But the tableland was coming to an end—in a few more hours he would reach the first outstretched tongue of the dunes and have to start climbing that steep, sandy height. How was he going to find him now?

The little rock cairns he'd been following since he left the canyon were still there, leading toward the foot of the dunes, but he had no idea whether they'd be much help once he reached that part of the journey. Wouldn't the sand cover the cairns fairly quickly?

Time will tell, he told himself. *All you can do is keep moving. And for crying out loud, show a little trust.*

The sun was nearly overhead by the time he neared the first dune and felt its massive presence looming over him.

At least a thousand feet high, it was such an awesome, immense object that it seemed to exert a sort of gravitational force of its own. In the end, though, he reminded himself that it was just a great heap of sand pushed together by the wind, one grain after another. There was a lesson in this somewhere, but he wasn't sure what it was. Perhaps that you could accomplish great things by concentrating on one tiny thing at a time. Grain by grain.

One uncertainty was resolved, at least. As he drew closer, he could see a line of tiny dots climbing the face of the dune and disappearing over its summit. The little piles of stones that had led him across the tableland all this time were still in place after all, still showing him the way. And there was more good news—the slope he was about to climb would be slowly swallowed in shadow as the sun continued its movement across the sky, so he'd be climbing in shade during the hottest part of the day. He'd climbed enough sand dunes to know that it was tough work even when you didn't have the sun beating down on you.

Breathing a prayer of gratitude, he took a long swig of warm water from his bottle, squinted upward, and started climbing. With each step his boots sank several inches into the sand, which made the climb much more tiring than if he'd been scrambling over soil or stone— but he knew the secret, which was to turn around every so often and sit down for a rest instead of trying to power through to the top in one heroic slog.

After taking three of these little breaks, he discovered that he was actually enjoying himself—especially once he'd begun to gain some altitude. Looking out over the sunbaked tableland he'd left behind, he could see the massive crack of the canyon from which he'd climbed the morning before. Beyond it rose a landscape of tortured stone—great domes, chimneys, and battlements of red, orange, and gray rock rising into the afternoon sky like the ruined and melted buildings of some fire-blasted city —and in the far distance, a range of blue mountains that seemed to encircle the rim of the world like a wall. It was majestic and scenic in its way, but he was glad to be leaving it behind.

Each time he stopped, he took note of how the shadow of the dune had advanced slowly outward below him as the day wore on, marking time like the sweep of a great sundial. Yet each stage in his ascent was bringing him closer to the summit, where the sun was still shining with all its force. Even in the shade, he could feel its warmth radiating down on him.

It took him a half dozen of these rest breaks to reach the top of the dune. As soon as he cleared the summit, the sun struck him in the face with its full heat and glare, but he didn't mind. Panting, he looked up and saw the westward view that had been hidden from him from the past several hours and was only now revealed to his eyes.

As he'd expected, this dune he had conquered was only the first and steepest of an entire range of pale, sandy summits, each topped by a sharp ridge—like the peak of a roofline dividing brilliant sunlight from dense shadow. One after another, they marched westward toward the mountains, growing ever higher as they went. It was a sobering and impressive sight. He could see that he had a great deal of work ahead of him.

The line of little cairns he'd been following was still there, leading from the knife edge of one dune to the knife edge of the next. And at the very pinnacle of that trail, so far away that he almost missed it, a human figure stood silhouetted against the bright-lit sand, arms akimbo, head thrown back, staring out over the desert.

Dan recognized that pose immediately. He'd seen it a thousand times. The figure was his father.

20

God is so great that we never finish our searching. He is always new. With God there is perpetual, unending encounter, with new discoveries and new joy. . . . I look forward to being reunited with my parents, my siblings, my friends, and I imagine it will be as lovely as it was at our family home.

—Pope Benedict XVI, *Last Testament*

He would have broken into a run if he hadn't been so tired already and if running in the loose sand would have gotten him there any sooner. He set off, immediately and deliberately, toward the distant dune. He would sometimes lose sight of his father as he dipped into the shadow of each ever-higher crest, but every time he reached the top of it, he could see that his father was still there. As though waiting.

Finally, after several ascents and descents, he saw that his dad had spotted him too. His father was waving energetically, and Dan thought he could even hear faint shouts —unintelligible but indisputably enthusiastic—carried on the fitful breeze. Soon they were hurrying toward each other at a respectable speed.

They met at the top of a high ridge, poised between light and shadow in a fierce, unhesitating embrace. Neither seemed surprised to see the other; it was obvious now that Pat had recognized his son as surely as Dan had recognized his father, and had been expecting and anticipating this meeting every bit as eagerly. After all this time, and through all these astonishing circumstances, it somehow felt as normal as anything Dan had ever done.

"Oh, Dad!" he exclaimed when they finally stepped back to study each other. "I can't tell you how wonderful it is to see you!"

"It's wonderful to see you too, son," said Pat, who was grinning joyfully. "I've waited a long time for this day."

"You look . . . great! And I'm not kidding. I mean . . . you look *really* great!"

And it was true. Dan wasn't sure exactly what he'd been expecting, but it wasn't this.

This was not the haunted, tormented ghost who had cast such a dark shadow over his adolescence. It wasn't the kindly, contrite grandfather of Dan's later years; or the sad, baffled old man his father had been at the end. This vigorous, animated, and startlingly youthful man was the Pat Geary he knew only from old photographs, whose image in his memory seemed almost mythical: young, tanned, and athletic, with twinkling eyes and a ready smile. He was wearing weathered khakis and a pair of battered hiking boots but was bare chested and shining with sweat.

"You look pretty wonderful yourself, Daniel," his father said. "Isn't it amazing, what's been happening to us?"

"I don't understand," Dan stammered. "To us? What are you talking about?"

"Ah. You've been too busy traveling to notice, I'll bet," his father said. "Me, I've pretty much been staying in one place for a long time and watching the people around me, and I've seen them all changing, one by one. I think it must be part of getting ready, part of what we're here for. All the shame and sorrow, all the resentments and grudges that have stuck themselves to us over the years —they're being scrubbed away, and this is what's been underneath. We're not entirely there yet, but this . . . this is closer to who we really are, who we were always meant to be."

Dan didn't know what to say. He hadn't noticed any changes in his own appearance. On the other hand, there were no mirrors in Purgatory, and he hadn't spent a lot of time reflecting on how he looked. *Maybe I should find a nice quiet pond to gaze into.*

His father clapped him on the shoulder. "Hey, forgive my terrible manners," he said. "You must be exhausted. Follow me—I've got a place up ahead where we can rest and catch up on things. It's not far, just a half mile or so. Can I carry your pack?"

"No thanks, Dad. I'm fine," said Dan. "Really. Just lead on, and I'll follow."

They headed out across the ridgeline, their feet making twin rows of dimples in the sand. Dan kept stealing glances at his father, whose younger, stronger appearance was still hard for him to get used to.

"I thought you were living back there in the canyon," he said. "Rose told me you were often gone for long trips, but—"

Pat brightened. "Ah, you talked to Rose, did you? Good. How is she?"

"She's fine. I tried to persuade her to come along with me, but she wasn't having any of it."

"Still waiting for that husband of hers, I'll bet."

Dan nodded.

"Don't worry," said Pat. "She'll figure it out. Some things are harder to let go of than others."

"But I have to ask—what in the world are you doing out here?"

"Waiting for you, of course. And working on my trail project, as you can see." He swept an arm behind them and around to the west, where the line of little cairns led over the last few dunes and disappeared into the forest beyond. "What do you think of it?"

Dan was astonished. "You laid out all these rock piles? All of them?"

His father nodded, grinning. "Every one. As you can tell, I've had a lot of time on my hands."

"But there must be thousands!"

"Yep, there are. And most of them had to be brought here from someplace else, two or three at a time. When I started, I was hauling them up from the canyon, and that wasn't a lot of fun. But now I have a good source on this end, so I'm doing less back-and-forth, and the trip doesn't take as long."

"Wow." Dan thought about his own journey from the canyon to this place, and all the markers he'd seen along the way. "This had to have taken years."

He shrugged. "Like I said, I had lots of time, and it's kept me busy. I wanted to make it easier for people to find their way across the wasteland. But mainly," he added, "I made it for you."

Dan stared. "For me?"

"Sure. For you. Don't look so surprised," he said, laughing. "But really, right now let's get you into some shade. There'll be plenty of time later for talking. My camp is just over the next dune."

"Okay," said Dan. "You're the boss."

"Actually, I'm not the boss," said Pat with a wry smile. "Really, that's kind of the whole point."

It didn't take long for them to follow the ridge westward to its intersection with the next dune. In the shadow it cast stood a bright blue canopy tent, where Dan could see a well-seasoned backpack, several full water bottles, and a small stockpile of rocks.

"My home away from home," said his father, ushering him in. "Sit down and take it easy. Can I offer you a drink?"

"Yes, please." Dan shrugged his own pack off and settled down on the sand. Pat handed him one of the water bottles, and he drank from it gratefully. This really was a comfortable spot, he thought as he looked around— well shaded but situated so that it caught the best of the breezes that blew across the dunes. Even the sand beneath him felt refreshingly cool.

"It's so good to see you, son," said Pat, retrieving a threadbare flannel shirt from his pack and buttoning it on. "I can't tell you how wonderful this feels. I've been waiting so long for this moment, and now that it's here, I'm having trouble dealing with it."

Dan laughed. He was finding his own feelings difficult to manage. "I know exactly what you mean," he said. "But look, I still don't understand any of this. I've been journeying here for God only knows how long—but how did I know you were here? How did I even know I had to find you? And how could you be here waiting for me —as if you knew all along that I would come?"

"I did know." Again, that smile. So unlike the man Dan had known in life. "I knew because I prayed for it, and because my prayer was pure I knew it would be answered."

Dan nodded, but his confusion showed on his face.

His father chuckled. "I can see that you want more of an explanation," he said. "But before we delve into that, why don't you take a rest? If you don't mind my saying so, you look like you could use a little shut-eye. We've got all kinds of time, Daniel. Nothing but time, in fact. Let me stretch out a bedroll for you."

Dan didn't argue. Quite suddenly, he discovered that he was exhausted. He watched as his father pulled a battered sleeping bag from his pack and spread it over the floor of the shelter for him. "Just lie down and rest. Don't worry about me. I know how to entertain myself."

Dan lay down, and before he knew it, he was asleep.

There were no dreams or visions to disturb his rest. He slept like a baby, and the next thing he knew he was waking up to the clatter of cooking pots, the smell of hot coffee, and the sound of his father humming "Oh, What a Beautiful Morning." He propped himself up on an elbow and watched his father at work over the camp stove.

"Are those . . . pancakes?"

"They are indeed. Good morning, by the way! Care for some coffee?"

"Yes, please. But I think I have to attend to some business first."

"I'm sure you do." Pat looked up briefly and grinned. "Downhill and around the corner."

"Thanks, Dad. And good morning to you, too."

The sky was already brightening in that swift way of the desert, pastel pinks fading away to light blue, slashed with a few brilliant streaks of predawn orange. Dan rose, grabbed a towel, water bottle, toothbrush, and soap, and padded down the night-cooled slope to make his morning ablutions. When he was done, he took advantage of the opportunity to offer a brief private prayer.

"Thanks, dear Lord, for this lovely morning. But even more, thanks for bringing my dad and me together here," he said. "I don't know what this is all about, but I ask that it may be a good thing, a healing thing." He looked down at the stony tableland he had crossed to get to this place, bathed in rosy light from the sunrise. "Amen."

Back at the shelter, his father was happily sliding pancakes onto plates.

"Come and get it! Hot pancakes are a lot better than cold ones!" He nodded toward the bedroll, where a steaming mug was nestled into the sand. "Your coffee is already poured and waiting; don't knock it over."

Dan eagerly took one of the plates. "This is great! I've missed your cooking."

"Not as much as I've missed being able to cook for someone besides myself."

They sat down across from each other on the sandy floor, said a brief but heartfelt blessing, and attacked the food with enthusiasm.

"Sorry for conking out on you last night," said Dan, shoveling a honey-soaked piece of pancake into his mouth and washing it down with a gulp of strong black coffee.

"No problem, son." His father chuckled. "I wasn't offended. You must have really needed that rest."

"But I took your bedroll. Where did you sleep?"

Pat shrugged and looked a little sheepish. "I didn't. I stayed awake, watching you."

"Oh." He couldn't think of anything to say. "Well, thank you."

"It was my pleasure." His father gazed at him over the rim of his coffee mug. "Believe me. It was."

They didn't engage in much small talk—it had never been their habit at breakfast—so it wasn't long before they'd eaten all the pancakes and drunk all the coffee. Dan volunteered to clean up the dishes, while Pat tidied up the shelter and put his well-used pack into better order.

"What's the plan now?" Dan asked as he dried the last plate and slid it into his father's tidy mess kit. He could already feel the warmth of the sun on his back as the morning heated up.

Pat pointed to the pile of rocks at the far edge of the shelter. "If it's all right with you, I thought we'd finish setting these out. I think we've got enough rocks here for five or six more cairns. There's no sense leaving them here when they might be able to do some good for somebody."

Dan nodded. "That sounds good to me," he said as he laced up his boots.

"Good!" Pat pulled a dusty canvas sack from the top of the pack and tossed it to Dan. "You can carry the rocks. But don't worry," he added mischievously. "It's not far."

Dan filled the sack—there wasn't much empty space in it when he was done—and lifted it experimentally to his shoulder. It wasn't light, but it was manageable, and he took a few clumsy steps in the sand to see if he'd be able to carry it without falling over. "Is this your usual load?" he asked.

"More or less. Follow me, now. This way, up and over."

Together they climbed the dune just beyond the shelter, where Pat had already placed enough cairns to show the way. This looked to be the highest dune of them all, and it would have been a tough climb even for someone who didn't happen to be lugging a hundred-pound sack of rocks on his back. As it was, Dan had to call several rest breaks before they reached the summit—but the view when they finally got to the last rock pile was well worth the effort.

21

And he will turn the hearts of fathers to their children
and the hearts of children to their fathers.

—Malachi 4:6

Below them lay an entirely different landscape than the
one they were leaving, so intensely colored with greens
and blues that Dan's eyes were almost overwhelmed.

Miles of tantalizing forest and fields stretched into the
distance—cool green spires of fir and spruce, meadows
filled with wildflowers, tempting glimpses of blue water
that had to be lakes and ponds—all rising gently westward
to the foothills of those impossibly splendid mountains,
whose every peak was a soaring tower of silvery rock
veined with waterfalls and capped by dazzling white.

At the foot of the dune on which they stood, a broad,
shallow stream cut its way through the last of the sand,
clear and gold and shimmering in the morning light. It
looked deliciously inviting, and Dan suddenly felt like
taking a swim.

"I know what you're thinking," said his father with a
laugh. "But first things first, son. It's time to lay down
some of those rocks." He pointed ahead. "There's no
need to put any more of them here on the dune; it's obvious that there's only one way to go. What we need to

do now is go down and mark the best crossing of that stream. There's a game trail through the sagebrush and manzanita on the other side—you can see it right there, just past that group of live oaks—but it's not nearly as easy to spot once you're at ground level. We want to make sure nobody misses it."

Dan decided it was time he and the sack of rocks took a more extended break from each other. He laid the bag down, sat beside it on the sharp summit of the dune, and looked up at his father.

"Sit down and take a rest, Dad," he said. "Let's talk."

"All right." Pat plunked himself down with a grunt. "Pretty good place for a break, isn't it?"

"It certainly is." Dan looked at him. "I was just thinking to myself that you seem to know this place really well."

"Yep, I do. Fact is, I've been back and forth over this part of Purgatory many times. Hundreds of times, I'll bet. Like I said, I've been here quite a while. Years, I think —although time doesn't seem to work here the way you might expect."

"Okay, so tell me now why you've been laying down all these stones. You're obviously expecting someone to use them."

"Well, I expected you to use them, of course. And you did, didn't you?"

Dan nodded. "I did. But somehow I think I'd have found you anyway."

"Maybe." He shrugged and smiled. "Okay then, probably. But this helped me feel I was doing something to make it happen. Showing that it was something I really wanted to happen."

Dan felt an unfamiliar surge of warmth in his heart. "Well, here I am," he said. "So I guess it must have worked."

Pat reached out and laid a hand on his shoulder. "I'm glad, Daniel. More than you can imagine."

They spent several minutes in silence, gazing out at the panorama before them. A flight of swans rose into the air from one of the half-hidden lakes, spiraling upward one after the next and heading north in a loose line. Faintly on the breeze, Dan could hear the beat of their massive wings.

"And I've been doing it for the others too," Pat continued. "The people back down in the canyon. I've gotten to know a lot of them—heck, I was one of them for a long while. They struggle, Dan. Sooner or later they'll get where they need to be, but it's hard for them."

Dan nodded. "I noticed that. It made me realize how dangerous it would have been for me to stay there any longer than I did."

"Exactly. There's a kind of exhaustion that sets in once you give up and start to lose hope. You become, well, not lazy exactly, but passive. Down there, everyone talks about the day when they're going to climb out and make that journey to the mountains. They really mean it, they really want it, and one by one, people do leave and make their way out. But for others that day never seems to come. Instead, they just sit there waiting for something to happen."

"I can't imagine *you* sitting around waiting," said Dan. "You, of all people."

"Well, I did. For a while, anyway." He sighed. "Look, son, I've been here long enough to see myself for what

I am and to see my life for what it was. You know what I'm talking about; you've been walking that road yourself. You've seen what your life was, and you realize what it could have been. You've seen all the missed opportunities for love, all the cheap substitutes for joy, all the careless cruelties and selfish choices."

"Yes, I have." Dan picked up a handful of sun-warmed sand and let it run though his fingers. "More than I ever wanted to see."

"Well, in this place everybody's dealing with his own variations on that particular theme. None of it is particularly special or unique. To some degree, every one of us failed to be what we could have been—and along the way some of us caused a lot of heartbreak to the people who loved us."

"Dad, we've already had this conversation a long, long time ago. All you need to know is that I love you and I'm glad to be here with you . . ."

"You're right," Pat said with a shake of his head. "I guess we don't need to go over that again. The point I'm trying to make is that when I climbed up here and saw those mountains from this spot, I realized that I was finally past all that. It was burned out of me; I was ready to move on. I'd been ready for a long time, in fact. Heaven was calling me, and I didn't want to wait anymore."

"But you *have* waited," said Dan. "Why are you still here?"

"I'll get to that, I promise. But while I was waiting, I couldn't help thinking about all those people down there in the settlement. Rose, with her fixation on that husband of hers, and all the people like her. All so easily discouraged. I couldn't budge them by talking to them, but it occurred to me that they might feel more confident if they could see that someone had already been this way and left a trail. So I started making little piles of rocks for them to follow."

Dan glanced back over his shoulder and saw the faint dots of the trail receding down, up and over the dune behind them. It wasn't exactly a superhighway. "So . . . how's it working out?"

His father shrugged. "I think it's helped a little. People have always been making their way up from below, either this way or some other way. Over the years, I think there have been more folks who've seen the trail and decided to take a chance. In the end, though, it's still their choice. They have to find the courage to trust it. And to trust him."

Dan didn't need to be told what that was like. Even now he could feel that call, ever stronger, but he could also feel his own insecurity and hesitation battling to hold him back.

Pat got up and brushed the sand from his pants. "Shall we get to work? Let's finish this thing."

"Sounds good to me." Dan shouldered the sack of rocks once more (after briefly entertaining the idea of dragging them instead), and they lumbered down the long, sandy slope to the stream. The water was cool but not cold; green streamers of weed waved in the shallows, and schools of tiny fish darted about as Dan and his father waded to the grove of evergreen oaks that grew on the opposite bank.

"Right here," said Pat. "We'll put a good-sized cairn on this bank and another on the other side, just to show that this is where people need to cross."

Dan squatted down and fished a half dozen good-sized stones from the sack, watching as his father laid them out carefully into a sort of platform that he used as the base for a sturdy little pyramid.

"Like this, see?" Pat said. "Now for the most important part." Solemnly, he crossed himself and began to pray.

"Lord, as we mark this crossing, we remember all those who are still suffering here," he said. "Bless them with courage, dear Jesus. And bless all those who wander, all those who are afraid or ashamed. Draw them to yourself. Help them—help all of us—to trust you more every day. Amen."

"Just a second, Dad," said Dan. Reaching into the pocket of his shirt, he pulled out the notepad he'd carried up from the canyon and read aloud the names of the people he'd met, trying to visualize each man or woman in turn. He could see his father reacting as he read, smiling and nodding at some of the names and raising surprised eyebrows at others.

"Amen," said Dan at last.

"Amen," said Pat. "That was a kindhearted thing, son."

They repeated the process in front of the live oaks that rose on the opposite bank of the stream, and still had enough rocks left over to lay several more cairns along the trail leading away into the bush. Each pile was stacked into its proper shape and received its own prayer. Finally, his father straightened up, dusting off his hands with a smile of satisfaction.

"I think that'll do it," he said. "How about a swim?"

That sounded perfect to Dan, who hadn't been in clean water for more time than he could remember. To his father's great amusement, he didn't even bother to take off his clothes, since they were just as much in need of a wash as he was—he simply emptied his pockets, dove into the stream, and sloshed about in the shallows, whooping and splashing and frightening the fish. A great blue heron that had been browsing among the reeds upstream gave him a look of annoyance and flapped peevishly away.

"This is awesome!" Dan shouted to his father, who decided after a brief hesitation that swimming and doing laundry at the same time wasn't such a bad idea. Soon they both were splashing, laughing, and dunking each other underwater like a pair of ten-year-olds, and stopped only when they ran out of breath. They peeled off their dripping clothes, hung them on the bushes and trees to dry, and jumped immediately back into the stream, where they happily stretched out on its shallow bottom and let the current rinse the ache out of their muscles.

"Pretty nice, eh?"

"Pretty darned nice, Dad. I had no idea a person could have so much, um, so much fun, in Purgatory. Doesn't it strike you as more than a little . . . I don't know . . . incongruous?"

"At first it did. But the more you think about it, why shouldn't there be joy here? You and I are together; that's certainly cause for celebration. We've been forgiven a lifetime of selfishness and stupidity, we've shucked off a lifetime of regrets, and we know that we're headed for something so amazing that it will make everything else—even all of this—seem like a tacky imitation of reality. If we could laugh and play and take delight when we were back in the world, with all its heartbreaks and failures and wickedness, why shouldn't we be happy here?"

"Hmm. I see your point."

"And I see yours, son. Don't think that I don't. Believe me, I've felt exactly the same way. It's hard not to keep punishing yourself once you realize what a lousy job you made of your life, right? Back in the world, a little guilt can help you mend your ways and fix the things you broke—the ones that can be fixed, anyway—but it doesn't serve any purpose here. In the end, you have to choose whether to keep clinging to it or just shut up and accept the gift."

Dan couldn't help himself; he started laughing. And it felt good. "You sound like Rafe, my angel friend."

Pat raised his eyebrows. "So you've met Rafe, have you? I should have known."

"We shared coffee," said Dan. "And a few beers. He's always talking about accepting the gift."

"And rightly so. Maybe that ought to be the motto of this place," said Pat.

"Sorry for laughing, though. I didn't mean to be rude."

"I don't mind a bit. Go ahead and laugh at your old dad. Laughing is good."

"You've always been able to deliver a good speech, Dad. But when did you get to be so wise?"

"Serious question?"

"Yep. Serious question. Completely non-sarcastic."

Pat stood up, water streaming from him in shining drops. "Okay, then. Here's the serious answer: I'm no wiser than I ever was. It's just that a lot of the things that were darkening my thoughts and my behavior are gone now. Taken away from me. I've said it before, and I'll say it again: Inside and outside, I'm more and more the man I was supposed to have been all along. The man I'm supposed to be from now on. Serious enough?"

226

"Yes, sir."

"The same thing has been happening to you, Daniel. I'm not sure you've noticed, but I can see it. You're not entirely who you used to be either. Or maybe the better way to say it is that you're becoming entirely yourself, for the first time."

Dan grinned up at him. "I appreciate the encouragement, Dad. But I'm afraid you're right—I still haven't noticed any big changes." He stood up too and let the water sluice off his body into the stream. "Anyway, here we are—all washed off and relaxed and done with discouragement. What's next on the agenda?"

"Well, if our clothes are dry enough, getting dressed might be a good idea," said his father. "Then maybe we can climb back up that dune and have some lunch at the shelter."

The clothes were still a little damp as they plucked them from the vegetation, but the sun and the desert air had already done most of their work, and by the time they reached Pat's bivouac in the dunes the garments were completely dry. Lunch was a simple meal of nuts, raisins, and energy bars from their packs, washed down with copious amounts of water—neither of them felt like cooking, and the day was already more than warm enough. Afterward they lay back in the shade, resting their heads on the packs and looking up at the blue afternoon sky.

"What now, Dad?" asked Dan, watching a single bird circling high above them. *Could be an eagle or a hawk*, he thought. *Or a vulture. Too far away to tell.*

Pat sat up and took a great breath. "Well," he said, "I suppose we could talk. I promised I would tell you why I wanted to have you here, didn't I?"

"Yes, you did. And here I was starting to think you just wanted the pleasure of my company."

His father started laughing. "Actually, I did. I do. The pleasure of your company is exactly what I wanted. That's exactly what I prayed for."

Dan raised himself up on one elbow and looked at him intently.

"Really? All these twists and turns and coincidences that have been leading me here—they're not part of some Great Divine Plan to prepare us both for Heaven? This isn't the turning point in the movie where everything gets fixed, all the questions get answered, all the knots get untangled?"

Pat held up his hands. "Honestly, I have no idea. It's God's movie, and I wouldn't venture to predict what he might have up his sleeve. All I wanted was to spend some time with you."

"Thank you, Dad," said Dan as he, too, sat upright. "That means a great deal to me. Right now, there's no place I'd rather be and nobody I'd rather be with." To his own surprise he discovered from the catch in his voice that he meant it. Deeply.

"Look, we've both spent more than enough time digging through our past failures and mistakes. It's the most painful thing about being here, and neither one of us wants to go over our litany of sins again. But the fact remains that I seriously messed up when you were a kid. My only job was to protect you, and instead I became something you needed to be protected from."

"Dad—"

"Let me finish. You already know how terrible I feel about that. I want you to know that I would give anything—anything—to have been the father I should have been back then. I robbed you of something precious. The thing is, I robbed myself of something precious too."

He reached over and ruffled his son's hair. A gesture Dan could not remember him ever having made before.

"It's not just that you and I spent so much time as enemies, Daniel. It's that we spent so little time as friends. You missed all the walks, the talks, the goofing around with your dad, the playing catch and catching fish. All those father-and-son times. Well, I missed them too. The loneliness and yearning that broke your heart? They broke my heart too—even though I showed it only in the most confused and hurtful ways."

"That's all behind us now," said Dan, distressed by his father's obvious pain. "I wasn't an easy kid to love either. But it was all a long time ago. You know now that I love you, and I know that you love me. We've already had this discussion. We had it years ago."

Pat nodded. His eyes were wet. "Yes, we did. And that was one of the best days of my life, Daniel."

"Mine too."

"I realize we can't undo the past; we can only forgive and accept forgiveness. But I think that sometimes, if we want it badly enough . . . sometimes we might recover at least a little of what we thought was gone forever." He cleared his throat. "That's why I've hoped and prayed for this meeting. Here I am now—here, in this place, finally the man I was supposed to be. And here you are too—the man *you* were supposed to be. I don't know what we'll be like when this journey is ended, but I'm convinced it will be wonderful. So . . . what I was thinking was that I'd like us to go the rest of the way together. Father and son. Pat and Dan. It doesn't have to be a big thing. Just the two of us spending some time together taking it easy, enjoying each other's company. Doing some of the things we should have done."

Pat looked up, and Dan could see the question in his eyes even before he asked it. "What do you think, son? Is that something you could see happening?"

"I think I'd like that very much," he said. "When do we get started?"

His father laughed with obvious relief.

"Part of me wants to say, 'As soon as we can get our gear packed and hit the trail.' But I think it might not be a bad idea to take our time, watch a last sunset over these dunes—I promise you, the sunsets are magnificent up here—and get a good night's sleep. If you're bored, I have a chessboard and a deck of cards in my pack."

"I'm not bored, Dad. And we don't need to have any deep discussions either. I'm just fine enjoying this time together."

The afternoon passed easily. Dan insisted on cooking dinner—from a packet of beef bourguignon he'd been saving for a special occasion—and the sunset, when it came, was everything his father had said it would be. As night fell, they lay happily, side by side, watching the stars brighten as the sand whispered around them and sang them to sleep.

22

The path to Heaven lies through Heaven, and all the way to Heaven is Heaven.

> —Dorothy Day,
>   quoting Saint Catherine of Siena

Dawn woke them, rosy and glowing, and Dan came awake with more energy than he had felt in weeks. After a cold breakfast—neither of them wanted to waste time washing dishes—he and his father rolled up their sleeping bags, took down the shelter tarp, and quickly packed everything for a day on the trail.

Once the work was done, they checked the site to make sure they hadn't left any sign of their stay, hoisted their packs to their shoulders, and said a brief prayer of thanksgiving and blessing. As Dan watched his father's bright face, he couldn't help wishing—only for an instant —that it could always have been like this. It was an unworthy thought, he admitted to himself; the important thing was that it was happening now. And that was one more thing to be grateful for.

"Ready?" asked Pat.

"Ready!"

Together they climbed the final dune, descended to the

stream to fill their depleted water bottles, crossed to the far bank, and took up the trail as it entered the dense, low chaparral beyond, heading west toward the distant mountains with the warm morning sun at their backs. The tallest peak, the unwavering goal by which they steered, towered now over the farthest trees, snow covered and bright against the brilliant morning sky.

Dan could feel it calling him, drawing him again, stronger than ever. Not the mountain itself, of course—he had come to realize that it, too, was a signpost pointing to a greater and more substantial reality, a potent reminder of their true goal and a message of encouragement. Like his father's trail of little rock piles. Gazing up at it, he remembered Heaven. And he could feel the strength of that call piercing through the old haze of mistrust and discouragement.

This is what Dad meant, he told himself. *This is what he was talking about. The haze burns off like fog in the sunlight, and then you see. Then you feel.*

After walking on stone and sand for so long, Dan found himself enjoying the springy, firm feel of the loamy earth beneath his feet and the chance to hike with a full stride once more. The sagebrush around them was damp and fragrant with morning dew, and he breathed its spicy aroma with pleasure. His father was leading the way, wearing his battered, sun-bleached pack as if it weighed nothing at all.

"This isn't the same approach I made before," said Dan. "The mountain looks different."

"It *is* different," said Pat, talking over his shoulder. "We're looking at the east face right now. In a while, the trail will swing around to the north again, and things will look more familiar to you."

Dan stopped in his tracks. "You said you've been out here before, but you never said how far. I'm curious, Dad —just how far did you get?"

His father stopped too, and turned to face him. "Well . . . pretty much to the foot of the mountain."

"And you came back?"

"Yep. I came back." He grinned. "I may have mentioned before how hard it was to turn around. By then I was more than ready. But the more I thought about it, the more I decided I'd rather stick around a few more years so we could do this together."

Dan stared. "Dad, I . . . don't know what to say."

"You can tell me you're glad I waited, I guess."

Without stopping to think, Dan hurried to his father and wrapped his arms around him. "Yes, I'm glad," he said. "Yes, yes, I'm glad. Thank you."

Pat squeezed back. "You're welcome, son. Now, let's get going, okay? We've still got a lot of ground to cover today, and there are some spots up ahead that I know you're going to love."

"I do have another question, though. That is, if you don't mind."

"Sure. Let's hear it."

"I think about Anna all the time, Dad, and I'm sure you think about Cindy. I keep thinking they'd love to share this with us too. Shouldn't we stick around and wait for *them*?"

His father nodded. "That's a good question," he said. "I really don't know the answer to it, but somehow I

233

get the feeling they'll be just fine without us. I think . . . I'm not exactly sure how to say it, but I think they'll be walking a different trail than this one. For all I know, they may already have reached the finish line ahead of us."

Dan spent some time chewing on this idea. He wasn't entirely sure he could wrap his mind around it, but it was worth considering. This place, this journey, was about getting prepared for an eternity of life in Heaven —straightening the crooked paths, moving the rocks and deadfalls that stood in one's way. There was little doubt that he and his father had a lot of work to do along those lines, but the situation was probably quite different for their wives.

"Okay," he said. "I'll buy that."

They resumed their walk. The trail sloped gently upward, and as they followed it Dan began to notice how the scrubby evergreen oaks and rabbit-brush gave way gradually to taller, shadier trees, how the scent of sage and juniper gave way to the familiar North Woods smell of spruce and pine. There were birds darting everywhere—wrens and jays, nuthatches, sparrows, and flycatchers—and a half dozen unseen woodpeckers were hammering overhead.

It was a beautiful day, in every sense of the word, and it seemed to get better every minute. It made Dan remember the best times of his childhood and the early hikes he and his father had taken together when he was just a youngster. These were good memories, true memories, and they warmed his heart.

"There's a nice lake up the trail a bit," said Pat. "Maybe five or six miles. Every time I stopped there, I'd think about how much you would like it. There's fine trout fishing and lots of good spots for the tents. If it's all right with you, I wouldn't mind staying there for a few days. Just for fun."

Dan nodded. "That sounds great, Dad."

Slowly, as they continued to climb upward, low outcroppings of gray, weathered rock began to appear on both sides of them, scattered randomly through the woods. Most were at waist or shoulder height, but a few were clumped together in rough palisades that rose fifteen or twenty feet. As they were passing near one of these, Pat suddenly stopped in his tracks, took a deep breath, and pointed upward.

"Look!" Pat said in an urgent whisper. "On the ledge just below the top of that rock."

Dan looked, and then stared openmouthed at the sight. A trio of mountain lions—two adults and a smaller adolescent—were sprawled on the rock, viewing the two of them with lofty indifference. One of the adults raised its muzzle slightly to sniff the wind, but otherwise the animals made no move. They were tawny and beautiful, and their silent stares conveyed a fierce, inhuman dignity.

Finally, he'd seen lions.

"That is . . . awesome," he said, as quietly as he could.

"Yes, it is." His father laid a hand on his shoulder. "It's a truly wonderful thing. And now it's time for us to move on and let them get on with their business."

Quietly, almost reverently, they made their way forward and up the trail. Neither spoke for several minutes, and when they did, their voices were still hushed.

"Thanks, Dad," said Dan. "They were so quiet, so still. I probably would have missed them if you hadn't pointed them out."

"God makes beautiful things, doesn't he?"

"Yes, he does."

"I don't want to bore you with all my regrets, but that's another thing I wish I could do over," said Pat. "Back there in the world, I wasted far too much time in my head, worrying and ruminating on things. I should have spent more of it outside, with you and with your brothers and sisters. I'd have been a happier man."

"Well, we're here now, right? And this place is pretty darned amazing." Dan looked around him at the forest, watching a pair of fat squirrels playing tag through the treetops. "I'm not sure what I expected Purgatory to be, but it sure wasn't this."

His father laughed. "Makes you wonder what Heaven will be like, doesn't it?"

"I honestly can't imagine," said Dan. "The truth is, I try not to think about it very much. I just know it's going to be better than anything I could dream up on my own."

He could see his father's brief nod. They lapsed into silence, and Dan was content to watch their surroundings, hoping to glimpse more wildlife. But although he saw birds, chipmunks, and squirrels galore, there were no more lions.

Eventually the trail began to rise more steeply. They hiked deliberately upward for nearly an hour, until it abruptly leveled out. He could tell by the sudden widening of the sky and the brightening of the light that they had reached the top of the rise. Beaming, Pat moved to one side of the path to make room for Dan, and in a few seconds they were standing together looking out over a stunning mountain lake.

"Pretty nice, eh?"

"Pretty amazing, I'd say."

The lake was a brilliant turquoise jewel, a mile across, tucked into the broad folds of a wide glacial bowl. Above it, a long, shining waterfall poured down from a wall of rugged ridges and peaks, and the meadows surrounding it were filled with wildflowers in a dozen shades and shapes. Even this far away, Dan could smell the honey-scented aroma of the blossoms.

Just beyond the far shore, a herd of at least a hundred elk browsed at the edge of a high snowfield, while scattered groups of bighorn sheep clambered across the rocks and ridges above them. In the lake itself, a small flotilla of geese moved noisily across the water. Even at this distance, Dan could hear the chaotic music of their honking. Overhead, the deep cobalt blue sky was sprinkled with fluffy clouds.

"We can camp up here at the edge of the woods, if you like, or move in a little closer to the lake," said Pat. "Your choice. There's not much cover down by the water, but I think I may have mentioned—in fact, I'm sure I did —that the fishing is excellent. Cutthroat and brookies, mostly, and they'll hit at anything you trail past them!"

Dan smiled. "Then let's set up camp by the lake. You obviously know where the good spots are."

"Right, then. I think we'll head right down *there*." Pat pointed off to the left, where the lake emptied into a lively mountain brook that tumbled noisily down into a narrow canyon. "Not too close to the stream, or we'll never get any sleep. But that ravine should give us a little protection if the wind comes up. Which it almost always does."

"Okay, Dad. You lead."

"Not so fast." Pat reached down to his side and drew a large camp knife from the sheath on his belt. "We'll need to cut ourselves a couple of good fishing poles while we're still up here under the trees." He looked at the vegetation with a critical eye. "Yes . . . these little saplings look nice and springy." Choosing a pair of small alders, he cut them free with a few sharp blows, stripped away the excess branches, and presented them to Dan. "Now we can go."

As they trooped down the meadow, Dan found himself marveling at this unexpected and matter-of-fact display of woodcraft. This was a side of his father that he hadn't seen in years and could only dimly remember from childhood. It obviously brought Pat a great deal of satisfaction and joy. Dan thought, *I wonder if this is where I learned to love the outdoors.*

It was at least a quarter of a mile to the stream, and once they reached it they looked at several possible sites before finally selecting one. It didn't take long to unpack and set up their tents, and soon they were sprawling in the grass, enjoying the luxury of stretching out under the mountain sun and watching the shadows lengthen slowly across the basin. It was still hours to sunset, but the afternoon was clearly edging toward evening.

"This is wonderful," said Dan after some time had passed. "So then . . . what's next? We get a good night's sleep and start fishing in the morning?"

His father chuckled mischievously. "Not at all. We're going to get a little warm food into ourselves and fish by starlight."

"Starlight? Really? I didn't know you could do that."

"Well, you can. I've done it lots of times. Let's rig these poles and grab some dinner while there's still some daylight left, and I'll show you how it's done. I think you're going to love it."

Sitting in the grass, they rummaged through their packs and pulled out pouches of hooks, lures, and monofilament line that were hiding in the side pockets. Dan had never noticed them before, and he wondered briefly what other surprises might be lurking in the unexplored corners of his pack.

His father patiently showed him how to turn the fresh-cut poles into improvised fishing rods, fastening the line and tying on hooks, sinkers, and lures. In return, Dan volunteered to cook supper. They settled on turkey and vegetables over noodles and wolfed it down enthusiastically when it was ready.

Once the dishes were washed and stowed away, Pat and Dan slipped down to the edge of the lake and walked along the shore to find a good spot to stand. The mountain sky had deepened above them; the sun was no longer shining on them directly, but its light filtered gently down from the peaks and spires around them, glowing with rose and gold.

"This looks like a good place," Pat said as they stood on a low knoll over the water, where the current from the lake seemed to speed up as it headed for the outlet. "If you want to fish here, I'll head down that way a bit. We don't want to be too close to each other. Somebody might make a wild cast and tangle our lines."

Dan snorted. "That would be me, of course."

"I'm not pointing any fingers, son. But I've seen you fish before."

"Dad. I think that was when I was in first grade."

"Point taken." Pat laid his own pole down on the grass. "Here, let's get you set up. Since there's no reel, there's no point in casting very far anyway. Just gently swing the line in from the side, like this, and let the sinker take it out for you. When you get a bite, you set the hook and just raise the pole upright to bring your fish into the shallows, where you can take it off and set it free. We already had dinner, so these guys will get a reprieve tonight."

"No bait?"

"Nope. Just that streamer. Here," he added, handing the pole to Dan. "It's all yours now. And don't be afraid to make lots of casts. It'll get their attention."

Dan began tentatively, tossing the lure more than casting it, and letting the current carry it into the shadowy spots, where he figured the trout would be lurking. His father set up his own spot a few yards up the shore, and they both stood like statues outlined against the luminous water as the sky first faded to lavender, then reddened to a pale apricot hue.

Truthfully, Dan didn't care if he caught a single fish. He was just enjoying the gentle sound of the water; the distant ruckus of the geese; the soft, intermittent plop of the tackle as one or the other made a new cast. More than anything, he was marveling at the way his father had just given him instructions without once expressing impatience or annoyance. *That* was a first.

Remarkably, it was Dan who caught the first fish. There was still light enough for him to see the slim, dark shadow dart from the bank, and his heart jumped with excitement as he felt it seize the hook, quickly responding with an answering tug of his own.

"Got one!" he yelled.

"Good for you!" said his father, much more quietly.

The brookie was a handsome specimen, dark green with a rusty belly and peppered with tiny blue-ringed dots on its flanks. It fought valiantly in its bid for freedom, and Dan let it tire itself before bringing it to shore. Reaching into the water to spare the trout any additional trauma, he gently slipped the barbless hook from its mouth and watched it flash away into deeper water.

"That was great!" he said, wiping his wet hands on the seat of his trousers.

"My turn!" His father's whoop was answered with a splash and a glimmer of thrashing fins from the water as a good-sized cutthroat yanked at his hook. Dan could see the pole bending in Pat's hands as he let the fish run for several minutes before bringing it in for release. From then on, they settled down to business, quietly hooking and releasing a few dozen fish over the next few hours.

Slowly, as the sky darkened, the waiting stars made their appearance, one by one, until the entire basin was covered with a blanket of pulsating light. There were tens of thousands of them, stretching above the valley in a river of light: some as bright as blue-white lamps, others forming a hazy phosphorescent mist that seemed to swirl and bend around them. There was more than enough light for fishing, and the trout themselves didn't seem remotely interested in going to bed. Finally, the two men looked at each other, nodded, and called a silent halt to the evening.

"Thanks, Dad," said Dan as they walked back to the campsite, glancing up every so often at the extravagant display of light and mystery above their heads. "That was magical! I had a great time."

Pat cleared his throat. "I'm the one who should be thanking you, Daniel," he said. "And really, we should both be thanking the one who made this possible."

And that is what they did.

23

The soul of the one who serves God always swims in joy, always keeps holiday, is always in her palace of jubilation, ever singing with fresh ardor and fresh pleasure, a new song of joy and love.

—Saint John of the Cross

They spent several days at the lake, relaxed and happy, and gradually their conversation grew less and less weighty, more and more easy. The fourth morning arrived just like the three that had preceded it: cool, clear, and filled with light. Dan awoke to the sounds and smells of breakfast.

He had been dreaming, and although he couldn't remember the dream, it had filled him with a quiet happiness that lingered as he unzipped his sleeping bag and stumbled out into the morning. The grass was still wet with dew, but his father had spread a dry tarp out and was frying pancakes.

"Good morning, sleepyhead," he said brightly. "Coffee's in the pot. Pour yourself a cup while it's still hot."

"Thanks. I'll be right with you."

Dan slipped a pair of flip-flops onto his feet and circled around to the other side of the tent. It was a beautiful morning, cool and clear, and the sun was already painting warm light on the craggy heights before them. There were ducks on the lake, mumbling softly to each other as they rode the ruffled water, and a lone coyote loped along the far shore, giving the birds an occasional interested glance.

A fishing trip through Purgatory, he thought. *Not exactly how I imagined this place.*

But why not, after all? He thought back to what Pat had said days before—back when they'd been swimming at the edge of the dunes—about how the enjoyment of simple pleasures might be just as much a part of one's preparation for Heaven as any somber asceticism could be, because purgation was about getting rid of the attachments and habits that still clung to you and held you back.

So yes, Dan could see that a painful dose of suffering had definitely helped him recognize the truths he'd been hiding from himself, and had definitely brought him around to real repentance. But to clean out the ugly nest of resentments and suspicions that had deformed his relationships with God and other people . . . for that, maybe a different approach was called for. Maybe a long-deferred father-and-son fishing trip was exactly the way to banish those last few demons.

"Come and get it!" called Pat, breaking into his reverie. "It's pancakes again, I'm afraid. Hope you don't mind."

Dan returned to the cookstove, poured himself a mug of coffee, took a healthy gulp, and sat down cross-legged on the tarp. "Don't mind? Dad, I've been eating instant oatmeal for breakfast since I got here. Trust me—hot pancakes are an absolute luxury. Even your instant coffee tastes better than what I've been making for myself."

His father handed him a plate and settled on the ground

beside him with his own plate in hand. "Things just taste better when you have someone to share them with."

They said a quick prayer of thanks, looking toward the brightening sky above the ridge, and set to work on the food. The pancakes were fluffy, steamy, and delicious, and when they had finished, Dan volunteered once again to wash, dry, and pack the cooking gear.

"What's the plan for the day?" he asked, returning the plates to the top of his father's pack. "More fishing?"

Pat nodded. "I suppose we might as well spend an hour or two harassing the trout while the sun dries the dew off our tents," he said. "But after that I think we ought to pack up and hit the trail. We've got a lot more territory to cover, and there's plenty more to see. Does that work for you?"

"Perfectly. And I think I'm finally starting to get the hang of this business. I've decided that fishing is a form of meditation." He stood up and was reaching for his pole when a thought struck him suddenly.

"Just a second," he said. "I almost forgot something."

Pulling the little notebook from his pocket, he silently read the names of all the people he'd encountered in the canyon, trying to connect each with a remembered face, and prayed that all of them would soon receive the strength to continue their journey.

"I love to see you doing that," his father said as they walked together to the lake. "I have a list of my own, up here in my head. It means a lot to them, Dan. More than you know."

The fishing, of course, was perfect; together they caught and released dozens of trout as the morning brightened and the sun finally made its appearance over the trees behind them. All too soon, they called a halt and returned to the campsite to pack the tents and resume their hike.

"We'll circle around the lake to the right and head for that saddle where those elk have been hanging out," Pat said, pointing up to a wide green rise between two rugged peaks. "There's a game trail up there that leads down into the next basin, and we can follow the drainage north from that point until we reach another forest."

They set off, rounding the lake and heading up toward the saddle. The climb was easy at first but grew steadily more strenuous as the morning wore on. For the last mile they stopped several times along the steep slope to rest, catch their breath, and look back at the landscape they were leaving behind. It was a lovely panorama: the lake and its basin, the wooded ridge where they'd stood so many days earlier, and a faint glimpse down the streambed to the tawny dunes and the stone tableland from which they'd started.

But the view as they topped the rise was even more spectacular. To the west, rows of jagged gray peaks thrust toward the sky, rising above deep canyons and forested ravines where shreds of mist still floated above the green spears of fir and spruce. And above it all, lit dramatically by the morning sun, the great mountain itself rose like a sleeping giant. Beckoning them onward.

"Oh!" said Dan, halting in his tracks to gaze at its glowing, massive splendor. "Oh man!"

The feeling that swept suddenly over him was almost more than he could bear, as though all the yearnings and hopes of his life were gathered into one powerful wave of eagerness and desire, untrammeled now by any trace of fear or shame. He looked over at his father, who nodded back at him and smiled but said nothing.

It was amazing how this ache of longing seemed to have lost none of its power to take him by surprise. By now he'd have expected to be hardened to it, at least a little. But here it was again, rising up in his heart stronger than ever, filling him with an overwhelming surge of mingled joy and glory. It stirred him deeply, like the banners and shouts of a great army or the mounting crescendo of a symphony.

He knew with absolute certainty that no mere mountain, no matter how majestic, could call up such a visceral response. This was about something else, *someone* else, entirely. He'd heard people talk about praying without words before, and now he found himself doing exactly that. No human speech could describe what was pouring into his heart. He could only stand above the abyss, legs spread and hands lifted to the sky, and let it all pour back out of him in a flood of speechless wonder and gratitude.

Eventually, the moment faded. He dropped his arms back to his sides, took a deep shuddering breath, and looked at his father, who had been studying him intently for some minutes.

"I'm okay," he said.

"Of course you are." Pat looked at him tenderly. "Of course you are. Do you need more time, or are you ready to move on?"

He nodded. "Let's go."

Pat pointed to the faint trail at their feet, which led downward and toward the right, into a deep and thickly forested valley. "There's the path," he said. "Watch your step. It's a little tricky up here at the top, but it'll get easier as we descend. The woods go on for ten or twelve miles, and after that the valley opens up into a nice meadow with a lot of wildlife. I hope we'll get to see some of it this afternoon."

They shifted their packs and headed carefully down the trail, picking their way through a litter of gravel and stones that made their footing shifty and undependable. After sending several small rocks tumbling down the slope, Dan could understand why his father had warned him to stay alert. "You've done this route a lot, haven't you?" he asked.

"A few times."

"Dad, how could you stand it?" he asked. "Coming so close and then turning back? The feeling is so strong in me now that I almost want to throw down my pack and run. All I can think of right now is that I was once even closer than this, and I lost my nerve like a fool. How could you do this over and over again?"

"Don't beat yourself up, Daniel. It's not about nerve; it's about trust. I've been there too, more times than I can tell. But we've both learned a lot since then. Everything that has happened has led us to this moment. Both of us. And this time neither one of us is turning back."

"But Dad—"

"Of course it hurt. It hurt every time I turned around. But now we're together and on our way, and everything is the way it ought to be. Thanks be to God."

"Amen," said Dan, wondering—not for the first time —how his screwed-up father could have turned into such a deep-souled man.

"Look!" Pat exclaimed, pointing upward suddenly. "Eagles! Dozens of them!"

They were golden eagles, larger and more majestic than the bald eagles Dan was more familiar with. They were kettling—soaring ever higher in a wide circle as they rode currents of warming air that would take them far into the sky and over the mountains. It was a beautiful, solemn sight.

"A convocation of eagles," said Pat. "That's what it's called, and it's a pretty rare thing to see. Solitary birds, eagles. They don't get together very often."

But Dan's attention had already been caught by a flash of movement from another direction. Below them, near the bottom of the slope, some animal was making its way up the trail toward them. It was too small to be a deer or a bear, and it didn't seem to be moving in the wary, careful way of creatures in the wild. In fact, there was something strangely familiar about that shape . . . and suddenly he recognized it.

"Buddy!" he shouted. "Hey, Buddy! Here, boy!"

The dog halted for an instant, uttered a pair of excited barks, and began bounding enthusiastically up the path.

"Somebody you know?" asked Pat.

"Heck yes! That's Buddy!"

His father nodded with a noncommittal smile, and Dan remembered that this particular canine had never been part of their shared life together.

"He was our family dog when my own kids were little," he explained. "He was here to meet me at the trailhead back when I first got here, and he stayed with me all the way to the foot of the mountain. He even tried to stop me from turning back, and when I didn't listen, he . . . sort of took off without me."

"Sounds like a smart dog." Pat peered down the trail. "I suppose we ought to get moving, then. I don't think you'll have much luck trying to stop him now, but we may be able to save him some unnecessary climbing."

Still choosing their steps with care, they picked up the

pace until the gear jostled and clanked in their packs, but Buddy was faster than either of them. In the end, the best they could do was to reach a relatively wide spot along the path where the dog could jump and whine and lick them without causing a landslide or a fall. Even then it was a close thing, because there was a great deal of jumping, whining, and licking when he arrived.

"Down, boy!" Dan scolded. Or tried to scold, anyway —he was so grateful to see Buddy again that his heart really wasn't in it. This felt like more than a reunion; it seemed almost like a kind of benediction, a token of forgiveness for his earlier failure of confidence, his lack of courage.

"Wonder why I didn't get a dog," said Pat, with what sounded a little like wistfulness, as Dan knelt down to scratch behind Buddy's ears.

"Maybe you didn't need one. Hey, calm down, Buddy!"

"Probably. But still . . . it might have been nice."

Dan grinned up at him. "Well, it looks like we've got this fellow back again, and I don't mind sharing. He can sleep in your tent tonight."

"We'll be sleeping out on this mountainside if we don't push on," said Pat. "Follow me."

Dan laughed. "That's not how it works, Dad. Like it or not, we follow Buddy now."

And that was how the three of them headed down the path: single file, dog first. Dan felt his spirits rising as they descended to the valley and entered the forest. Sunlight hadn't yet reached this deep cleft between the ridges, and Dan suspected the woods wouldn't get more than an hour of direct sun even at midday. There was plenty of indirect light reflected from the surrounding peaks, though, and they hiked forward contentedly under the canopy of evergreens.

On the high saddle they'd just crossed there had been no sound except for the singing of the wind and the crunch of their boots. Off to their left, a modest stream accompanied them, coming occasionally in and out of sight but always making its presence known by a constant, cheerful gurgling. It was a gentle descent on springy turf, and the hours passed pleasantly enough without any need for conversation.

By the middle of the afternoon, they reached the clearing Pat had promised. The gradient of the trail had gradually flattened out, the trees and mountains had fallen away on either side, and they now found themselves traveling through a narrow sun-drenched meadow filled with grasses and flowers; huge dragonflies zoomed back and forth over the vegetation, their wings glinting like glass. All around them, rugged crags rose up like ruined towers, somber and bleak, but they didn't intimidate Buddy in the least. He bounded ahead, led on by some scent he alone could detect, and they followed, amused by his enthusiasm.

"This is a big place," said Dan.

"It is," his father agreed. "And there's really not a bad campsite in the entire valley. So what's your preference? We can follow the trail as far as you want to go, or start looking for a place to settle in."

"Actually, I'm still feeling pretty fresh. Since there's plenty of daylight, let's put on a few more miles before we call it a day."

"Sounds good."

They headed down the path in good spirits, keeping

an eye out for larger animals that might be lurking in the brush near the stream. At one point they heard a loud thrashing in the bushes that Pat identified as a bear—or possibly several bears.

"Time to make a little noise ourselves," he said. "Just to avoid any embarrassing encounters."

With that, he burst unexpectedly into song. It was "Volare," of all things—a standard from . . . when was it, 1958?

> No wonder my happy heart sings
> Your love has given me wings . . .

It was a happy, ridiculous song, and Pat's carefree baritone carried Dan immediately back to the Time Before It All Went Bad, when his father had been the kind of man to burst frequently and unexpectedly into song— around the house, out in the yard, while driving. This had been one of his favorite tunes.

Suddenly Dan found himself weeping. The tears just sprang out of him silently, streaming down his face. He was glad Pat was walking in front and couldn't see them.

He hadn't cried like this since . . . well, in a long time. It wasn't as though he were ashamed or miserable now. It was nothing like that. There was just something so sweet and beautiful about the moment, and here it had sneaked up and smacked him between the eyes. As if none of the other things had ever happened, even though he knew they had.

Whatever had been making the noise in the bushes, Pat's singing must have put it in a more thoughtful mood, because it became very quiet. They walked on, and Dan surreptitiously wiped his face, letting the dry mountain air do the rest. He felt strangely peaceful now, strangely happy. Something important had happened. He wasn't certain exactly what it was, but he didn't want to spoil it by thinking about it too much.

"Look up ahead and to the right, Daniel," said his father. "About halfway up the cliff. Are those mountain goats?"

They had to be, Dan thought. Nothing else could leap around so fearlessly on such a steep, sheer rockface. There were a half dozen of them, tiny in the distance but brilliant white against the gray rock, dancing from one narrow ledge to another as if they had all the room in the world. Pat and Dan stopped, fascinated, and watched the performance for several minutes before resuming their hike.

They walked on for another hour or two, as the valley continued to broaden on either side and revealed more and more of the surrounding mountain ranges. Buddy wandered back every so on to check on them, then would resume his tireless canine patrol. Finally, as the light visibly gentled toward evening, they reached a spot that seemed made for camping—a wide, level lawn near the stream, sheltered in a stand of young aspen whose tiny leaves shimmered in the breeze.

By common consent Dan and his father laid down their packs, set up camp, and put on fleeces and jackets to counter the growing chill in the air. Dan volunteered to cook dinner, and Pat took the opportunity to explore their surroundings. He reported back just as Dan was setting out plates and cups.

"Good-sized trout in this stream," he said happily. "We should have a nice leisurely time catching them tonight if you like."

"I'd like that a lot," said Dan. "Just by coincidence, I made us a tuna noodle casserole for dinner. Well, something with tuna and noodles in it, anyway."

"As long as it's hot."

Gratefully, they filled their plates, asked God to bless the meal, and sat down on the trunk of a fallen tree to eat. Buddy had returned to the campsite, but as was his custom he seemed more interested in their company than their food, settling down between them with a contented sigh. Together they watched the water tumble over the rocks, watched shadows creep across the tallest peaks where the sun was still shining, watched a flock of birds winging down the valley across the cloud-flecked sky.

"Another momentous day, Dad," said Dan. "Thank you."

Pat shook his head. "No, Daniel. Thank *you*. And thank God. I'm so glad we didn't miss all of this."

"Me too."

That was all the conversation they had for a while. It was interesting, Dan thought, considering how much they had talked during those first few days among the dunes. This easy silence seemed to have become their default setting. But after all, what more was there to say that couldn't be better expressed with a smile, a nod, a hand on the shoulder? After so many years and so much unease, they had finally become comfortable with each other.

They fished until dark, casting with their homemade tackle as the light dimmed and the stream became a ribbon of rose, a shimmering banner of orange, and finally a sheet of moonlit silver. Pat caught several of the wary brookies, but they completely outwitted Dan. It didn't matter. He was entirely content to stand on the rocky bank, pole in hand, enjoying the flawlessness of the moment.

He's right, he thought. *Thank God we didn't miss this.*

At last, feeling his eyelids getting heavy, he gathered in his line and wound it carefully around the pole. "I think I'm going to turn in," he said.

"Buddy and I will be along soon," said his father, looking down at the dog, who lay at his feet. "I think we'll wait to see the stars come out."

Dan nodded.

"He's all yours tonight, Buddy," he told the dog. "Take good care of him."

24

Our lives are involved with one another; through innumerable interactions they are linked together. No one lives alone. No one sins alone. No one is saved alone.

—Pope Benedict XVI, *Spe Salvi*

The next day was every bit as lovely, and so were all the days that followed. Each morning Dan awoke to a beauty, a contentment, and a sense of gratitude that he had never known before, not even in the best moments of his life, and a growing conviction that even this was a pale shadow of what awaited them.

As if the landscape itself were mirroring his thoughts, the country through which they traveled seemed to become more and more beautiful with each passing day. There were steep climbs to lofty ridges with tantalizing views of the great peak toward which they journeyed, long treks across grassy plateaus where the entire world seemed spread out below them, careful descents to forested ravines and mysterious canyons of weathered stone. But for all its ups and downs, the trail carried them ever higher.

Life teemed around them in all its manifold vigor and multiplicity, from the lofty mountain trees that clung tenaciously to the steepest crags to the tough alpine grasses, shrubs, and flowering plants that covered the high meadows. Each day they spied animals from the trail— elk, bear, bighorn, fox, pikas and marmots, clouds of butterflies among the endless flowers—and each night the coyotes and wolves sang the two travelers to sleep.

They camped beside streams and waterfalls, in dry canyons and open meadows, fishing when they chose and hiking when the spirit moved them. They journeyed through all kinds of weather: brilliant sunlight, eerie fogs, torrential afternoon rains, and one brief high-altitude blizzard in which they lost all sense of where they were. There were splendid sunrises and vivid sunsets, and Pat and Dan marked each wonder with prayers of thankfulness and praise.

In quiet moments, Dan found himself returning over and over to his tiny notebook, reviewing the names he'd scribbled in it during his brief stay in the canyon and adding others as they occurred to him. Carefully, he tried to remember each face and prayed silently that all of them would be given strength, courage, and joy for the road ahead. After a time, the notebook began to look tattered and grubby—several pages even came loose—but by that time he'd come to know every name in it by heart.

Each day his prayers grew more fervent, his desire more piercing, his impatience more difficult to contain. Yet he knew that this, too, was part of his growing excitement —that somehow the pain of his earlier longing was being transmuted into a poignant, exuberant eagerness, all the sweeter for its stinging.

Patience, he reminded himself. *Patience, Dan. This, too, is part of the journey.*

And then, quite suddenly, everything changed.

The runners arrived late one morning, just as Dan and his father were breaking camp. Dan and Pat had chosen a spot beside another small alpine lake, higher than they'd ever been before; the night had been clear and cold, and they'd awakened to find a thin, smooth sheath of ice over their gear and all their surroundings, including the surface of the water. It melted quickly in the sun, but they'd had to wait several hours for the tents to dry before packing up.

It was Buddy who first heard the sounds. Pricking up his ears, he stationed himself silently in the middle of the trail they'd climbed the day before. Soon Dan and Pat could hear it too: the faint murmur of happy voices, the urgent rhythm of running feet. Dan remembered it well, although he hadn't heard it in weeks, possibly months. It was the sound of Heaven-bound runners, heading their way.

He looked up at his father, who was listening intently with a faint smile on his face. He seemed to have had some experience of his own with these purgatorial athletes.

"Sounds like we're about to have company," he said. "We'd better hurry up and finish packing."

It was the work of a few minutes to get their gear squared away, but Dan already knew how fast these runners could move. They barely had enough time to pack their gear and tidy up the campsite before the first of their visitors emerged from the ice-glazed vegetation and came to a halt in the clearing.

Dan stared as more and more runners arrived, wide grins on their faces.

He knew these people.

"Well, if it isn't the Geary boys!" said an exuberant Rose, panting a little but otherwise unscathed by what must have been a very strenuous run. "Good morning, Daniel. And Patrick! I'm so glad to see that you found each other at last! And now we've found you too!"

They were all there, clustered together around them: Rose and Maria, Robert and Shirley, Daoud, Anthony, Felicia, Ted, and at least a dozen others. They all looked fit and eager, flushed with confidence and not even the slightest bit winded. Buddy raced around them, barking joyfully, and several members of the group bent down to scratch his head and let their hands be sniffed.

"Good morning!" said Dan. "What a wonderful surprise!"

His father, on the other hand, didn't seem the least bit surprised. "It's good to see you all," he said. "Have you had a good run so far?"

Everyone nodded. Some were dancing from one foot to another—not exactly running in place, but still full of restless energy. Dan struggled to remind himself that these were the same souls who had been so fainthearted and uncertain back in that crowded canyon. Not only had they found the wherewithal to climb those forbidding cliffs, but they'd somehow been running at such a furious pace that they'd caught up with him and his father.

"Okay, I'll admit it. I'm really impressed by you folks," he said wonderingly. "How in the world did you do this?"

"Well, for one thing, Daniel, we're not *in* the world!" piped up someone (Shirley, he thought) from the back of the pack, bringing a brief flurry of laughter. *These people are really in a good mood*, he thought.

"Really, it was thanks to you two," said Rose quietly.

"Thanks for laying out all those cairns to show the way," said Anthony. "As soon as we saw them, we realized what you'd been doing during all your trips away from us. That was a very helpful and encouraging thing for you to have done, Patrick."

"Yes, it was!" Again, there were nods and murmurs of agreement.

"But it was your prayers that got us moving in the first place," Rose continued. "I can't speak for everyone here, but I know that every day I could feel myself getting more courageous, more eager, more convinced of God's love. And I know that was because you were asking him to give me those things. You boys have no idea what you did."

"And there are more people behind us!" added Ted. "We just wanted to be first."

"Well, it's wonderful to see you all here," said Dan, still amused that Rose had referred to him and his father as boys. He noticed that she hadn't once mentioned the name of her missing husband, either.

"We were just stowing away our gear," said Pat, gesturing toward the nearby tree where they'd propped up their packs. "But it wouldn't take any time at all to make you some breakfast. Some coffee, at the very least."

"No, no, no," said the runners, waving off his invitation. "That's very nice, but we can't stop now."

"We're on our way!"

"Come and join us! Run with us!"

Dan looked at his father. "Well? What do you think, Dad? Are we ready to end our fishing trip and join up with these people?"

Pat shrugged and smiled back at him. "Why not? I think it would be fun."

His ready agreement came as a surprise to Dan, who discovered to his chagrin that he was feeling a spasm of hesitation. He'd always hated to make split-second decisions, and now he could sense a familiar urge to dig his heels in. One of the runners, a younger man he hadn't noticed before, detached himself from the group and came up to him. He was wearing a red hooded sweatshirt that looked as if it had seen better days.

"Come with us, Daniel," he said quietly. "You won't regret it."

"I don't know," Dan said. "I've never been a runner —and even if I were, I couldn't run with a backpack strapped to my shoulders."

"What backpack?" the young man asked, looking past him.

Dan turned to look at the tree where he and his father had stashed their gear. The packs were gone, and so was his hiking stick. In fact, there was no sign that they had ever been there.

"You're not going to need those anymore," said his companion with a mischievous grin, stretching out a hand to him in invitation. Looking down, Daniel saw to his horror and amazement that the hand had been deeply, terribly wounded. The injury looked raw and fresh. He stared openmouthed, gaping like a fish, and finally raised his eyes to those gentle, all-knowing eyes. "Lord, I . . . I don't . . ."

"Not a word," said the runner, holding a finger up to his lips and winking playfully. "And no excuses this time either. Run with me this time, Dan. Run with me today."

"Okay," he said, feeling bewildered, tongue-tied, and stupid, not knowing whether to drop to his knees or start shouting and waving about. "I mean . . . I mean, yes! Yes, Lord!"

Jesus laughed and clapped him on the shoulder. "That's the spirit," he said. "No turning back, remember?"

"I remember, Lord. No turning back. Not anymore."

"Everybody ready?" asked Rose happily. "Then let's go!"

And off they went. All of them, including Dan and Pat. Buddy, of course, outpaced them all—sprinting ahead, then running back to check on them in the way of all happy dogs. Rose was in the lead, setting a pace that he would never have believed from anyone dressed and coiffed so perfectly, but to his own surprise he found that neither he nor anyone else in that motley group was having trouble keeping up. Their feet were kissing the ground lightly, to be sure, but it felt as though they were flying.

The ice-glazed branches around them clattered in the breeze as they passed, glinting with rainbows of refracted light as though clothed in millions of crystal prisms. And when the sun grew warm enough, the melting ice fell from them in a brief, sparkling rain.

Jesus soon left Dan's side and began moving among the other runners, exchanging words of encouragement here and there, chatting with them about things that didn't seem particularly celestial—stories about old friends, favorite foods, vacations that had taken place years before. From his spot near the back of the group, Dan saw that there was writing on the back of the Savior's faded red hoodie. It said *Follow Me*.

On and on they ran, heads high and eyes bright, their feet beating the same steady rhythm as they navigated alpine forests, zigzagged up switchbacks, traversed high snowfields and flowered meadows, forded icy streams, and made their way across treacherous slopes of talus as though they were no obstacle at all. Sometimes individual runners would point excitedly at a particularly spectacular waterfall or rock formation, and once the entire group halted to admire a pack of hunting wolves for several minutes before setting off again.

In tight spaces they ran in single file, but across the wide flats and meadows they would spread out in twos and threes for conversation and companionship. Rose, motherly as ever, gave up her spot at the front of the group to drop back and check on all the members of her flock, including Dan and his father.

"How are you doing, Daniel?" she asked.

"I'm great," he said. "It's amazing how easy this feels. How about you?"

"I'm doing very, very well. We're on our way at last!" She patted his arm gently as they ran. "I meant what I said, Dan. You did a good thing, remembering us."

"I was glad to. Really, I was."

"Well, then. That makes it even better." And with that, she moved off to chat with another runner. It sounded to him as though they were exchanging recipes.

His father had moved up toward the front of the group, and Dan increased his own pace to catch up with him. "How's it going, Dad?" he asked.

Pat grinned. "It's going great! I never ran this fast in my life, and I'm not even winded. I feel like an Olympic sprinter!"

264

They laughed, running side by side across the meadow. Up at the front of the group someone had begun to sing.

"Did you get a chance to talk to him?" Dan asked. "To Jesus, I mean."

"I've sent up a few prayers, if that's what you mean. How could I keep from praying?"

"No, I mean personally. In person. He's here, running with us. The young guy in the red hoodie."

His father looked at him strangely. "Red hoodie? What are you talking about?"

Dan searched the group for a sight of that sweatshirt, but it had disappeared. "He was here just a minute ago. I talked to him . . ."

"He's always running with us, son," said Pat. "Always has been. Always will be."

The trail took them up and down across the corrugated landscape, but their progress was steadily upward. Soon they were well above timberline, running through an austere world of rock and sky punctuated by vast carpets of flowering turf and walls of shining ice. Here it seemed as though an entire world lay spread out below them on every side, in folds of moving light and shadow that stretched out to the edge of the sky. But Dan didn't feel the least bit bothered by the altitude or the temperature, and none of the other runners seemed to mind either.

Buddy, who had been running tirelessly up and down the line like some sort of four-legged track coach, suddenly gave out a series of happy yelps. Dan looked around to see what the fuss was all about and saw that two more runners had joined the group. Unlike everyone else, they were wearing sleek new white running suits and didn't seem to have a hair out of place—but he recognized them immediately.

"Hi, Dan!" said Rafe, moving in to run alongside him on the right. "I see you've found your way back to the trail again!"

"Hi, Dad!" said Amy from his left. "I'm so happy!"

"We thought we'd come and run with you on this last leg of the journey," said the angel.

Dan was literally speechless. He gulped a few times and wiped more tears from his eyes. Amy reached over to give his hand a quick, warm squeeze, and his heart felt huge with gratitude. "Thank you," he said finally. "Thank you both, so much."

"Wouldn't have missed it for the world," said Rafe. "Hey, Buddy! It's good to see you again too, old pal!"

Hours passed. The sun climbed to the top of the sky and slowly made its way down again, and still they ran. Higher and higher, faster and faster. Now Dan understood why the runners he'd encountered before had been reluctant to stop for so much as a moment's conversation. It was so exhilarating, so thrilling. All that unrequited longing, all that suppressed desire was being released, all their pain turned to pure eagerness.

They were free. They were going home. That was what that singer was singing about, up at the front of the pack.

> There's no sickness, no toil or danger
> In that bright land to which I go . . .
> I'm only going over Jordan,
> I'm only going over home.

Evening came, kindling a fire of tropical red, gold, and orange that spread across the sky and bathed the peaks

266

with light. One by one the stars appeared, wheeling over-head in their radiant thousands. And the runners kept on running, heedless of the night and of the vast chasms to either side, of all the dangers that wait in darkness for unwary mountain travelers. They were past all that, well past it, and now they knew it.

The miles flew by. The group ran under pure starlight, and eventually it was as though they were surrounded by stars on all sides. Below, innumerable points of light gleamed up at them from the canyons and the valleys and across the endless rolling world. Not icy white but warm orange and umber, like the lights of homes and campfires, candles, and hearths. They spoke of companionship and fellowship, of all that was welcoming, healing, and kind.

A great radiance appeared on the horizon and grew slowly as they approached, spreading out across the sky. There was a distant throb of sweet, swelling music and a rising whisper of voices that sounded like the cheering of a vast and joyful crowd. They were running through pure warm light now, and Dan felt an answering light within himself that seemed to expand unbearably, blissfully to meet it. He thought his heart would burst with the joy and splendor of it all.

"It's so beautiful!" he breathed. "It's perfect!"

Amy giggled.

"Oh, Daddy," she said. "You have no idea."

Acknowledgments

Ingratitude is a terrible sin, and I have often been guilty of it. I cannot count the number of people—parents, siblings, children, teachers, clerics, mentors, friends, colleagues, and others—who have given me love, advice, and support over the course of my life. I'm afraid they rarely received the recognition or thanks they deserved, and there isn't enough room here to list those many names. But I have not forgotten you. Nor will I ever forget.

Chief among these unsung heroes—and the one who cannot escape being mentioned—is my dear wife, Karen. For nearly four decades, she has been my love, the mother of our children, my constant hiking companion, and the best editor a writer ever had. Tireless, brave, and patient, possessed of a deceptively gentle wit and a profound sense of the sacred, she has prayed for me constantly, inspired all my best impulses, and smothered most of the worst.

Thanks, Sparky!